SOMETIMES DEATH IS A BLESSING

CJ GRANT

RUNNING WILD

To my family. Always my family.

CHAPTER ONE

It was my first out of state assignment, and I'd be lying if I said I was completely ready for it. No matter. The office gave me a job, and they expected it done. I got on the road at 0400 for the eight-plus-hour ride from my home outside Falls Church, Virginia to Toledo, Ohio. My Honda Shadow 450 was big enough for speed yet small enough I could handle it, even if I ever laid it down. It had nothing flashy about it—black, quiet, custom muffler, minimal chrome. I had put an Ohio plate on it before I left.

I hunted the bad people of the world. Not arrested. Eliminated. Having experienced my own share of violent crime—the bodies bloody, maimed, and unrecognizable, drove me to excel at my job, even if I wasn't quite comfortable with the way I earned my living.

My route avoided tolls, and I paid cash for food and gas. The less trail the better, and life was easier when I flew under the radar. I timed my arrival for 1400 and cruised by the mark's place, a three-acre corner lot enclosed with an eight-foot fence. The large house sat toward the front of the property and had a large back-yard. The office led me to believe the grounds were small–less than two acres total–and more secluded. Shitty intelligence.

After scoping out the house, I checked into one of those scummy motels that rented by the hour and expected cash-paying customers. The job was due after midnight, but I still had prep work to complete before going in.

It was a straightforward assignment. Just the day before, Chief had said, "Routine job, Raine. Follow protocol, stay sharp, and you'll be fine."

Yeah, right. Maybe routine for someone seasoned, but I was still learning. And one thing I knew for sure—don't ever get complacent. There was no such thing as over-prepared.

The report said the target had moved to just outside Toledo seven years ago under an assumed identity. Surveillance showed he lived alone since his latest woman left him, and he'd become relaxed in his routines and security. Guess he believed himself not only untouchable but forgotten. No effing way. Government agents never forgot when you killed three of theirs. It may take a while—it had with him—but they'd find you.

I got a closer look at the property and the area at 1600 when I went for an innocent jog past the house. My main objective was to scope out the best place to hide my motorcycle and myself later. Across the road stood the sole surviving barn up against the sprawl of mini-mansions set on two to three-acre lots. The hayloft's opening had a direct line of sight to the mark's property. The property itself had a lot of landscaping, and satellite photos showed that thick bushes ringed the inside perimeter of the wooden fence. Good. More cover for me.

Back at the motel, I ate the food I packed then got some rest. After it got dark, it was time to dress for the mission. I pulled on mottled gray and black: tactical trousers, a long-sleeved T-shirt, and a black, tactical jacket that fell past my hips, the better to hide the two guns I carried. An unregistered Glock, my throw-away gun, sat in a holster on the front of my waist. My favorite Glock 17 at the back. I put my hair in a braid and under a knit cap to keep it out of the way.

Once dressed, I stared at myself in the full-length mirror. Who was that girl looking back at me? She looked confident, strong. Nobody to mess with. Inside, my nerves built to something near a panic. I was hundreds of miles from home, in a place I'd never been to before. How had I found myself in this position? How was this really me? I was prepared to end a life—on orders, with sanction ... but still. I closed my eyes and fought for calmness. I was not going to mess this up. This was not my first job, and it wouldn't be my last. After a few minutes of some breathing exercises and mental tough talk, I calmed down.

At 2300, I pushed my motorcycle behind some trees and brush on the roadside about a half-mile away from the place. From there, I took up a position inside the hayloft. For the most part, I wasn't a patient person. I fidgeted in lines and drifted off during small talk, but when watching and waiting on the job, I was able to sit and concentrate. My life depended on it.

Through the hayloft opening, I viewed two sides of his house and watched the target move about turning lights on and off in various rooms. A half-moon lit the sky, and I took care its glare didn't bounce off my micro binoculars and give me away.

The mark's bedroom light went off after 2330, yet I remained in the barn until after 0100, Tuesday, October 27. My twenty-first birthday. It didn't matter since I wasn't the cake and party type anyway.

To settle my racing mind, I made one more inventory of my equipment starting from the top down. Throw-away Glock, best Glock, first knife, second knife, switchblade, suppressor—not silencer like most civilians called it—bike keys, Swiss Army knife, and penlight. Binoculars would go in my left zipper pocket. My personal weapon fit snugly at the small of my back in a custom holster. The rare occasions when I didn't wear it made me feel naked and vulnerable. Other girls, that is normal girls, seemed to always wear a special necklace or ring, but not me. I had my Glock.

I also carried two handcuff keys—one hidden in my waistband and the other in my pants hem. My waistband and hems also held lock picking tools, capsules of activated charcoal, and other useful tools. I left my identification and cell phone with my bike—phone turned off. Thin leather gloves protected my hands.

At 0130, I made my move, fluffing and scattering the hay, removing my butt mark, and smearing my boot prints. Trees and bushes on the side of the road provided cover when I left the barn and snuck closer to the property.

I would enter the yard from the back corner nearest the road. It would only take me seconds to get over the fence and into the bushes. I made a running start, used my feet to run up the fence's side, and threw my left arm over the top to pull myself over when I heard a snarl—the kind that came from a large dog.

Doing my best to abort my leap, I didn't pull my arm back quickly enough. I caught the briefest flash of shiny, white fangs before jaws clamped on to my forearm just above the wrist. Pain shot up my arm.

On instinct, I pushed off the fence with both feet before that monster got a good grip on me. I wrenched my arm free and hit the ground, falling first on my ass then my back. I put my hand to my gun but hesitated. With at least six homes in proximity, a gunshot would make too much noise. Besides, I didn't want to shoot a dog—call me a sap or whatever. Running my hand over my sleeve, I found it wet with slobber but intact. Even so, the ache meant a bruise was forming.

The beast made two sharp barks and a continuous low rumbling emanated from its chest. I put my eye to a crack in the fence. Doberman. Well, crap. Why wasn't I told about the dog? Where in the fucking report did I miss seeing that? More shitty intelligence. I moved into the brush across the road to regroup.

Had I known about the Doberman ahead of time, I would have packed a tranquilizer gun. I could abort. There was reason enough except I traveled all that way. To leave in defeat didn't sit right. Instead, I ran back to my bike and retrieved my taser and a roll of duct tape from my saddlebag.

Back outside the fence, the Doberman growled his warning, then barked. I needed to get this done fast. I took a running start and got one hand and one foot to the top of the fence. I suspended there just long enough for the dog to jump at me again and for me to hit it with the taser. The dog got off a short yelp and fell to the ground stunned. I popped over the fence and gave him one more tag to keep him twitching. With the certainty of dog bites to propel me, I wound duct tape around its muzzle, then around the front legs. The animal was just coming around when I taped its back legs together. Another few seconds and I dragged it into the bushes.

Hell. I lost ten damn minutes dealing with that shit. So much for that being a straightforward and routine assignment. I took a moment to calm and regroup while catching my breath. I should have known about the dog. When I got back to D.C., somebody's ass was going to feel my boot.

I crossed the grounds and passed the pool, huge patio, and outdoor kitchen under a pergola to get to the backdoor. By that point, I wasn't feeling confident about the alarm code I memorized. After dealing with all the other shit intelligence, if it didn't work the first time, I'd abort. At the back door, I kept my face in my hood's shadows in case any cameras were still online and pressed five numbers into the security pad. The red light blinked three times then turned green.

Well, gee. Somebody got something right.

Once inside, I paused in the kitchen to put covers over my boots that were wet from the trek across the lawn. I then used a rag to wipe the wet prints. After stowing the rag, I screwed on the gun's suppressor and recalled the route through the house. Get in, take care of business, and get out.

Moving into the rest of the home, I could tell the mark thought a lot of himself. Photos, trophies, awards. The furnishings looked expensive—and they should with all the money he made off state secrets. Through the downstairs to the foyer. So far, easy peasy. Ascended the stairs. Hallway at the top, five closed doors, one room with an occupant. I made for the door centered at the far end.

Thick carpeting muffled my steps. At the door, I squatted to the side, reached one finger, and pushed down on the handle. Locked. Flimsy door—could kick it in, but then I'd have to burst in and make a kill shot on a wary guy who probably kept a gun on his bedside table. Stealth was smarter. I put my ear to the crack and heard soft snoring. My gut twisted as I thought of him sleeping and vulnerable. The twist went away when I reminded myself of the damage he did, the people who died because of him, and the kids who lost their parents in the firebomb attack on one of our military bases in Germany.

It was then I allowed my brain to slip into that dark place. The one where only me and my target lived. Deep in my own mind, I focused only on my quarry. How to hunt them, how to kill them. In that place, I didn't feel awkward about it, and I didn't think about guilt. Only the hunt mattered.

With my penlight in my mouth, I inserted a tool from a Swiss Army knife into the lock on the door handle. With a soft snick, the lock released. Still low, I opened the door. Bed on the far wall between two windows. My eyes, already adjusted to the dark, took in his form well defined under the duvet—and snoring. Tucked low, I crossed to the bed, stood, made a positive ID, and fired two shots. He never knew what happened.

I retreated, changing out my leather gloves for nitrile ones and swiping my hands across the carpeting to remove my boot prints, then paused at the door to relock it. Repeated my hand sweeps along the hall carpet and stairs.

In less than ten minutes, I returned to the dog still in the bushes. I didn't feel any hate for the animal. It was a nice-looking dog and just doing his job. Though he growled through the tape, I positioned myself behind him to free it and make my escape. I cut through the tape on the back legs. Then pressing on its head, I cut the tape on the muzzle knowing it could chew through the tape on its forelegs. Before the dog could swing its neck and get me with those teeth, I hopped the fence.

Keeping to the shadows, I jogged a few minutes to my motorcycle and rode into the night, only slowing when crossing the Maumee River to toss the unregistered Glock off the bridge. Stopping for gas at 0800, I took a minute to send Chief the text he waited for—*Problem solved*—then found a cheap motel. The report I sent Chief said I'd be in the office by 1600. Some sleep, another four hours on the bike, and I arrived in D.C.

Paycheck earned and on to my next assignment.

CHAPTER TWO

Right on time, I steered my motorcycle into the parking garage located across the street from the office. In the back of the garage, a wall marked with a private entry sign hid a secure ramp that led down two stories to a fortified level. I pressed my thumb to a scanner for access then guided my motorcycle down the ramp and parked in my assigned space. When I got off the bike, my body still vibrated with the feel of the engine, so I took a moment to stretch and work some flexibility back into my limbs.

I worked for Domestic Security Services, or DSS for short, a civilian contract office mainly getting work from the FBI, CIA, Army Intelligence, and the NSA. Sometimes we did stuff for Homeland Security. As I understood it, a board made up of a general or two, a few members of Congress, and a few more 'special people' called the shots. The DSS took care of the domestic jobs the other agencies didn't want to dirty their hands over. Sometimes we worked with their personnel, but mostly we didn't. The DSS had money and excellent technology. I had no idea where any of that came from. Maybe Army Intelligence or something like that.

"Welcome home, Thompson," said a male voice through a speaker. Someone was always watching.

"Thanks," I said to the air, knowing the hidden speakers would pick up my voice.

"Remain with your motorcycle and wait for further instructions," said the voice.

I stiffened and wondered what that really meant. "Can I change the plate back to the legal one while I wait?"

"Affirmative."

On the wall near the door was a key safe and a cupboard. Inside the cupboard was my real plate and a screwdriver, and I began switching the plates.

Just as I finished my task, I heard a car approaching from the far side of the garage. A black Dodge Charger came to a stop in front of the door that was monitored with a thumbprint and facial/voice/retinal recognition scans. That door accessed a tunnel under the street that led to our building. The tunnel was a long corridor with a white ceiling and walls of sectioned panels. Other than that, it looked like any old hallway with a speckled linoleum floor and fluorescent lights. In an attack situation, the tunnel would fill with sleeping gas and bullets. Cameras and automatic weapons fired from a remote location, and I suspected more precautions protected both the garage and its tunnel. At the end of the tunnel, an elevator to the office.

One of the DSS mechanics got out of the Dodge but left the door open. A moment later, an agent I had trained with, Tony Delgado, burst through the door and jumped in the Dodge's driver's seat. He raced off, engine growling, and tires squealing. Jeez. What was that all about? The mechanic had already started walking back to the shop and never looked in my direction. I stood there a moment longer before I called to the watchers.

"Hey, can I go in now?"

"Go straight to the fifth floor," a different voice said.

The actual Domestic Security Services building appeared as ten stories from the outside but was really nine on the inside, because the operations theater took up a lot of space, equivalent to two stories. I didn't know how many more stories were below ground. It had only been in the last few weeks that the office allowed me to visit anywhere other than the training labs in the sub-levels. I guess until I had proved myself they didn't want to show me the operational areas or have me get to know anyone other than Chief Capshaw.

Though a highly paid employee, I was more equipment than person. Useful, but expendable. There was no doubt in anyone's mind that if I stepped out of line, I was done. As in dead.

At the end of the hallway, the elevator opened as I approached it. Eyes upstairs still watching my every move. I boarded, and as if on its own, the elevator ascended to let me out on the fifth-floor mezzanine.

Chief's domain.

The mezzanine opened to the front part of the floor—the theater. The space was darkened to make the computer screens in front of the analysts glow brighter, distorting their faces into weird shadows. A set of stairs in front of Chief's office descended through the middle into the operational area.

The theater held six rows each with six stations of techs and analysts with the most senior at the upper level. Chief kept his station at the top center right. A twenty-foot screen took up almost the entire front wall and showed between one and eight displays, depending on what the analysts needed. There, we watched live feeds of satellites, drones, body cameras, video, maps, analytics on possible routes—all kinds of stuff. Of course, the smell of coffee permeated the air. I swear if that stuff disappeared one day, the world would probably end.

Right then, the screen showed a drone view of the Dodge Charger swerving through the city, maybe the 495 Beltway.

Another part of the screen showed a van presumably on the same highway further along. The letter T indicated the agent on that job. That had to be Tony Delgado. I didn't know what was happening since we weren't supposed to talk about our cases. A fair bit of urgency occupied the analysts and techs as they tapped on their keyboards and spoke into headsets, but since Chief wasn't out there, I assumed it wasn't critical.

I moved to the top of the stairs, studying the screen, but didn't go any further. An analyst in the top row noticed my presence and stood to face me.

"This is a restricted area. You must proceed to the waiting area."

I didn't take kindly to his snarky tone and took my time turning my head to him, my expression less than cordial. I stared at him, unblinking.

He shifted his feet then spoke sternly and pointed to the chairs outside Chief's office. "Leave the area immediately."

Other analysts heard him and also turned to look. No way was I slinking away like a scolded child. I held his gaze and said, "You realize those chairs are only about ten feet away and with no barrier? I can see and hear just as well from there as from here."

The man clenched his jaw and fists. The guy in the seat next to him whispered something.

He muttered, "Whatever," and sat, breaking eye contact. Others in the theater still stared at me. I shrugged and went toward Chief's office.

The chairs outside Chief's office were uncomfortable. Black plastic bits held together with thin wire-like legs running up from the floor to hold the back panel in place. Five minutes passed while I picked at my nails. I had arrived exactly on time. Chief was in his office but was running late—like always.

I never expected to have a job like that. It's not something any normal person would set out to do, and if someone said they wanted it, they were disqualified. You can't study for it. Either you had what it takes, or you didn't.

I had the job for over a year, and it consumed my life—body, mind, and even soul. First, months of study and practice, then assignments of increasing responsibility and danger. With only a high school education and no marketable skills, I had no idea what I'd be doing if I weren't with the DSS. Probably some hourly crap job.

I glanced again at the door with its ugly, brown nameplate. Chief Lonnie Capshaw. No one ever called him Lonnie—not even the suits upstairs. It was always Chief. Three of his office walls were glass but with a push of a button, they went from clear to black in seconds. Right then, they were black. I couldn't see in, but if he were looking, he could see out at me just fine, fidgeting in the chair.

"He'll only be a few more minutes, Raine."

Chief's admin, Andrea, in her desk to my left, smiled at me. I only gave her my attention when I had to because she was a know-it-all who babbled too much, which grated on my nerves. I gave Andrea my usual look back. The one Chief said was both blank and hostile at the same time.

"You know," he once said to me, "the people here in the office are on your side. We're all on the same team. No need to be so prickly with everyone."

Yeah, right. I wasn't the easiest person to get along with, and I didn't bother with friends. Too much responsibility and effort. I learned long ago not to trust anyone. Pappy never did and neither did I.

"Been another mass shooting," Andrea said, peering at her computer screen through her thick-framed eyeglasses. "Some bastard fired into a crowd waiting to enter a megachurch." She shook her head. "I don't know what the world is coming to."

I shifted my gaze to her but didn't offer an opinion. A chubby

woman prone to wearing floral stuff with colorful bolero sweaters, she was a great admin but not someone I'd ever hang with. Romance novels and shopping weren't high on my list of fun things to do. They didn't even make the list.

She lowered her voice a little. "Bet you'd love to get that job, wouldn't you? I mean, go after the shooter and kill him? I know I would. Why, if it weren't for my health issues, I would have followed in my father's footsteps here at the DSS."

I still didn't say anything but damn, the bitch sounded a little too eager when she said that. She told me all the time how her parents had worked here—her father as a problem solver and her mother as a field agent. Until they were killed on the job.

"Of course, with your skills, you could just take care of it, and no one would know it was you or what happened, right? Not that you would, of course." A patronizing smile followed her words.

Idiot woman. Either she was trying to test me, which meant maybe the suits upstairs were trying to test me, or she was just that stupid. I kinda agreed with her, but I lived the sanction rule. I didn't make the live or die decision. I followed orders. Andrea, knowing I wouldn't answer, went back to her computer screen.

Glancing into the theater, I saw the empty station next to Chief's finally had an occupant, an analyst who had been around a lot longer than me. I forgot her name, but I'd seen her before. Female, blonde, maybe mid-forties, blue suit, and she glanced at me while typing.

She looked like one of those put together types. Hair, make-up, clothes. Probably always said the right thing. Probably always cool and composed. Nothing like me. I'm messy. Been called surly. I didn't wear clean clothes every day. Right then, I sat with one leg bent up on the chair, with my heel next to my right butt cheek, and the other leg stretched in front of me.

The blonde kept twisting her head to look at me. Maybe she wanted to tell me to get my feet off the furniture. I switched legs to retie my boot. I didn't much care how I looked but preferred Doc Marten boots and black leather jackets. Other than that, jeans and a fitted black T-shirt would do. I usually wore my hair loose, but sometimes put it in a braid when I didn't want it to get in my way. Some black eyeliner, and I was set.

When I caught the analyst looking at me again, I turned to stare right at her with my best 'fuck off' look. She smiled, and her eyes crinkled. She didn't turn red and look away like most. What was up with that?

I broke the stare and went back to picking my nails, wishing I could see out a window. There had been one, but the office covered it when it became too much of a security risk.

Chief opened his door, still on his cell phone, and waved me inside his office. He still maintained his slim form and military stance. Thick salt and pepper hair covered his head which was always moving, surveying his surroundings. Though not in the field much anymore, Chief hadn't lost his edge.

The chairs in front of his large, cheap-ass government desk had fabric cushioning, but that didn't stop me from sitting with one foot on the chair. He kept his office neat to the point of being bare, everything stowed away. The only photo was of him and his girl-friend, Gina.

Chief wrapped up his call with a lot of uh-hums and yeahs. He kept a Rubik's Cube on his desk and fidgeted with it when deep in thought. Chief didn't twist the toy to solve it—it was something to do with his hands. That meant all the colors were in the wrong place, which irritated me. I grabbed the toy off his desk to fix it, again, twisting the cube while replaying the last job in my mind. I thought it went off clean, and Chief didn't appear to be irritated, so it probably did. In less than a minute, the colors were back in their correct places.

Chief ended his call and grunted at the cube. "I'm gonna mess it up again anyway." He tapped his keyboard to open a file. "I read your report. Good work. No one's found him yet. Any difficulties?"

And there it was. The moment I had to relive the job, spew out all the details, and keep professional about it. The idea of taking a life, on purpose, even with sanction, even when I knew the person was a criminal, still shook me. Maybe someday I'd get over it. Then again, what kind of person gets over something like killing?

Though a prickly warmth spread over my body, I swallowed any discomfort. No whining. The memory of walking across the mark's bedroom carpet the previous night and raising my weapon came unbidden to the front of my mind, and goosebumps rose on the back of my neck and upper arms.

Drawing a deep breath, I said, "Incorrect property dimensions and the Doberman no one told me about. Thanks for that. Had to figure out how to neutralize it on the spot, which messed up my timing." Inadvertently, I rubbed at the place where the dog got me. Last night in the shower, the purple bruise from the bite stood out on my pale skin. It ached like shit too. "Whose ass am I going to kick about that?"

"There'll be no ass kicking," he said in his boss-voice while slapping his desktop. Chief raised his eyes to me over the tablet screen; his bushy, gray-speckled brows came together like a fuzzy caterpillar. He held my gaze until I acknowledged his tone by dropping my eyes.

Chief was the only one who could scold me and make me care. A little. Despite my tetchy personality, I respected him and his ways. A patient teacher, he taught me lots of stuff about the covert world. He put up with me without much attitude, cut me slack when he could, and didn't wear me down too much. That, and he could have left me to rot in jail instead of teaching me the business.

Twitching the corner of my mouth at him in acknowledgement of the rebuke, I asked, "Do you expect fallout from his death?"

"Depends on who his contacts think killed him. He made enemies all over the place."

"What about retaliation?"

"Don't expect any in this direction. More likely, they'll look to the CIA. No big deal. They're aware and can handle it."

Then I asked the question I always asked. The one that ached so much. "Where are we with the Russian case?" The office had several Russian cases going at any given time, but Chief knew which one I meant. I had wanted to move on the Zhiglov gang since I started there. Over the last fourteen months, he had never given the answer I wanted, and I didn't expect it that day either. Asking had become a habit.

"Actually, I got something for you about that."

Straightening my spine, I put both feet flat on the floor. I heard my own breathing and forced my mind to settle down so I could process what Chief was saying.

"Got intelligence to share with you. No assignment yet, just info." Chief pushed his tablet my way—on screen, a file with twenty or more crime scene photos. I swiped through them. "We hacked these from the Metro PD," he said.

As soon as Chief spoke, my heart thumped hard, forcing me to draw in more air. The photos showed two white males—dead—under a highway overpass maybe? Gray trousers and black, polo-type shirts over large, muscular bodies. Raw hamburger where their faces had been, probably blown away by several large caliber bullets. Hands chopped off. Why? To make ID harder? That might have meant they were new meat in the country illegally.

Though freaking out on the inside, I managed a calm and professional voice. "When?"

"Early this morning. Time of death possibly around 0200. Bodies found around 0530."

"Where?"

"Near the I-395 North Exit for the US Capitol."

I zoomed in close to the wounds. "Somebody's making a point. Forty-five caliber?"

"Yep, though they were killed elsewhere and dumped there. The scene was too clean. No blood splatters, no shells, no fresh bullet marks in the concrete bridge supports, no body parts or tissues laying around. No witnesses either, at least none who'll come forward. Very professional. I doubt we'll get a hit on any DNA test."

"How were the hands removed?"

"Preliminary analysis, maybe a hatchet. We'll know more after the autopsy."

Hatchet. Small and easy to conceal under a coat, especially for a large man. A forty-five-caliber weapon, either rifle or handgun, was a big thing to handle and took some skill and strength. I re-swiped through the photos.

"The Metro PD has no idea who they are, but we do." Chief reached over the desk to swipe through the photos to a morgue shot. He pinched the screen to zoom in on a specific part of the body. "Recognize the tattoos?"

The Russian underworld developed one of the more highly evolved systems of tattoos for communication and identification. A while ago, I spent the better part of a week studying and memorizing the intel the office gathered. A shit ton of tattoos decorated the bodies in the photos, but two, both on their chests, jumped out at me. A light sweat creeped over my scalp.

"The Russian Prince of Thieves Cross directly over their heart. The high-level shits have these." The other tattoo that caught my eye was very telling. "This other one," I pointed to the corpse's right-side chest on his upper pectoral muscle, "only one Russian mafia family uses this symbol, and only lieutenants and up have these." Tattooed there was the old Imperial Russian flag, not the communist one, with an outline of a pistol overlaid on the flag. I set down the tablet and looked at Chief.

"The Ovechkin family headed by Fedor Ovechkin. Who's strong or stupid enough to go up against them?"

"You really asking me that?"

I took a deep breath and let it out. "The Zhiglovs are reforming here in D.C., trying to reclaim their territory, and pushing out the Ovechkin's."

"That's how I read it," Chief said. "Got analysts on it."

"Forensics report?"

"Yeah, preliminary. I'll make it available to you."

My brain buzzed. That was what I'd been waiting for—one of the reasons why I accepted a job with Chief and the office—not that I really had a choice. I'd gone up against those Zhiglov shits before and killed five upper-level members, including the local leader, crippling their operations in the US. Because of my bullets, the gang's strength suffered major damage, and they had faded back into Russia to regroup. The Ovechkin family filled the vacuum.

I knew the Zhiglovs would be back. They were a small, tight-knit family without leaks. No agency, not us, not the FBI, the DHS, CIA, or anybody else found a way to infiltrate them. Fourteen months ago, Chief showed me the forensics reports on my five kills. That's when I learned the Zhiglovs wore a stylized tattoo of a Russian bear on their chest. Five small bears formed a geometric shape around their right nipple. Freakin' weird. We nicknamed them the bears.

I couldn't follow them into Russia to finish them. Back then I was too green, too untrained, and didn't speak Russian. Now they were back. On my turf. Just over a long year and a half later, two dead Ovechkins dumped under a highway overpass signaled their resurrection. Best part of all, no one, them or any agency, had any idea it was me who had offed the five members. The DSS kept that intel to themselves, hoping to use it to good advantage later.

The buzzing in my ears grew louder, and my hand twitched to reach for my gun even though there was no one in sight to shoot.

Chief's presence dropped away, and my mind left the office to replay the sounds of gunshots, the sight of dead bodies, the metallic smell of blood. He called me back.

"Raine, I feel bad energy coming off you. I've trained you better than that. This is going to be a slow train coming, right? We need to do our homework first. You gonna hold it together with me?"

I wanted them. I wanted them bad for what they did. Had I less respect for Chief, I'd have ignored him, grabbed five or six magazines for my Glock, and left to go bear hunting. No. Chief was good to me. Taking a deep breath, I forced myself to release tension.

"I didn't kill the right people back then, and I didn't get them all. Victor was the local boss, but someone else was calling the shots. They're gonna be back on top in no time."

"No, you killed the right people. They deserved death. It would have been nice to have finished them then ... but considering the circumstances, the five you did get was an important victory. This time, we'll work smarter. We'll destroy them."

Nodding at Chief I said, "I'll do it your way and follow your lead. Your analysts and experience are my best chance. But this is my job." I stared right into his eyes and repeated, "Mine." It had to be because of what they did. I swallowed hard and gritted my teeth, still angry with how things had played out.

Chief stared at me a moment as if assessing my mindset, then relaxed. "Okay, Raine. You're tired, distracted, and had a long ride. Go home, relax. I'll see you tomorrow morning at eight. Got something else for you then, too."

CHAPTER THREE

I arrived home calmer than when I started. Chief was right. Gather intel then make the right move at the right time. I would do things the DSS way, having learned much over the last fourteen months. I'd finally have my vengeance.

My one-bedroom apartment was in a four-story building in Falls Church, Virginia. I chose that apartment right after I joined the office. It wasn't too expensive, it was out of the city, and it came with a small washer and dryer in the kitchen. I had the back half of the first floor, and Cathy, the property manager, had the front. Storage and mechanical systems made up the rest of the first floor.

One night after I first moved in, I swiped Cathy's manager keys and made copies. I could go anywhere in the building I wanted—even the roof–and had several escape plans. It helped me sleep better. I also built a false wall in the back of my apartment's hall closet that slid up two feet to hide a cut out into the mechanical room. On the mechanical room side, the wall looked as if it had a patch job. If I could get to the closet before an enemy breached my door, I'd have a way of either escaping or ambushing my attacker. Mostly older folks lived there. They all seemed to know me by name, but I didn't much bother getting to know many of them except for one or two. I avoided Cathy as much as I could, paying the rent on the first of the month by automatic bank transfer. That way, if I was out of town, I didn't have to come home to complaints.

I parked my bike in the shed that cost extra, double locked its door, and walked toward the front of the building. Almost at the street, I tensed at the sound of squealing car brakes and then a long, wailing scream. My gun appeared in my hand without my having to think about it, and I threw myself against the building. Sliding to the corner, I let one eye peek to the street.

The property manager kneeled in the gutter crying and pointing to a car, watching it back up before it took off. I noted the vehicle's details while running to Cathy, thinking it had hit her.

Cathy's orange tabby lay in the road—still alive, but not for long —poor stupid thing. It made pitiful, faint sounds. I squatted next to Cathy and put my hand on her arm to stop her from picking it up. "Don't. You'll cause him more pain."

"Raine, I think he's dying." Her wail turned to sobs.

No point in messing around. "Yes, he is," I said, making an effort to interject some sympathetic feeling into my voice.

"Maybe we can move him onto a board or tray and get him to a vet."

I got closer and studied the injuries. "I think his spine is broken. A vet won't be able to help."

"I have to do something!"

"You have to let him go. He's too hurt."

"How do I let him go? I don't know what to do!" She wailed again.

"You slit his throat or cover his airway," I said. "You help him die."

"No! I can't do it. I can't."

"Then he'll die slowly in pain."

"Can you help, Raine? Please? I can't do it." More tears streamed down her face.

The cat panted and twitched its front paws as if in agony. Cathy seemed just as pained having to watch him without being able to do something. The few people who had stopped to look drifted away leaving me alone with her.

"Yeah, I can help. He'll die quickly. No more pain."

I knew how to slip a knife into an animal's heart from my pappy and his hunting lessons. We didn't go hungry too often because me and Pappy hunted deer, wild turkey, and rabbits. Pappy taught me that if my bullet didn't make a quick kill, it was only right to slit the throat or puncture the heart and give the animal a good death. I didn't want to slit the cat's throat because I guessed Cathy would want some sort of funeral. If I went for the heart, a towel could hide the hole in its chest.

Cathy gave a shuddering breath, and the cat mewed with pain. "Do it," she said. "Please do it quickly."

I took out my knife and put one hand on the cat's shoulders and touched the knife's tip to the cat's fur under its breastbone. The cat felt warm, soft, and so alive under my hand. "Are you sure?" The cat made another cry of pain.

"Yes. Please. Hurry, Raine."

I slipped the knife into its chest, puncturing its heart and causing more blood to leak into the gutter. The cat shuddered and closed its eyes while traffic whizzed by uncaring, unaware. Movement in my peripheral alerted me that another neighbor, Mr. Ziegler, approached us with a dark blue towel.

"Here," he said. "Use this."

I bundled up the cat like an infant so only its head showed. "There, Cathy. Now he looks like he's sleeping."

Still crying, Cathy took the bundle, pressed it to her heart, and staggered to her apartment. I remained squatting on the ground looking at the bloody gutter thinking about how I went and hurt two innocent animals in less than twenty-four hours. Shit. I was going to hell for sure, never mind that I killed a man too.

Mr. Ziegler cleared his throat and said, "That was a mighty brave thing you did, young lady."

I nodded without looking at him.

"Sometimes killing is right," he said. "If you got reason. No sense letting the poor thing suffer. Sometimes, death is a blessing."

If he only knew. Without raising my eyes, I said, "Thanks, Mr. Z."

I left the curb and entered the building, walking the dim hall with its worn carpet to my apartment. Cautious by nature, I unlocked my door, pushed it open, listened, and waited. After grabbing my Glock from the small of my back, I entered, and methodically moved through the main room, the bedroom, the bath, and the closets. All clear.

It was habit for me to do that after I'd been away for a few days even though I probably didn't need to. I assumed the office had placed a bug or two in my apartment to alert them if I stepped out of line. My SUV and motorcycle had trackers, the office having so kindly let me know about them, and asserted it was so they could find me in an emergency. If I disabled anything, I'd best be prepared to explain myself in a hurry. It was part of the job, which I accepted. Not like I had a choice anyway.

Putting my gun back in its holster, I looked at the fridge. Without having to open it, I knew it was empty except for some bottled water and a few beers. After a moment of deliberation, I reached for my cell and dialed the diner across the street, a small place mainly used by locals. Sometimes, I went there and sat in a booth to eat. That night, I was too wrung out.

"Give me Elroy," I said when someone answered. A moment later, Elroy, the owner, got on the line. Though I didn't know him well, I found his voice soothing. Deep south, bass, and smooth as warm honey.

"Yeah?"

"Hey, it's Raine. You guys got steak?"

"Yeah, and they're good tonight." Mentally, I shook my head. Unlike most people in the restaurant business, Elroy was so honest he told me when something wasn't up to his standards. I had a special arrangement with him. Even though the diner didn't deliver, for an extra ten dollars, Elroy brought me my food.

"Good. Steak, any kind of potato you got, and dessert. How long?"

"Give me like, a half hour."

"Pound hard on the door in case I'm still in the shower."

He said yeah and hung up. That was something I liked about Elroy. He didn't waste my time talking a lot.

I opened a beer and stripped, kicking my clothes into the closet. I locked the bathroom door even though I was alone, got under the spray, and drank my beer in the shower. Not much danger of missing the thirty-minute deadline. The building only gave me about twelve minutes of hot water.

Someday, I'd have an apartment with a large bathtub and at least a half hour of hot water. The office paid me a decent salary, more than I'd make at any other job, but I resisted spending the extra dollars. I saved most of my money for in case. No specific in case in mind, but I figured a healthy savings and investment port-folio was a smart idea. I had no college, no other training, and no people skills. When I left my job, I'd need something to fall back on —assuming I left the job alive.

By the time Elroy knocked on my door, I had on sweats and was running a towel over my hair. Opening the door, I positioned myself to block him from entering.

"Hey, Elroy. Thanks," I said, handing him ten dollars cash over the cost of the food.

"I put some broccoli in there too. You need some vegetables, you know." His expression dared me to argue with him.

I suppressed an eye roll. "Thanks. What's for dessert?"

"Chocolate cake. Had some myself. It's good."

Of course, Elroy had some cake. At fifty some years of age, he suffered from 'dicky do' disease. As in 'his belly sticks out farther than his dicky do'. From the doorway, Elroy's eyes roamed through my apartment. He looked like he was judging my décor—or lack thereof.

"I'm a minimalist," I said, scowling at him. His eyes slid over the kitchen table with two chairs, a sofa, a table with a lamp, and a small table with a tiny TV. No rugs, nothing on the walls, no junk lying around. The bedroom had a queen-sized bed, a table with a lamp, and a dresser. The walls were white and most everything else was brown. The sofa was plush velour, deep and comfortable. It was my one indulgence except for the Egyptian cotton sheets the website said were superior because of their gazillion thread count. Expensive, but worth every penny. I had everything I needed.

"One woman's minimalist is another man's sparse, I guess," he replied.

"If you say so. See you next time."

After more or less pushing him out the door, I locked it behind him. Next time, I'd go across the street and pick up my own damn food. People all up in my space made me itchy.

I learned to clean up my stuff early on, even the seemingly innocent crap. When I first moved in, there was a problem with my pipes, and Cathy sent in a plumber. He was in and out of my apartment for the better part of three hours. A book on anatomy lay open on my sofa. The guy saw it and asked if I was studying to become a doctor. I answered no. He asked why I had the book. I couldn't tell him I was using it to learn the best places to knife someone for a silent kill or a quick bleed-out. So, I lied. A med student friend left it. I was looking through it until she stopped back to pick it up. I learned to be a good on-the-spot liar.

I ate the steak and potatoes with another beer and trashed the broccoli. For a few minutes, I debated on whether I should head out to a bar but then decided to stay home and study the file on the murders.

With a glass of whiskey in hand, I read the reports and went over the photos inch by inch. The arm stumps had clean edges as if someone removed all four hands with one swing of the hatchet. Even with a keenly sharpened blade, it took a lot of strength to make a cut that clean. The autopsy report confirmed they were alive when their hands were cut off. A shudder went through me at the idea of dying without my hands. Imagine looking at your stumps, watching your blood leak out and knowing there was nothing you could do about it. When my death came, I hoped it would be quick. Eventually, I learned all I could from the report and let a little more alcohol help me drift off.

That night, I dreamed about Daniel.

Daniel, sometimes Dan, never Danny. I met him when I was nineteen and he was thirty-three. He never said what he did for a living, but I figured out it was illegal. And I was so young and naive, that I didn't care.

We met at a bar, and I moved into his place three days later. Right from the start, I was in love. Daniel taught me how to pick locks, circumvent simple alarms, ride a motorcycle, and shoot whiskey. He used me as a look out for his jobs. Sometimes, I even got to wear an earpiece and mic. I thought it was so cool.

I dreamed I was on his motorcycle, my arms wrapped around him, pressed against his back, breathing in his scent. I felt the wind, the sun, even the vibration of the bike. It was so real.

The bike sped up going faster and faster until it wobbled and tipped over. I awoke, gasping, afraid, and reaching across the bed for Daniel. But like so many other times, I had this dream, he wasn't there. More than a year after his murder, I still missed him.

CHAPTER FOUR

Within the DSS, certain criteria existed before a hit was ordered. The target must present a past, present, and future threat to national security that would result in catastrophic damage. No one fully defined catastrophic damage for me. I suspected it had to do with death rates and irreparable harm to national security. Next, there must be evidence of the threat beyond doubt, confirmed from more than one source of the target's threat. DSS analysts also affirmed that the effort of capturing the mark would either be a futile attempt and result in serious loss of life by the arresting agents or soldiers involved, or not worth the hassle. I probably paraphrased that shit too much and more went into a decision than that, but it's not like I had a choice. Either I did my job, or I became someone else's job.

Once those standards were met, a kill would happen. The upstairs office suits decided that, and I had no part in it. Except when I argued the need of such action with Chief—which would probably come back to bite me in the ass someday.

The next morning, after submitting to a retinal scan, I rode the elevator with a guy named Michael Shepherd, a forensics expert, and one of his team members, Carley Flynn. Shepherd was one of the few black men in the DSS—at least as far as I'd seen. He had a lab one up from Chief's floor. Nice looking guy, mid-thirties, clean cut, and often in a suit. His walk had a funny gait, though; I wasn't sure why. Bum knee maybe.

Flynn looked about my size, had a blonde pixie cut and wore a Glock like mine on her waist. I'd never had a conversation with her, but she looked cool. She gave me a chirpy, "Morning," in a singsong voice while tapping at the music app on her phone. "What's up, Thompson?" She smiled in my direction while bopping her head to whatever was coming through her earbuds.

I said *hey* to both then ignored them.

Once on five, I didn't have to sit in my waiting chair for Chief. He stood at his theater station, speaking to the analyst who had stared at me yesterday. He tilted his head toward me and said, "Go on in, Raine. I'll only be a moment."

Slouched in a visitor's chair, I once again re-fixed the Rubik's Cube. Chief came in all business. "Okay back to yesterday's job. I'm sorry about the property dimensions and the dog. I spoke with the analyst assigned to prepare the file, and it was an oversight. It won't happen again. Anyway, Charlotte will take care of things going forward. She's been out sick but is back now and working on your next job."

"Which one's Charlotte again?" Up till then, I hadn't spent much time on the fifth floor. Mostly, Chief put me through the wringer in the training rooms, or I worked from home, taking orders for jobs directly from him. Back when, Chief had said I'd have to prove myself before he'd allow me to move about the office and get to know others. Security and all.

"You know, the analyst who sat on the other side of the room? The blonde you saw me speaking with at station two? I assigned her to you because she's the best."

Hmmm. The best for the best, or more likely the best for the worst because I needed the extra support? I wasn't sure I wanted to know which.

"Nice woman," Chief said. "You'll get to know her better starting today, because you'll work with her directly from now on. It's time I cut the apron strings."

My eyes narrowed, picturing the woman who had stared at me yesterday and smiled. I didn't like that or any change. "Why? I'd rather speak to you."

"Because I said so and because I have to concentrate on some other shit."

Whatever. I'd give it some thought later. "Any questions about my report?"

"Nope. Your usual thorough stuff, as expected. Ready for another assignment?"

"Yeah."

A voice from behind caused me to whip my head around to look at the door. That Charlotte woman. She leaned in, holding a computer tablet and a three-ring binder. Her gray suit with pearls, short, blonde hair, and muted but perfect makeup made me again think she was the stuffy, prissy type.

"Sorry, I didn't mean to interrupt. Shall I come back in a few minutes?"

"No," Chief said. "Come in. Raine, I asked Charlotte to join us."

I'd only ever dealt with Chief, and for the moment, he had my trust. I looked at the woman from the corner of my eye, not troubling to hide my scowl. Charlotte sat in the other chair and crossed her legs at the ankle. So demure.

She leaned a little in my direction and said, "I'm sorry you didn't know about the dog, Raine. I reviewed the file. The intel was available, but the analyst didn't do enough digging into the landscaper's info."

"The landscaper?" I raised one eyebrow at her. I liked I could do that. It threw people off, except it didn't throw Charlotte off. Her face didn't change expression and she continued while staring straight into my eyes. Hers were a pretty shade of gray.

"If you look at the landscaper's invoices, it shows extra charges for poop pick-up and mentions the animal's ferocity. The intel was there but hadn't been processed and passed on to you."

Chief laughed and said, "See? Charlotte is our best. She leaves no stone unturned."

They both smiled at me; I couldn't bring myself to smile back. "Okay," I said in my driest tone, "What's my next job?"

"Something to do with the Zhiglovs," Chief said. I stiffened in my chair. "Don't get too excited. It's an indirect operation—one that should make their lives a little more difficult, hopefully force them into making some mistakes."

"Yeah?" I said. "Like what?"

"The Zhiglovs worked with an arms dealer out of Venezuela until a year and a half ago." Chief gave me a half-smile. "Then the Ovechkins started working with him. Now that the Zhiglovs are moving back in, it seems he's in town to meet with them. Nobody wants that to happen, and someone high, high up gave orders."

I noted the emphasis he gave to the words, high, high up.

"You have sanction. Eliminate the problem. If nothing else, it'll ruin the Zhiglov's day, and we'll rid the world of a stinkin' gun runner."

"Fine. Details?" I asked.

"I have some urgent stuff to take care of." Chief paused to gather his tablet and some files. "I've got to run to a meeting upstairs, so Charlotte will give you the briefing and materials."

With that, he secured his desk and left the room. My eyes followed him all the way to the elevator. Chief always prepped my jobs. Who was this Charlotte anyway? I hid my annoyance and held my peace, choosing to hear her out. If I didn't like how she arranged things, I'd wait for Chief before proceeding.

When Charlotte tapped her tablet screen and opened a file, a familiar face appeared in a photo pasted to one side. I alerted like a hound to a pheasant. That was one real bad dude.

"Diego Rolando Martinez. Arms smuggler out of Venezuela," I said. The office had kept tabs on him for a while. Right after I started with the DSS, they had me stake out a house in Georgetown for sixteen hours. I sat across the street on a sloping rooftop, in the pouring rain, between two brick chimneys. They didn't tell me at the time, but he had killed two of ours a few days before. Intel came in he was never actually in that house and escaped back to Venezuela before anyone could move on him.

"Among other things," Charlotte said. "We expect him in the area this Friday for just the weekend. He has reservations for the Presidential suite at the Hyatt Grand Regency under his new ID—Francisco Gutierrez, import/export dealer. Of course, you know he's cozy with the Venezuelan embassy."

"Guess they're the ones who gave him the new documentation."

"Unconfirmed, but most likely. I set up your cover as a fire inspector, which gives you access anywhere in the hotel. You'll need to read up on how they go about their business." She pushed a thick three-ring binder across the desk to me. "There's an ID and badge for you at my desk. If hotel security challenges you, we've set up a phone number they can call to verify your credentials." She handed me a short stack of business cards. "See Miss Chickie in wardrobe for your uniform. She'll fit you after our meeting."

Miss Chickie was an older Chinese woman who worked magic with a needle and thread. She could make anything, even a warm, yet sexy Baby New Year outfit for me to blend in at the New Year's celebration in Baltimore last year while helping to keep an eye on security.

"The rest of the dossier details his presumed schedule," Charlotte continued, "and lists the associates and others we think he'll meet with. It appears he accepted invitations for two receptions."

Receptions and other formal occasions weren't my thing. Gowns, polite talk, heels. I'd stand out like a fox in a chicken coop. No, I operated in the shadows. Leave the glamor—and the receptions—to someone else.

"He usually travels with two to three bodyguards," Charlotte said. "Also, he has a predilection for dark-haired hookers. Actually, what he really likes is dark-haired young teens. Thirteen, fourteen."

A pedophile. I hated them most of all.

"At twenty-one, you're a little old for his taste, but you're slim, brunette, and pretty, so given the chance, he'll still try to use you. If you don't like the fire inspector cover, it's only Tuesday. I still have time to set you up as a prostitute by Friday."

The corner of my mouth twitched. Okay, she almost got a smile out of me. "No. Fire inspector is fine. I can work with it." I had used a prostitute cover before, but for obvious reasons, it wasn't my favorite. Not that I've ever had to or would go all the way to prove my cover, but still.

"The rest of the intel is in this file, and I have the information on your cloud. Any questions?"

"Not yet." The intel she compiled was well put together. I still wasn't sure about her, but I had a couple of days to study it and run it by Chief first.

After shoving the fire inspector binder into my backpack, I followed Charlotte to her station. Her tidy space had a floral coffee mug, a small vase with silk flowers, and a photo of a teen boy who resembled her.

"That's my son," she said, following my gaze.

I kept any comments to myself. Saying stuff led to conversations, conversations led to personal questions, and the next thing you knew, a person was trying to be your friend. I avoided that. I didn't ever make friends anymore and hadn't had a close friend since high school. Even then, I never allowed anyone too close. I had my reasons.

Charlotte cleared me to go down to the third floor for my fitting. Miss Chickie ruled an area about the size of maybe ten offices. Shelves overflowed with all kinds of fabric and accessories, and the six tailoring mannequins made the space feel crowded with people. Tables and racks held a jumble of clothes, three sewing machines each held a different project, and a rainbow of snipped threads and fabric scraps littered the floor. It was a mess, but Miss Chickie knew where everything was at any given moment.

The first time I met her she said I had a good look for the job. Five-eight, lean and strong, an attractive but not too attractive face. My long hair was a dark brunette, and my eyes honey brown or hazel in certain light. Nothing about me really stood out. The DSS required I drop my Appalachian twang and adopt a neutral accent. Just one of the many lessons they gave me.

A trainer showed me it was easy to change my looks when needed with make-up, wigs, or prosthetics. I didn't have any tattoos or piercings other than my ears. Nothing to remember me by. When I needed a tattoo to look a certain part, I wore a fake.

She rubbed her hands together when I arrived. Like always, she was wearing trousers with a long tunic–this time in bright pink. The sleeves were close fitting so they wouldn't get caught up in one of her sewing machines. "Oh, I did a good job on this uniform," she said, bringing out the navy-blue trousers and a coat of a cheap looking serge material. It looked like most any minor official work- ers' get up.

"Thanks." I put it on behind a screen and stood in front of the three-paneled mirror to inspect myself. Miss Chickie topped out about two inches below my shoulder. As she came up behind me to tug and pull at the uniform, she had to peer around me to meet my eyes in the mirror. She had tailored the uniform perfectly. Too perfect. It wouldn't have anyone looking at me twice. "This guy likes to fuck," I said. "I need to look better than this."

"Don't all men like to fuck?" Miss Chickie said giggling. She came over and began pinning. "I'll make the shirt a little better for your waist."

"What I mean is, he's a real pervert. If I give this asshole an eyeful, he'll be easier to distract."

Miss Chickie giggled again. "What do you have in mind?"

"Tighten the trousers around the butt and make the buttons between my breasts gape a little." In my experience, men got distracted by any hint of boob, especially the sort I went after.

Miss Chickie giggled some more. "And you wear a lacey padded bra under the shirt. Put on a thong too."

Padded. Because thirty-four B was nothing special. "When can I pick it up?"

"It'll take me twenty minutes. Sit and play on your phone."

Thirty minutes later, I was on my way with my disguise.

CHAPTER FIVE

From the office, I drove to the I-395 overpass where the homeless people found the two dead Ovechkins. Something about being on-site helped my brain fit things together better than with photos.

The location was hard to get to, and I had to study overhead photos to figure out how to find it. First, I had to park my bike in an empty lot under one part of the overpass with used syringes and condoms littering the edges. The report didn't say which direction the bears came from to dump the bodies, but since that lot led to the path of least resistance, I assumed they also parked there, so no one would have to carry the dead weight too far.

From there, I walked a chain-link lined path that led to a short tile-lined tunnel. Even though I saw the steps leading out and light on the other side, the tunnel looked sketchy, so I put my gun in my pocket with my hand on it. The tunnel's other end forced me to turn left at a wall for the highway above then along another chain-linked path. The left side of the fence opened into a woody area accessed by a gate with no lock. Just beyond that space was another empty parking lot.

There was a tent in the back corner of the lot. I didn't see anyone around, but maybe they had gone still inside their tent. Probably best if I was quick. The police had removed all evidence of the murders and the investigation–even the crime scene tape had been cleaned up. I paused just inside the gate to get a sweeping view fixed in my head.

A garbage stench permeated the air, and a steady stream of traffic roared overhead, blocking most other sounds except for the steady moan of cold wind that whipped dirt and bits of dried leaves into my eyes. That day, the air carried the salty scent of the tidal flats. Before I left my home in Western Virginia, I had never smelled anything like that.

I looked at the long-range photos on my phone to pinpoint the spot where the bodies had lain. The vegetation helped me zero in on the place to the right of the gate. Good spot for that kind of thing. Forensics indicated the victims were shot elsewhere and dumped there. For bodies that size, going down and then up steps, at least two Zhiglovs must have carried them. The FBI had taken over the case from the Metro Police, and while I was sure they swept the site carefully, I began a methodical search for any evidence. Nothing. I walked past the patch of ground where the bodies had been and scoured in the other direction.

Ten minutes later, I gave up but gave the blue tent in the back a good long look. Maybe the owner was watching me at that moment. Maybe they saw something, and if so, I needed their cooperation. I'd get nowhere approaching them now, considering the way I invaded their space. As a gesture of good will, I placed a twenty-dollar bill under a rock in plain sight, hoping to return and get some intel.

There wasn't much else for me to do there. Like Chief said, it was a professional job. No one expected the DNA tests on the bodies to come up with a match. Probably illegals imported directly from Russia. Disappointed, I left the overpass.

Next stop was the grocery and liquor stores to fill my empty refrigerator. Couldn't eat every meal at the diner. Back home, I found a plate of homemade chocolate chip cookies outside my door and a note from Cathy. *"Thank you for your help yesterday. You were a true friend. Please come over for a cup of tea sometime."*

She called me a friend? Crazy woman. Chocolate chip wasn't my most favorite, but a close second. I considered knocking to say thanks, but then I'd disappoint her when I refused tea. Never mind. Didn't want to start a precedent.

I only ever had one other real conversation with her back when I signed the rental agreement, and I lied my way through it. Cathy asked what I did for a living. The office set me up to say I was an insurance fraud investigator. That's why I traveled a lot and didn't keep a regular schedule. When she called the phone number I gave her, she heard my office considered me an outstanding investigator and an honest person.

I set up a study session at my kitchen table and dug into the materials Charlotte put together. It seemed like a straightforward job, though fire inspector skills were new to me. In addition to the reading material, I found several YouTube videos with real fire inspectors giving safety lessons which I watched to see how they presented themselves. I stopped for dinner at 1800, and I was only halfway through the binder.

I heated and ate the pepper steak and rice from the grocery deli counter, pushed aside the peppers, and munched four cookies while trying to settle back to work. It was no good. My apartment was too quiet, and sitting on my ass all afternoon, studying a boring topic made me restless and horny. Time to go find somebody. Or some body.

I said somebody like it didn't matter who when really it did. I didn't much like strangers. I didn't much like clingy. I didn't much like talkative either. Having grown up an only child on a small farm, I spent a lot of time on my own and never did crave having someone around all the time. At least not until Daniel, and no one since him.

I got back on my motorcycle, took I-66 east, and drove to a smaller club just outside of Georgetown where a guy named Connor Desjardins and other locals hung out. At the door, I paused to let my eyes adjust to the dim interior. The bar was too trendy for my taste and served fruity, little drinks to women. The lighting flashed pink and purple waves of color while the loud music was shitty pop/techno. Not much of a crowd that night. Connor sat at the far end of the bar, getting cozy with some blonde with boobs spilling out of her tight red shirt.

He used to be a doctor, but Connor lost his license for writing too many prescriptions for Demerol, Vicodin, and the like. He not only wrote them for himself but for many of the politico wives in and around D.C. One senator's wife OD'd. She survived, but the senator hunted Connor like a heat-seeking missile. He lost his license to practice though his plea deal, and his agreement to squash the story from the press, kept him out of jail. It was too bad because Connor was a great doctor and surgeon, though he never completed a surgical residency. Another DSS employee gave me Connor's name and number. Those of us who didn't want to go to the ER and attract the attention of the authorities used him. Expensive—cash only, no questions, no problems.

The man was good looking as hell too. Blond hair, curly, kept close to his scalp. A hard body and killer smile. The bimbo next to him? I'd make her history in a minute. She didn't know him like I did and would never have the guts to give him what he and I both liked from sex. His eyes locked on mine as I came around the end of the bar. I put myself right between him and his arm candy.

"Hey!" the woman said. The bitch started to talk tough and smack my shoulder.

Ignoring her, I raised one eyebrow at Connor. He chuckled and called to the bartender, "Two whiskeys. Neat." Then to me he said,

"I see an empty booth. C'mon." Connor held my arm until we sat. "Haven't seen you for a while." His eyes never left mine, nor mine his.

"Been out of town. Busy with work."

When we first met, I told Connor about my being an insurance investigator. When my injuries didn't match my job, I told him I did free-lance investigative stuff. Connor was smart enough not to question too much. He took care of me when a bullet grazed my upper arm two months into the job and a few months later when I had a concussion. No hospital if I could help it. It was safer under the radar.

"Good to see you," he said. "You staying around or leaving again soon?"

"I expect to be around the next two weeks."

Our drinks arrived, and we threw back our whiskeys. "Want another?" he asked.

"Not really. Your place?" Why waste time?

"Why not your place?"

"It's a mess." Never my place. I didn't want anyone to know where I lived. It was where I left the office, the job, and the blood behind. It was where I could hide from the world and not have to watch my mouth or worry about anyone else's feelings. It was the one place where I felt a measure of safety and peace.

I followed his BMW to his Georgetown apartment building. We were on each other the minute the elevator doors closed. Connor liked to appear suave and cool, but deep down—he was savage. I liked that. A security camera sat in the elevator's upper left corner, and the security people got a free show, but I didn't care. We kissed the way the preacher back home called sinful. Not sweet, not gentle. Fierce and hungry. Nipping, sucking, licking, our tongues mimicking thrusting and receiving. I tasted the whiskey flavoring his mouth, the smooth, smoky essence of it. Connor held my jaw, his thumb digging into my cheek. It hurt. Hurt so good.

We kept it at an R-rating until Connor opened his apartment door. He threw his coat to the floor and peeled my jacket off me the moment the door shut. I had already moved my gun from my waistband to the special inner pocket Miss Chickie made for me. When he grabbed me by the shoulders, pushed me back, and banged my head against the door, my need for his body surged to the point where if he stepped away, I would have screamed with anger. Connor pinned me, grabbed a chunk of hair over my ear, and forced my head to my shoulder kissing and sucking on my neck. His grip stung my scalp so good, so right. I dug the fingernails of one hand into his neck. He groaned as I knew he would. After almost a year of casual sex, we knew each other's likes.

Not many appreciated pain with pleasure like we did, and few could get it right. Just enough pain to make the pleasure sweeter—too much and it became a distraction. For the first round, we didn't make it as far as the bed. We threw off our clothes and screwed on the sofa, biting, grabbing, squeezing. Damn, he was good. For round two, we went to his bed, wrecking the sheets in the best possible way. My handprint showed red on his thigh and even twenty minutes later, my palm felt the slap's sting.

Some tension released, I fell asleep for a bit, woke at 0200, and used the bathroom. In the mirror, I saw new bruises forming on my upper arms and thumbprints on my breasts, courtesy of Connor's powerful grip. I smiled and twisted to the side. The impression of Connor's teeth showed red on my ass, which would turn to a bruise in a few hours. I'd have fun checking Connor's body for where I left bruises, scratches, and teeth marks. No bondage, choking, or humiliation shit for us. Just sweaty sex that left us a little sore but sated for a while.

Connor watched me walk from the bathroom and said, "God, you look good naked. Makes me wish I were eighteen again."

"Why eighteen?"

"Because at eighteen, I'd be ready for a third go with you. My thirty-one-year-old body, not so much. It's a damn shame."

"Ahhh, but what you lack in multiplicity, you make up for in technique." I meant that. He and I were two of a kind. "I bet eighteen-year-old you wasn't half as good a lover. I like you just as you are now."

I leaned in to kiss him. I'd always preferred men in their thirties —even when I was eighteen. My hands grazed the spot on his shoulder where I left a bite mark then pushed on it enough to get a grunt out of Connor. I broke the kiss and walked into the living room to gather my clothes.

"You're not leaving now?" Connor asked, following me into the room. "Wait for morning. It's not safe for you to be out on the road this late."

"You say that as if I'm some delicate flower," I answered, pulling on my underwear.

He took me in his arms. "Just once, I want to have breakfast with you."

"Maybe someday." I licked his ear then nipped it. I lied. I wanted the hell out of there and inside my apartment alone—no spending the night. Ever. A rule of mine. Connor was fun and all but in small doses. I only tolerated people in small doses. Spend too much time with someone, and they began to get ideas.

Connor put on sweats while I dressed. That senator may have stripped Connor of his medical license but not his money. I had the impression he came from moneyed people, which meant he was slumming with me. His condo had a lot more color than my apartment. Paint on the walls, rugs, artwork. The décor blended traditional with contemporary. Expensive but not in a 'don't touch' way. Funny enough, his sofa was almost the same as mine, deep brown, plush, and perfect for sex.

He held my jacket for me, and then I took my Glock from the inside pocket to put it into my waistband holster so it nestled there and fit into the curve of my back just right. I felt safer when it was in place.

"Are you always armed?" he asked.

"Yep." Miss Chickie created a knife pocket inside my jacket along with lots of other discreet internal pockets, and I had two shivs embedded into the inside soles of my boots. This guy in one of the worst D.C. neighborhoods altered shoes and boots to hold all kinds of things—operating cash only, of course–and I let him think I was a bodyguard to a drug dealer.

I leaned to kiss Connor goodbye. "Okay if I call again while I'm in town?"

"Sure," he said as he walked me to the door. One more kiss, and the door closed behind me. At the elevator, I had a strange compulsion to go back to Connor and ask to stay. I paused, held my finger in front of the elevator button, then squashed the notion. I was better off on my own. Besides, I had a lead to check on.

CHAPTER SIX

Instead of driving home, I went to the office, spoke to the analyst on duty, and asked for the use of a drone. Technically, they were illegal in D.C., but the DSS didn't always follow the rules. I wanted to look at the woody lot where I left the twenty dollars to see who used the spot for shelter and if they'd picked up the twenty. The on-duty analyst authorized my request and sent me to CAIT—the Computer-Aided Investigative Team—our hackers, although calling them hackers was a bit of an understatement. Those people were at the top of the game. Located on what was technically the fourth floor under the mezzanine, CAIT didn't have windows either. The team sat behind bullet-proof glass, had an extra-secure door, and even had their own bathrooms and kitchen.

A hacker named Harry let me in the room and said he'd be my pilot that night. He pointed to a chair next to his computer and said, "Fasten your seatbelt and stow your tray tables for takeoff." A map of the city showed on his computer monitor, and he pointed to it and asked, "Where we going?"

I manipulated the map and zoomed in at the location next to

the I-395 exit. "I need to get a look at the homeless people living there."

"Why?"

I gave him a blank look.

He rolled his eyes. "I have more security clearance than you do. Maybe I can help you better if I know what's going on."

He had a point, so I explained my theory. Harry pulled up the drone flight program, got one in the air, then directed it to the area I indicated. The travel time was just enough for me to grab a cup of coffee. Once at the place, he hovered the drone just inside the lot and swept the vicinity. My hunch was right. Two bodies lay inside the unzipped tent next to a small camp stove for warmth. Two over-flowing shopping carts sat parked on either side of the tent.

"Can you get in closer? I want to see their faces," I said.

"If they're not asleep, they may notice the drone," Harry said.

By that time, a few overnight CAIT team members had gathered around Harry's desk because apparently nighttime drone flights were entertaining. I waited a moment more. Neither target moved.

"Even if they notice, they don't know who we are. I need to see a face."

Harry maneuvered the drone closer. It seemed the motion or the buzzing caught one of the men's attention. He pushed up to his elbow and stared directly at our camera.

"Good enough," I said. "Go ahead and leave in case he decides to throw something at it."

"Right-o," Harry said, and he manipulated the joystick to return our drone home.

"Send the footage to my cloud and copy Chief and Charlotte, okay?" I asked.

"You got it, Thompson."

I needed to noodle on how I could approach those men for information.

. . .

I slept in some the morning after my fun with Connor and the drone flight. When I awoke, I went to the dojang for a Taekwondo lesson and a workout since I wasn't due in the office until 1300. My best defense against someone larger and more skilled was distance and big weapons. When I didn't have distance and big weapons, I needed to get up close and move fast. Strike as many times as I could get in before his next strike. Block, heel of hand, elbow, knee, and block again. To survive, I needed at least three strikes to every one of theirs, meaning I had to work harder, faster, and smarter until either subduing my enemy or gaining distance and a big weapon. A lot of my time went toward practicing defensive arts. My usual instructor and occasional hook-up, Ricky, wasn't there that morning, but I had a good lesson.

Late morning, I had an idea for how to approach the guys who may have been there when the Ovechkin bodies were dumped. At the grocery store, I bought some canned chili, tuna, chicken, and fruit along with a can opener. I also got a small first aid kit and made sure I had fifty dollars on me in smaller bills.

At their lot, I went to them on foot, holding the first aid kit in front of me as if I were an outreach worker. The two men let me approach, though they eyeballed me hard. It was the larger of the two who had spotted the drone.

To put them at ease, I took on a bit of a southern accent. Somehow, southern accents seemed less threatening to most folks. "Hey. Got some food and first aid supplies for y'all." I set the bag near them and backed off a couple of steps.

"Thanks," said the larger man.

Both were older. Maybe in their sixties. Back when I was homeless for a time, at least I had Pappy's old pickup truck to shelter me. There they were out in the open. When the cold weather really hit, maybe they'd go to a shelter. That wasn't my immediate concern though. I squatted to look harmless and asked, "How are y'all making out? You okay here?"

"We're okay," the same man said.

Neither were very talkative, and rather than waste time, I took the plunge into what I wanted. "I'm not a cop, but I have some questions about what went down here night before last. I need to know what you saw."

Neither man spoke nor looked directly at me. "I left twenty dollars for you yesterday. I help those who help me," I said gesturing my chin toward the food and letting that sink in. "Those bodies were dead when they got dumped here. How many men brought them?" No answer. I took a can of tuna from the bag and put it in my pocket. "How many?"

The big man stared at my pocket then back at the bag of food before he answered, "Three. Big 'uns. Two carrying, and one giving orders."

"Did they see you? Did they speak to you?" No answer. I took a can of chicken from the bag and added it to my pocket. "Answer me now, y'hear?"

The second man whispered something to his friend, and the first man gave me more info. "Yeah, they seen us. They said we don't talk to no one. They hit me, and they kicked Pasqual real hard." Pasqual nodded. All I could really see of him through his layers of clothing and scarves were his sad, rheumy eyes.

I put the can of chicken back in their bag. "Did you see anything else? Did they do or leave anything else?" I pulled the can of tuna from my pocket and held it out as bait, feeling like an ass for manipulating them like that, but I wanted immediate answers.

"They gave us some cigarettes. Funny foreign ones."

"Still got them?" His hand went to his pocket, but he didn't pull anything out. "You can keep the cigarettes. I just want to see the pack." I put the can of tuna back into the bag and pulled out a twenty.

He fetched the pack from his pocket. Marlboro—Russian label. I checked his hands. Like me, he wore gloves. "Have you touched the pack with your bare hands or just with the gloves?"

"I don't never take my gloves off," he said. "If I did, they'd get stolen."

I put the twenty in the food bag and pulled a zipper storage bag from my pocket. "I'll buy the pack from you—you keep the butts, okay?"

He put the remaining cigarettes in the storage bag and gave the pack to me which I put in a second zipper bag. They both eyed me again.

"Anything else you want to tell me?" They shook their heads no. I placed the remaining thirty dollars in the food bag. "I take care of those who help me. I don't hit or kick them." With that, I left confident I could come back with more questions if I needed to. So long as I brought more food and cash, which was fair enough.

I arrived at the office a little early, and as soon as I got to the fifth floor, I went straight to Chief at his station in the theater. "I got something new on the Zhiglovs."

Chief jerked his head toward his office where I gave him a quick rundown and showed him the cigarette pack.

"Good work. I'll send it to forensics," he said. "Get some coffee. You've got a few minutes." He glanced at the theater screen. "Tony just entered the garage."

In the kitchen, I found a mid-twenties, rumpled guy who walked toward me. White with dark, wavy hair overdue for a cut, khakis, a size too big, white oxford shirt coming untucked. He looked up and met my gaze. His eyes widened, and he stumbled back a little. He said, "Uhh, uhhh," turned red, then hurried out of the kitchen.

Feeling guilty about something? Hmmm?

So that was Anderson—the man who didn't let me know about the Doberman. I'd deal with him later.

Chief had scheduled Tony and me for some training. All the agents constantly went to classes. Weapons, equipment, interrogation, investigation, and vehicle operation. It seemed like technology updated every week, and there was always something new to learn.

I loved the aggressive/defensive driving courses. My office used the FBI training tracks, but a guy from military intelligence was my teacher. In the beginning, I needed six days of eight-hours each to learn enough to pass the basic test, although my teacher said I was a natural. Good thing my pappy's old pick-up and tractors were all manual. At least I had that much knowledge.

The instructor put me in all types of vehicles. My favorite, the Porsche 911. Buttery soft leather interior and six-on-the-floor. I also tried out everything from a Kawasaki Ninja ZX 14 to a minivan. Because I didn't have college or military experience, Chief had to show me everything from scratch. That made me a less valuable employee, so I took any training seriously. Good thing I like learning that stuff.

That day was tech gear in the lab, but before we left his office, Chief said, "Raine, the tech people will train you on the equipment, however, the reason I've got you and Tony together is so Tony can offer his perspective on how to use the stuff in the field. Give him every question, every scenario you can think of." He put us on the elevator, pressed his thumbprint to the security scanner, and punched eight. Someone from the lab staff greeted us when the doors opened.

"This is a secure floor," the woman in dark-framed glasses and a white lab coat said, "and you two don't have clearance to move about at will."

She looked at me and Tony like we were mud-covered hogs tearing through the house. Maybe that tight bun on her head was painful or cutting off her blood flow.

"Stay put," she continued with cranky teacher sternness. "Only use the bathrooms over there." She pointed to the doors next to the elevator. "Go nowhere else." She clacked away with quick, short steps full of self-importance. Whatever.

Tony just shrugged at me. The first tech, Josh, waved us over to a worktable. That time around we concentrated on new listening and recording devices—their apps and limitations. One of my favorites was a conduction transmitter/receiver, like conduction headphones but better. Not those things they sell on Amazon. These were cutting edge, high-tech stuff that allowed me to communicate with the office discreetly. One of the techs let slip they came over from Army Intelligence.

I tried out the transmitter/receiver thing, which fit inside my mouth on my upper gums over my molars. The paper-thin, soft plastic material molded to my gum line and stayed put. I didn't have any problems speaking around it and after a few minutes, I didn't feel it anymore. Sound filled my head, but nothing blocked my ears, so I heard everything around me too.

Bitchin'.

No one would know I was getting instructions, warnings—whatever. The receiver was built into it, but to record, the techs added an app to my cell phone to work the tech wirelessly.

The lab also fitted me and Tony for sunglasses that not only had conduction technology but video capabilities too. They told me three times I wasn't allowed to break them. Like I ever broke anything on purpose. Accidents happen.

"Tony! Put that down." One of the techs got exasperated with Tony and me manhandling all the stuff. But crap, it was asking for trouble to have all those cool things out and not let us play with them.

Tony put down a thing that looked like a tape measure but could be used to create a smoke screen and turned to me. "Hey,

Thompson, guess what I picked up last weekend? Got me a brand-new Harley Sportster Forty-Eight."

My heart sped up. I loved that bike. "How's it ride?"

"Real nice. I'll take you out on it when I get it back from the shop."

I never hung out with Tony before—or any other investigator from the office. No one told me I couldn't, so I guessed it would be all right. "Cool."

He added, "I'm having some custom work done including getting rid of the chrome."

"Yeah. Hard to be stealth with light firing off your chrome."

He pinched my cheek and added, "Maybe when you grow up, you'll upgrade from your cute little Honda."

"Don't be making fun of my Honda," I said with a laugh.

Behind two security doors in a secure building, I relaxed. Maybe sex with Tony would be fun. But nah. It wasn't a road I'd go down. I doubted Chief would be okay with us sleeping together even if it was all sex and no strings. Besides, Tony had sorta been giving off a big brother vibe, and that too was kind of nice. He picked up another object, and we tried to figure it out before someone slapped it out of our hands.

The tech stepped away to gather more equipment, and when he was out of earshot, Tony turned serious. "Hear you're working on shit with the Zhiglov gang. How's that going?"

Hmm. He knew about that? I huffed some air. "Not great. They're careful. We haven't gotten verifiable intel yet."

"Yeah. The entire Russian mafia has gotten careful—and better with technology. I'm working with our guy in California—something on the Dvornikov cartel. Now, that's a ruthless family. Both Homeland Security and the CIA are involved."

And that sort of explained how he knew about my case. "Is that normal?"

"Not really, but the Dvornikovs are engaged in some real nasty shit. I can't say what, though if you hear anything weird about biologics from your investigation, let Chief know immediately. I mean, like, wake him up in the middle of the night urgent."

Tony played with his new sunglasses when he said that and didn't look at me, which got me spooked. "If I didn't know better, I'd say you were worried." I expected Tony to make some smart-assed remark to put me at ease. He didn't.

"Keep your ears open, Thompson."

He dropped the subject when another tech came over with a tablet and a new kind of biodegradable listening device. We gave her our full attention for the rest of the afternoon.

I lazed around the rest of the day until well into the evening, sitting on my sofa and brooding for hours. I fought the urge to start drinking even though I yearned for that numb feeling to wash over me. Sitting there alone, just me and my depression, I wondered if it was worth living this life at all. I pulled my gun from its holster and set it on my lap, running my fingers over it. Would that be the best way to die? I stared at that Glock, wondering if I had the guts to go through with it. To shoot myself in the head and end my existence. To stop the feelings. Guilt, failure, loneliness.

Maybe there was a better way. Poison? The office taught me a lot about drugs and poisons. It would be easy. or I could ditch my helmet and rocket my motorcycle into a bridge support—my hair loose and streaming behind me until ... nothing.

That wasn't the first time I had those thoughts. Usually, I was drunk on whiskey when I entertained those notions. At those times, the whiskey let me sleep before things got out of control. That night, I was stone-cold sober. My thoughts turned to the Zhiglovs. Who was I fooling? I wasn't going to exit this world until after I'd taken them down or died trying.

Even though it wasn't an active case on my roster, I occasionally staked out Nick's Bar where the Zhiglovs used to meet. Located just to the east of D.C in Hyattsville, MD, Nick's Bar sat right in the middle of a blue-collar neighborhood. I always sent Chief a report on whatever I observed even if nothing happened. That night, I went to see if anything was happening since we believed the Zhiglovs were back in business.

Sometimes, I used an abandoned building across the street for cover, and other times I watched from a car from the office pool. That night, I sat in a car and looked at the bar across the street. It was more run down than a year and a half ago when I last visited. Dirt smeared the bricks and windows, and the K in the neon sign had burned out.

Over the past year, I had seen nothing concrete. Some men who looked like muscle went in and out. Lights on the second floor, but no real activity. Chatter on the street rarely mentioned the Zhiglovs, and even then, they spoke in the past tense. I didn't think Nick's Bar was headquarters anymore but hoped to get a clue by photographing and following people then creating a map of their destinations. The intel went into a special encrypted journal that Chief had access to. In case I died, he'd be able to use the notes to continue the work.

That night, I sat in the car and watched from a block away. Shadows passed the second floor's front window at 2330. In the past, that meant they were getting ready to leave, so I phoned the office and asked for the analyst on duty.

"It's Thompson. Who's this?"

"Uhh, yeah, I'm Anderson," he said.

Great. The guy who messed up the intel with that dog that bit me. I hoped he wouldn't screw things up this time. "I'm outside Nick's Bar. The address is ahhh ..." I trailed off as I fumbled for the information.

"I got it," he said in a rush. Eager to be helpful?

"Right. Are our cameras across the street and next door operational?"

"Yeah. You need them?"

"Some bears coming out in a minute. Get me video." I hung up while he was still answering. A moment later, I nearly freaked out and had to cover my mouth to stifle a scream.

Victor Zhiglov stood on the sidewalk.

A loud buzzing sounded in my head, and a cold sweat covered my scalp. But Victor was dead. Though it was over a year ago, my mind's eye saw him sitting at that table. I felt the kickback of the handgun again, saw the spray of blood ... three bullets to make sure he was good and dead.

I took a cleansing breath. The man on the sidewalk paused to look at his phone which gave me time to calm down and study him. Not Victor, but someone close enough in looks to be his brother. Sonia's dead husband, Victor, had been a masculine man and gorgeous with cut cheekbones, thick blond hair, and piercing blue eyes. Could have been a model. The new dude was a bit taller, a bit wider in the shoulders. Two bodyguards accompanied him and shit, a woman. I raised my binoculars and redialed Anderson.

"You seeing this?"

"Yes, four people."

"See the hot, blond guy and the woman?"

"I don't have a good angle from either camera. I'll try and zoom in."

"Is it Sonia? Who's the dude?" The woman looked like Victor's trophy wife, Sonia. She had been a beauty queen a decade ago in Russia, wore fur from October to April, always in spike heels, and her platinum hair stood two feet over her head. She mostly dressed in tight skirts that barely covered her ass. After I killed Victor, she had fled to Russia. Back then, Sonia had a little, white dog she carried everywhere just like the one the woman on the sidewalk carried.

Anderson didn't answer me, but I heard the click of his keyboard. In moments, he came back on the line. "Yeah. I think it is her. I'll run facial recognition scans to verify."

The bodyguards swiveled to scan the street, and I lowered my binoculars and ducked before they could spot me.

"Okay. See what you can find out about the guy too."

"Sure. Thompson, what are you going to do now?"

"Don't worry about it."

"You're not assigned to be there. You're not supposed to follow without orders."

Whiny thing. "So, I'll get orders." I disconnected from Anderson and dialed Chief. He didn't answer, so I left a message. *"I think I just saw Sonia Zhiglova back in D.C. Checking out where she's staying."*

It looked like Sonia got herself hooked up with Victor's replacement. The guy helped her into the car and then entered the back too. It might have been reckless to chase after a bunch of Zhiglovs without Chief's blessing and without identity confirmation, but I was on the hunt like a hound on a rabbit trail. Adrenalin raced through me—I felt alert, alive, and focused. No matter how many other jobs I did for the office, that was the only one I really cared about.

That time, I drove the Ford Taurus from the pool. A basic Taurus on the outside, but inside, the engine was extreme, and it had all kinds of tech built in. Company cars, even our own personal cars, didn't have daytime running lights, no panel or door lights or tones, not even seatbelt chimes. Can't have something so small give you away.

I turned on the car's video, authorizing a feed to the office. A confirmation message showed that Anderson picked up the transmissions. I left my headlights off, easing from the curb to follow, and then I turned them on once traffic increased. The car headed south in the direction of where Sonia and Victor's home had been, a house in the nicer suburbs of Alexandria beyond the Capital Belt-way. Since Victor's death, it hadn't been sold or occupied.

Were they heading to the same place? Records showed a holding company held by a conglomerate, and then more layers of corporations, owned the place. The car took the exit I suspected was their destination. I took the same exit but turned in the oppo-site direction. A few hundred feet later, I turned around in a parking lot and re-entered the road in their direction, not bothering to catch up. I didn't want to. If they were at the same house, I'd know in a minute, and if I lost them, oh well. I or someone else would follow them another time.

I came to the neighborhood and cruised the street to see if lights were on in the house. Yup, and their car was probably in the garage. There wasn't much else I could do right then. Maybe Chief would give me the okay to go in and place bugs and cameras. Problem with that was those assholes swept their places almost daily and would find them—a bug would tip them off that someone was watching. Chief wouldn't want to make that move until he collected more intel.

Past forays taught me that neighborhood was active with kids outside all day, moms with strollers, old ladies in their little walking outfits, landscapers working on lawns. Even late into the evening, people walked dogs, went for runs, came home from work or parties. They all seemed to know one another, meaning a stranger couldn't blend in.

And what's that? my brain asked as I slid by the house. The place next door had un-mowed grass, brown and matted down, a yard full of unraked leaves, and a notice on the door. Vacant? Excellent.

The next day, after clearing my plan with Chief, I went back. Finally, I had something to do to move the case forward. I used a beat up, yellow, 2008 Volkswagen Beetle and wore a long, red wig, make-up that paled me, freckles, and a dental prosthesis that gave me a major overbite. Two of those cheap magnetic signs stuck to either car door read *Flower World*. I wore wrinkled khakis, a Taylor Swift T-shirt, a cheap nylon coat with a tear at the hem, and dirty sneakers—no socks. Your basic incompetent, teen, flower delivery idiot. That was the part of the job I didn't mind. Investigation, a bit of a con, a test of my skills.

I cruised past the vacant house like I didn't know where I was going, backed up, and got out with a floral arrangement. Next, I spent too long ringing the doorbell which gave me time to read the door notice. Bank foreclosure. I got a happy tingle as I thought about how the situation could help me. The alarm keypad told me what kind of system it was, and I filed that information away while taking the arrangement next door, but not to my quarry's house. I went to the house on the other side. A woman answered the door.

"Hiya," I said in a chirpy voice. "These are for next door," I said gesturing to the empty place, "but they're not home. Do you know when they'll be back?"

The woman had a mean smile and took her time looking at the expensive arrangement. "Mmmm, not sure," she said.

Lying bitch. She knew damn well the place was abandoned and was probably the first to complain about the grass being too high. I finished blowing a pink bubble and asked, "Can I leave this with you, and you'll give it to them when they come home?"

"Sure, I will," she said, grabbing for the bowl. If she snatched it any quicker, my hands would have come off. I popped another bubble in her face then thrust the handheld computer at her and asked for a signature. She made an unintelligible scrawl then slammed the door before I blew another bubble. Just for spite, I spit my gum into the flower bed next to the door.

So, the house next door was definitely abandoned. Guess who was gonna use that? As I drove away, I asked Chief for permission to break in and set up cameras.

"Got an alarm system?" he asked.

"Basic set up. I'll be in and out before the bank sends a security tech."

"Yeah, okay. I'll call upstairs, and they'll give you what you need."

"Can we get a floor plan of the Zhiglovs' place, for just in case?"

"Sure, I'll get Anderson on it."

At least we'd see who came and went. I entered the neighborhood the next night, disabled the alarm, and picked the lock to the back door. In under fifteen minutes, I placed my cameras, then a CAIT tech confirmed they were collecting the feed. I put another camera on the curbside mailbox to collect the license plates of any cars. It wasn't much, but I felt better for having done something.

CHAPTER SEVEN

Around 1400 the next day, my phone rang. It was Andrea, Chief's admin, saying he needed me to come in. An hour later, I was back in that stupid plastic chair, waiting for Chief because he was running late again. Andrea tried to make some small talk while she used a box cutter to open a package. A moment later, she squealed. I shifted my eyes to see her holding an open, velvet jewelry box.

"Oh my gosh," she said in a breathy gasp. "It's beautiful. Come see, Raine." She pulled a pearl ring set in gold from the box.

"I can see fine from here," I answered, barely making an effort.

Andrea didn't seem to notice my brush off. She was busy trying on the ring. "It fits perfectly," she said in a gushing kind of voice while stretching her sausage fingers toward me and admiring it. She held her hand out there for too long, and I finally accepted the hint.

"It's really nice."

She beamed and replied, "It sure is."

She kept her eyes on me, and I guess I was supposed to ask who it was from. I didn't feel like it, so I took out my phone and began scrolling through my photos. She gave up and sat to continue admiring the ring. By the fuss she was making, it obviously came from a guy she liked. Yeah, whatever. Good for her.

My thumb slipped while scrolling through some photos, and the app went all the way to the oldest ones. Without any warning or preparation, I was suddenly staring at Daniel's face. Memories flooded my head without my permission just as they had many times the past eighteen months.

My eyes burned, and I blinked fast to avoid tears. I hated that I couldn't make those memories go away. That I couldn't control them. I closed the photo app and leaned back in the chair to take deep breaths. Chief stuck his head out his door, interrupting my memories. With one more cleansing breath, I pushed away from the chair and stood. The office was no place for emotions.

"Raine, Charlotte has the new intel. She'll take care of you. Okay?"

I frowned. Up till then, I always dealt with Chief directly.

He said, "It's okay, Raine. Trust Charlotte. She's been working with me to take good care of you since you joined us. Now, I gotta handle something else urgent." With that, he pointed to the theater. "Go see Charlotte."

I descended the steps to Charlotte's station. A cup of coffee steamed on Charlotte's desk, but her chair was empty. Probably in the bathroom. I turned my attention to the theater screen. It displayed the front entrance of an office building on one side, and the ticket counter of Delta—Miami International the tag read—on the other. The letter 'B' identified the agent. I didn't know anything about that situation.

The DSS employed a bunch of agents for field and investigative work, but only a few of us for wet work—insider's slang for those who dealt with blood—who killed for a living. I didn't know how many of us did wet work and only met two others, Jack and Tony. Just because the DSS called us problem solvers instead of wet boys or assassins didn't make the task any easier or less intimidating.

As a teen, I'd heard plenty of adults say that the death penalty should be used more or that we'd all be better off with this or that criminal dead, and sometimes I nodded my head with them. Now, though ... being the one to make that happen ... it was hard. Part of me believed that the world was better off with those people dead. I just never expected it would be me that pulled the trigger. Given the choice, I'd run home to the farm and never look back.

Movement to my left caught my eye. Charlotte appeared and did her smile thing again when she saw me. "Raine, I'm sorry I wasn't here to greet you. Let's go into the conference room where we can talk privately."

Tucking some files under her arm, Charlotte picked up her coffee cup with two hands. Either she walked slowly, or I was used to moving fast, but the pace felt excruciatingly slow. In the conference room, a box of donuts sat on the counter. Because I didn't know where they came from, I left them alone, though my mouth watered. It was my home office, but I didn't really consider myself safe there—not enough to relax my guard. In my experience, people turned on each other all the time. Friends turned out not to be friends, and it was everyone for themselves.

Charlotte drew my attention back to the new job Chief had given me ... to take out that gun runner Martinez. She briefed me on changes to Martinez's schedule and his bodyguards. "He has three newer guys with him this time. Here are some photos." She tapped her screen and sent a group of photos to my tablet. "From what we can tell, they have less experience. Don't count on it being easy, though."

"I never do," I replied, sliding my thumb over the screen and looked at the photos. I glanced up to see her give me what I thought could be a motherly smile. Because I couldn't remember my mother, I wasn't sure.

"Yes. You aren't reckless. I appreciate that."

Huh? What did she mean? My face must have shown confusion because she said, "Even though we just met face to face, I feel I know you. I've prepped assignments for you for the past year and read all your reports. I respect you won't go through with a job if kids are present."

Shit. She read my reports? I didn't like that, and I didn't like feeling exposed that way. She knew me well, but I knew next to nothing about her. That wasn't how I operated. "Why am I just meeting you now?"

She tilted her head to one side. "Well, you've had to notice Chief's a little protective of you. He likes to review the intel before you get it. Make sure everything's accurate and that you're fully prepped."

Chief kept extra tabs on me? What the hell?

"I also take care of your expense reports."

"You? I thought they went to accounting."

"An analyst checks everyone's expense report. You know, for discrepancies, anomalies."

"You think I lie about my expenses," I said, getting all heated up. I kept track of every receipt, watched every penny, gave a detailed report when I had to use bribe money. I was no thief. Not anymore, anyway.

Despite my angry tone, Charlotte maintained the same cool, calm voice. "No. We check everyone's expenses to make sure you were where you said you were, when you said you were, for the amount of time you claim. I know you understand this is a business built on paranoia—for good reason."

"I guess," I said, calming down some.

"Because you're so accurate, we'd catch any misstep you made. The minute you became vague or leave a gap, an analyst would investigate it. You're just so damn honest."

Crap. It was like my whole life was on display. While I turned

Charlotte's statement around in my head, she picked up a pen to make some notes but dropped it to the floor. She retrieved it, and as soon as she straightened, she dropped it again. That time, I grabbed the pen for her. I must have made her nervous even if her face didn't show it. Wet work employees like me had that effect on regular people.

"Thanks," she said. A red tinge colored her cheeks. Charlotte swallowed hard then finished the briefing's details. I left with new intel and spent the next couple of hours scouting the exterior of Martinez's hotel. That wasn't good enough—I needed more.

Back at the office, I called the hotel and made a reservation for myself for that night using one of the four fake ID's the office set up for me. After, I went to see Miss Chickie. The sewing machine was going full speed when I arrived, so I stood back and waited for her to finish whatever she was working on.

She spied me, and after cutting some threads, she said, "Hey, come to visit me?" She wore metallic olive green with red glasses and red flats. I think she had at least a dozen sets of half glasses in different colors to match her outfits.

"Yeah. Need some help." Something was different about her. Her normally straight bob was curly. "You have a new hairstyle," I said.

She giggled some and touched her head. "Got a perm last night. Me and my friend are hitting the casinos this weekend. Maybe even pick up a guy."

I raised one eyebrow at her and said, "You're going to pick up a guy?"

"Maybe a young one ... like in his fifties," she said with a wink.

Okay, time to move the conversation on. The sex life of old people wasn't high on my list of interests. "Anyway, got an assignment, and I want to look like an account executive in town for one night. Can you give me a wig, suit, decent suitcase, briefcase, and whatever else a person like that would have?"

Miss Chickie pulled her half glasses off her nose and let them dangle on their chain. Then she giggled and rubbed her hands together. "I'll make you look real good. Take off your clothes," she ordered while she rummaged through the racks and pulled out a suit and blouse. She squinted her eyes and peered at my bare arms. "What are those bruises? Oooh, did you get in a fight? Tell me all about it."

No way would I tell her about Connor and the fun we had. Instead, I snatched the blouse from her and said, "Sort of."

"I have something to help your bruises. From China. It has ginger, peanut oil, and secret stuff. It's good, but if you add some of your own pee to it, it's better. Just rub it in your bruises. I'll go get it."

Eww. No way. "Uhh, thanks. Maybe next time."

Forty minutes later, I was blonde with a bob cut in a stylish black suit and had a shit ton of make-up beyond black eyeliner. I wore black, Kate Spade heels, had an actual purse, Coach I think, and a briefcase, along with a floral-patterned suitcase. Everything was just expensive enough to make me seem successful, but not uber-rich. I made a face at the flowery suitcase, and Miss Chickie laughed at me.

"Remember, you are not you." She pointed to my altered reflection in the mirror. "That girl likes flowers." She giggled again. "Now, show me your saleswoman-smile-face."

I took a deep breath, channeled a vapid corporate robot into my mind, and gave Miss Chickie a dazzling smile. "Well, hey there, honey," I said in a southern accent to match my Georgia ID. "I'm just delighted to make your acquaintance." I put my hand out palm down for a girly handshake and tilted my head to the side still smiling.

"Oh, very good," Miss Chickie said clapping for my performance. "Do it exactly like that. But go home and clean and file your fingernails. Pretty saleswomen don't have ragged nails. Put pink polish on them."

"Thanks," I said, patting her arm before packing my own clothes into the suitcase. "I'll have this stuff back in a couple of days."

I went up two flights to Chief's floor and found him at the water cooler. I wheeled my suitcase to him, and when he turned, he almost bumped into me.

"Oh, pardon me, sir." I said in my sweetest voice.

"My fault," Chief said, glancing at me then furrowing his brow. A millisecond later he exclaimed, "Raine? Shit, girl!"

Amused, I allowed a grin. "I'm checking into the hotel for the night so I can scout it from the inside. I've got a room on the same floor as Martinez's suite."

"Okay, but don't go crazy with the liquor bill. It'll never get approved."

"Same old story. I'm taking a car from the pool," I said and went on my way.

That night, I reclined on clean sheets, enjoyed room service, and watched a movie until things quieted down around 0100. Security was tight in the hallways with working cameras at the end of each corridor. I put on the fluffy bathrobe and slippers Miss Chickie packed for me, put my gun in the pocket, and grabbed a book and the ice bucket. My room was in the corridor's middle, and the ice machine and elevators were to the left. Upon leaving my room though, I turned right in the direction of the Presidential Suite.

Sticking my nose in the book as if engrossed, I shuffled along the hallway, pausing at the T. Two cameras. Left, a door onto the service stairs. I turned right. Twenty feet to the suite's entrance and no other doors in that part of the corridor. Still seemingly absorbed in my book, I counted twelve steps to the door.

I stopped and examined the area. Left, hall chair and table with a silk flower arrangement. Right, another table with a mirror above it both in ugly, fake gilt. Thick carpeting to muffle footsteps. In front of me, a heavy security door with a peephole. While I studied the handle mechanism, the door opened, and I back peddled as someone in the hotel's uniform exited.

"May I help you?" she asked in a friendly yet suspicious way. The woman pulled the door closed behind her, not letting me get a look inside. No matter. Charlotte gave me the room's floor plan, dimensions, and some photos from the hotel's website. Main room, conference room, two bedrooms, open kitchenette, and three bathrooms. The bath for the master suite, huge.

"Oh, my stars, how you startled me!" I said in my southern accent. "I'm afraid I'm all turned around." I held out my bucket. "I'm looking for the ice machine."

"It's at the other end of the corridor near the elevators," the woman said. "I'll walk you there."

"That's sooo nice of you. This is such a lovely hotel."

I followed and thanked her again at the ice machine. She watched me until I fetched my ice and returned to my room. The hotel staff was on the ball. No biggie. I'd work around them.

The next morning, I used the service stairs to return to the lobby, just to get their feel, lingered over my free breakfast, and watched how things worked in and around the front desk. Both security people leaned on a wall and watched the floor or their phones more than the guests. I sent a text to Chief asking him to get me intel on the security staff. How many per shift, how well trained. It was Charlotte who texted back she'd have the info for me by lunch and that we had gotten an agent inside on the maintenance staff. I guess Chief meant it when he said I had to work with Charlotte. I went home to prepare some more.

CHAPTER EIGHT

Hollywood films seemed to think my job included scaling the sides of buildings with suction cups or crawling through duct work. Both stupid. Duct work was flexible, and it was impossible to move through them silently. Besides, most were too small for anyone older than a four-year-old, and they were filthy with dust and mold. But why complicate things when most of the time I could walk through a door?

Saturday afternoon found me wearing the fire inspector uniform with a silver badge that twinkled on my chest. I parked the company-issued, nondescript sedan near the hotel's side entrance. Another employee left me a second car out back–just in case. Keys to the car in the side lot were clipped to my belt loop. Keys to the one out back in my left pocket. I entered the hotel lobby by the side door closest to the elevators, wheeling an important-looking black case. In my left hand, I carried a clipboard and pens. My hair was in a loose bun with a few tendrils framing my face. I had dark-framed eyeglasses, and red lipstick. On my feet, I wore the world's ugliest black uniform oxfords. The tight trousers caused my thong to ride up into my crack. And shit—I couldn't stop to pluck at it.

No one challenged me about getting on the elevator and taking it to the top floor where I walked to the suite like I had a right to be there. Twelve hours earlier, the inside person reported Martinez checked in with his three bodyguards. Get in, get it done, and get out.

I had two methods ready. First option for its stealth: a dose of poison hidden in a pen tucked into my breast pocket next to my tactical pen. The stuff was tasteless on food or in drink. Second option: gun with a suppressor hidden in the case. It was only a .22 and would do the job, but it wouldn't be much protection in a firefight. I also carried a knife. That wasn't my favorite work tool, but in a tough spot could make all the difference to getting out alive. The tight fit of the shirt and jacket meant I had to do without my Glock because I couldn't risk letting them see it on my waist or in a shoulder holster. That was irritating. The Glock had become a part of me, and I felt vulnerable without it. Despite my nervousness, I rapped on the door loud and forceful because, after all, a fire inspector is a public authority figure. Even through the heavy door, I heard the blare of the TV.

A male answered. "Yeah?"

"Fire Inspector."

The door opened an inch and a dark eye under dark hair looked at me. "Qué?"

I held up my ID next to my silver badge. "Fire inspector. I have a legal right to enter this room for inspection. If you do not comply, I will notify the police."

The man said, "Occupado."

"Are you refusing to cooperate with me?"

"Occ – u – pa – do."

So, no English. Great. I didn't want to let on I had some Spanish.

Another voice reached my ears, and the first man made way for a second man to come to the door. "I help you?" That one opened the door a bit wider. His voice, while accented, was clear.

"I am the fire inspector. I must inspect this room today, or I will have to shut down the room and evacuate the floor. The City of Washington D.C. takes its fire codes and inspections very seriously." Unrealistic, but being foreign, would they really know?

"Oh, for shit's sake," came a third voice. "Let her in. Let's get a look at her."

The man stepped back and opened the door all the way. I entered the suite's main room with my official-looking case. Three men in suits stared at me. A fourth man, Martinez, was bare but for a towel wrapped around his waist. No food or drinks in sight. That would have been too easy, right? A soccer game was on the big screen TV, and a second TV had a different soccer game.

"Fire inspector?" he said looking me up and down pausing at my chest. The button between my padded breasts strained to contain me. "Sure," he said. "Come in and inspect anything you like." He smiled like a wolf and gestured to his towel letting me know I was welcome to make a move on him.

I spent a little too long looking at his towel, making a hint of a smile at the corner of my mouth. I shook myself, cleared my throat, and said, "Thank you for your cooperation. Why don't I start in the en suite bathroom?" My mind raced, trying to decide how to get him away from his henchmen. The office said to leave the bodyguards alone if I could.

"Why don't you?" Martinez said. He followed me through the master bedroom into the palatial bath. The door of the suite had a direct line of sight to the door of the bathroom, and Martinez had left the bedroom door open when he entered. Damn it. In the bath, steam rose from the full tub of water. Enormous—big enough for two. If only I had a bath like that at home.

"I won't be long," I said. I put my clipboard and glasses on the vanity, looked at the outlet there, pushed the breaker switch, then made notes on my clipboard. The tub and the toilet couldn't be seen from the main room. Maneuvering Martinez there might be my best chance. Behind me, Martinez turned on some lively salsa music. Excellent.

He took off his towel and got into the bath. In the mirror, I watched his ass. Nice one. Not too hairy. I stared long enough to make sure he caught me peeking.

"Don't mind me," he said. "You know, why don't you close the door? You're letting all the heat out."

Damn, he made it easy. I went to the door, and the three stupid bodyguards grinned at me from the main room. I heard the word *puta*. Whore. Well, crap. I chose the fire inspector cover but ended up a prostitute anyway. After closing and locking the bathroom door, I pretended to work another minute, letting Martinez see my glances in the mirror in his direction.

He made a sly grin and said, "How about you come over here and rub my neck for me? I'm so tense."

Well, why the hell not? Once again, a man who should be afraid of strangers, had real and compelling reasons to be wary, dismissed a young woman as being no threat. And there was the real secret to my success in that job.

"Um, okay."

He closed his eyes and leaned back. Taking a moment to put the clip board back in the case, I took the .22 with the suppressor from the hidden compartment. At the tub, I sat on the edge with my body hiding the gun and reached for Martinez's face. He sat up, and his hand squeezed my tit as his face came at mine for a kiss. In one fluid motion my right hand put the end of the gun to his head, and I squeezed. No hesitation. That was the second secret to my success—no false starts, no wavering. Aim. Fire. I never gave them a chance to react or defend.

Martinez slumped into the water. I observed the small hole that went into his brain and reached to turn his head. No exit wound.

Bubbles rose to the surface from his mouth, and the water turned red. Three seconds more and a few more bubbles rose. Ten seconds later, no more bubbles, therefore, no need for a second bullet. The salsa music played on.

Job done, but I still had to get out of there. First, I put away the suppressor then put the gun on the counter within easy reach. Blood stained my white shirt and face. I took the shirt off, bunched it into the bottom of the case, and rinsed my face. Then I put on the fresh shirt I brought with me. I took a chance and put the gun in my waistband under my jacket in case I needed it quickly. It took ten seconds to pack up the rest of my shit and put the glasses back on my face.

If I opened the door too soon, the bodyguards would be suspicious. I looked over my shoulder at Martinez. How long did he usually last during a blow job? Ten minutes? Seemed reasonable. While ticking off the remaining minutes, I wiped my fingerprints from the surfaces I had touched, undid my bun, and left my hair in a messy ponytail. I smeared my lipstick and rumpled the shirt.

At the ten-minute mark, I slipped through the bathroom door looking back as if listening to Martinez. "Yes, I understand." I nodded toward the tub, shut the door, then moved through the bedroom and into the room closing that door behind me too.

"Señor Martinez and I have come to an understanding," I said to the bodyguards. I tried to blush, but I'd never been successful turning red on command. Instead, I looked at the floor and squirmed. From under my lashes, I watched them take in my appearance and noted their nasty grins. "I gave him my number. He wants me to come back and says he'll call when he's ready.

"I bet he did, princess," the English-speaking man said. He translated for the other two, and they laughed. I heard the word *puta* again.

"He said he doesn't want to be disturbed. I promised to go now." I edged to the door. No one tried to stop me. Amateurs.

In the hall. No time to breathe. Keep moving. I pushed open the door to the service stairs when a voice called out, "Chica! Wait." I looked back to the suite while resisting the urge to reach for the gun under my jacket. The one bodyguard who'd been silent until just then leaned out the door. "Since el jefe is taking a nap, you come have fun with us, no?" He grinned, displaying a mouthful of crooked teeth.

"Señor Martinez told me no. I'm not allowed to do that."

"He'll never know. He's sleeping. Come back." He walked toward me.

Shit, I did not need that complication. "Can't. Gotta get back to work." I let the service door close behind me, knowing he was following.

In the seconds before a fight, a thrum built in my blood. A shift happened—all else faded but the enemy. A strange excitement, a weird eagerness for the fight. Am I worthy of this opponent? Will I come out of it alive? In one piece? The thrum extended to the tips of my fingers, tingling, itchy to strike, to test, to win.

I moved fast but not too quickly. Cameras watched me, and I didn't want to raise suspicion among the hotel staff if I could help it. Above me, the dude entered the stairwell and ran the steps to catch up. I made it to the ninth floor before he overtook me and grabbed my arm. I shook him off.

"Beat it." I pushed him off me and went down another flight, running through options of how to handle him. Best case was I made it to the lobby.

He jumped half a flight and pushed me against the wall wrapping his hands around my waist. The ass felt the gun in my waistband, damnit, his face going from surprise to furious in a millisecond. The shit pushed off me and pulled his gun before I could get mine. Defensive training took over my brain. I grabbed his gun, pushed it to the side, and made a throat punch.

He took it well and wrestled with me to get his gun back in

place to shoot me. I slammed my knee into his groin, grabbed and twisted his arm behind his back, spun him around, and pushed him down a flight of stairs to the seventh floor. He lay there with his eyes wide open and his head at an unnatural angle. Grabbing my gun, I raced down the steps, jumped over his body, and checked for a pulse. Nothing.

Feet running on the stairs. Not from above—below. Damn it. Security? I leaned over the railing to look, ready to bolt. It was Tony Delgado, coming to help.

"It's cool," I called down to him.

He ran the last few steps up to the seventh-floor landing, assessed the man's broken neck, and grinned. "You didn't need me after all, Thompson."

I jerked my head to the security lens in the upper corner of the wall. "Hotel security isn't responding. Are we on camera?"

"Nah." He pulled a tablet out of his shirt. "I took care of that."

I relaxed a little. "I'd rather not leave him here. Any ideas?"

"Yeah." Tony handed me the tablet and said, "I know a place we can stash him for a while." I grabbed the bodyguard's gun and ran up one flight to retrieve my case, while Tony put the dude over his shoulders in a fireman's carry and descended the stairs. "If anyone asks, he's passed out," Tony said as I caught up with him.

"Right." Even though his head swung too loose to be normal.

On the first level, Tony entered the mechanical room off the stairwell and dumped the body up against the wall. Outside the room, I peered through the stairwell door's window to the lobby and saw security gathering at the main doors and front desk. For me? No easy way to know.

"What's going on in the lobby?" I asked.

Tony checked his tablet feed. "Not sure. The cameras are still blocked, but let's not take any chances. Follow me out back."

Good thing about that second car option. Tony led me through a maze of back corridors and out a service door. The tan Kia waited a few yards away.

"Thanks, Tony."

A moment later, I pulled out of the parking lot and went on my way. At the first red light, I texted Chief. *Problem solved with complications. All good. Report to follow.*

Two problems solved in two weeks. I needed a rest.

CHAPTER NINE

My official title was Junior Investigator, but my unofficial title was Problem Solver. They stopped calling me rookie after a year though I still heard it from time to time. When I wasn't solving problems, I gathered intelligence or obtained evidence. I helped build cases, but I didn't arrest anyone. Much of my job was all about intel and staying under the radar.

Once I asked, "Why doesn't the government arrest and try these people?" Chief told me that using legal means to gather enough of the right kind of evidence was a long and expensive process, and so were trials. Even though I drew a nice salary, it was nothing compared to what a trial costs. When the government did try some of those people, it was always very publicly. It drew the public's attention away from other stuff, and it showed the nation they were vigilant, but too much of that, and the public got scared. They clamored for war, the stock market tanked, and weirdos came out of the woodwork. It made our allies nervous, and enemies saw chinks in our armor. Or that's how he explained it to me.

At home, I showered, packed my disguise to return to Miss Chickie, and wrote my report. Chief texted me to arrive on

Monday at 1000 for debrief. I planned to tell him I needed a week off before my next assignment.

While dressing, I wondered if the bodyguards found Martinez yet but shook the thought from my brain when my stomach grumbled. It was time for dinner.

A few nights ago, I had emptied the pockets of my jacket and found a bunch of change. I glanced at the coins, and one was a 1954D Wheat penny. I had no idea if it was worth anything, but I had set it aside for Elroy.

He was always going on about *this coin was worth this much* and *that one was so rare*. All day long he checked the change in the cash drawer looking for the one coin that would make him rich. I fingered the penny in my pocket while walking across the street. Elroy lifted his head at me when I came into the diner and pointed to my favorite booth. Good man, that Elroy.

I ordered the special and settled in to read my book. I had a thing for epic fantasy. Maybe because it was so far removed from my real life.

Elroy brought my dinner. "I see you ordered the cherry pie, but I got you the blueberry. The cherry ain't so good this time." He put down a second slice of blueberry pie for himself and sat across from me. "Hope you don't mind, but I got to get off my feet a minute."

I shrugged, pushed the penny I found across the table, and started on my pork chop. "Why did you put green beans on my plate?"

"You need a vegetable," Elroy said, peering at the coin. "Eating only meat and potatoes gives you constipation."

Well, shit. Literally. "I'm fine."

"You say that now, but in a few years, you're gonna sing a different song."

I shrugged again, my go-to gesture. "The coin worth anything?"

He grunted. "Not really. It's not in mint condition. Might be worth fifteen cents. If it were mint, might be worth three dollars or so."

"Too bad. You can keep it if you want."

"Thanks for thinking of me." Elroy pocketed the penny, and I ate a few beans to keep Elroy off my back. He finished his pie then leaned back with a contented smile and half-lidded eyes.

"You got a boyfriend?" he asked.

What the hell? That came out of nowhere. "No, and don't want one."

"'Cause I got a nephew. Been to restaurant management and culinary school. Gonna make himself a nice living."

Elroy thought I'd be suitable for his nephew, the chef? "No thanks. Can I have a coffee to go?"

"Sure 'nuff, Raine." He stood. "I'll have it ready at the register for you."

I went home and started drinking. The more I drank, the sadder I got, and the sadder I got, the more I thought about Daniel. I lost all control over my mind. Daniel dead, me crying over his body. His blood soaked my clothing and one side of my face. Someone was yelling for the police. In a panic, I grabbed Daniel's wallet and keys, and then I ran.

I didn't know much, but I knew better than to stay in Daniel's condo inside a block of converted Victorian buildings. I was in and out in ten minutes, gathering only Daniel's spare gun, the emergency cash he had hidden in the wall, and a backpack with some clothes. I picked the lock to the condo next door which windows to the street out front. It had been vacant since old Mr. Wilczynski died a month before. After a quick shower to wash away the blood and change my clothes, I watched out the front window. Within minutes the Zhiglovs arrived.

From the fire escape, I watched as those Russians ransacked Daniel's place. I memorized their faces, their cars, the license plates. When they left, I went down the fire escape and got on the motorcycle Daniel had just bought me. I followed the Russians to Nick's Bar, a three-story, stand-alone building, in Hyattsville, MD with the bar on the first floor. It looked like the kind of place only regulars went into. A few minutes after they entered, lights showed on the second floor. I backed off to think about my next move.

A few hours later, again hiding in Mr. Wilczynski's empty condo, I watched a different group of people enter Daniel's place. They looked just as rough but treated his things with more respect. They took some items away with them, including some of my stuff, and they lifted our fingerprints. One guy even took samples of hair from the furniture. I memorized their faces too.

It took me almost two weeks to accomplish what the office later taught me to do in a couple of days. I commandeered Daniel's second stash of weapons, ammo, and money hidden in the basement of the building. I studied the bar where the Russians hung out, all the faces, all the exits, how many went in, how many went out, what time of day, and for how long. I was going to kill them.

Those memories slammed me hard. I kept drinking until I passed out, spending the rest of the weekend nursing a hangover in a self-pitying sulk. Trying to pull myself out of it, I texted Connor, but he didn't text back. As a last resort, I crawled into bed and stayed there until Monday morning.

When I made my way to Chief's office on Monday at 1000, I found Tony Delgado sitting in my waiting chair. He had a good rep around the office and was great with tech. I wasn't sure how long he'd been with the DSS, but he looked like he was early thirties, dark hair, brown eyes, and a V-shaped extra-fit body type. Andrea leaned forward listening to him with her new pearl ring on her finger, and Chief stood in his doorway. Even Charlotte stood next to Andrea's desk.

Tony saw me first and said, "Hey, Thompson! Guess how long

it took those three dumb motherfuckers to find out their boss was dead? Guess!"

"I can't."

"Three hours! They let him lay in that tub for three hours!" Tony held his sides laughing. "That's what the fool gets for hiring inexperienced bodyguards."

"You erased the security footage with me? Right?"

"Of course, Thompson. Local PD is all kinds of confused about that. I was in the lobby when those two assholes got off the elevator with their suitcases. They jumped in a taxi and took off. Housekeeping found Martinez when they went in for evening turndown. Maintenance found the other guy about midnight."

So, it went off clean. Good.

Chief shook his head. "Thanks for coming in, Tony. Raine, Charlotte, come in my office for the debrief."

Chief, Charlotte, and I took an hour for the debrief. "Upstairs is very pleased," Chief said. "They really wanted that guy."

"So happy the suits approve of my work. Do you have more on the connection between him and the Zhiglovs?"

Charlotte leaned forward. "Some. They were pretty upset when he didn't show up for their meeting. By now, news has reached them of his death. We're waiting on their next move."

Chief shifted in his chair, turned to me, and said, "Tell me about the three bodyguards. We have their photos. Their names— Lamas, Cortez, and Vidal. Vidal is the dead one. Not much background. What are your impressions?"

"Inexperienced and sloppy. Nobody to worry about." We moved on to the event's implication and repercussions.

"Have the Zhiglovs said or done anything about this yet?"

"A lot of cussing. Talk about choosing another dealer. If nothing else, we ruined their day. Give it some time to shake out," Chief said, and then he wrapped up the debrief.

When we finished, I asked to speak with Chief alone. Charlotte's comment about him being protective and not confident in my work ate at me. I had tried to come up with a way to ease into the conversation, but in front of him, I blurted, "Do you prep my cases for me because you don't trust me to do a job?"

"What do you mean? I tell you when you've done a good job."

"Charlotte said I had been working directly with you and not her because you had to double check everything, like I can't figure things out for myself."

Chief leaned back in his chair. "Not at all."

"You give me all the cakewalk jobs."

"Of course. You're a rookie. Still learning."

"So, everyone knows I can't handle the tough stuff. They can't count on me."

He bobbed his head a few times while gathering his thoughts. "Thing is, Raine, you're the youngest agent I've ever trained. And the greenest. You didn't have any experience—no military or other knowledge of covert operations—when you began. With you, I started from scratch." Chief leaned back in his chair. "I guess, even though you've come a long way, I fell into a habit of double-checking everything for you. Obviously, with this last job, I eased up a little."

"So, my work is okay?"

"Your work is excellent. I'm happy with the way you've grown into your position."

"Still, Tony was there in case I messed up."

"Tony was there to back you up and to handle the tech. In due time, you'll be sent to back up Tony."

I looked at the floor while digesting that new information. He seemed straight with me. "Okay. Anything more on the Russians? Any leads for me?"

"Not yet. I told you it would be a slow process."

"Yeah. So, since you have nothing new for me on the Russians, you think I could have a little time off? Like four or five days?"

"Sure. You have time coming. Anything wrong?"

"No. A little tired. Need to unwind." I was actually ready to jump out of my own skin with tension but played it cool in front of Chief. Although I had been working for DSS for over a year, the idea of what I did for a living—that I ended people's lives— still didn't sit right with me. It made me feel like a criminal even as the office praised me for a job well done.

"If I need you for a briefing, I may have to call you in—you know—because you're taking off with short notice."

"I won't be far. Probably stay around here. If it's about the Zhiglovs, I'll be in."

"Sounds good. Stop by Charlotte's station and let her know so she can switch her priorities. Keep in touch."

At Charlotte's desk, she smiled when I said I was taking some time. "Good for you. You deserve it." She pushed her chair back from her station and twisted to face me. "Tell you what, since I missed your birthday and to celebrate the start of your vacation, let me take you to lunch."

Birthday? Lunch? I froze. She looked so happy and nice. The best way to say no was ...

"Yeah, sure." Damn. What the hell just came out of my mouth?

Charlotte's face broke into a smile, eyes wide like she didn't expect me to accept either. "Give me a moment to call in a table, and we'll go. I'll drive. I don't think my skirt would do well on your motorcycle."

"Okay." What was wrong with me? I really needed a vacation.

Twenty minutes later, we were on the sidewalk outside a fancy French restaurant where a uniformed man opened the door. Not my kind of place at all, but Charlotte looked right at home in her gray suit and pearls. Me, not at all in my leather jacket and boots.

"I asked for a table near the back wall," Charlotte said in a whisper as the maître d' led us to our seats. "I thought you'd be more comfortable there than at the windows."

What could I say? She got that right.

The place was hushed, the carpeting deep, the furniture white with gold trim and delicate looking. Real china on the tables, and the silverware felt heavy enough to be, well, silver.

I knew enough French to recognize chicken on the menu and ordered that. It was a weird sort of lunch. The other diners looked at me like Charlotte brought her diseased, exotic pet with her. I thought about blowing my nose in the cloth napkin just to give them something to talk about, but that would have embarrassed Charlotte. She carried the conversation and didn't seem to notice the stares. After, she pointed to the park across the street and asked me to walk with her for a bit. Since she paid for lunch, I said sure.

The paved path she chose wound under trees losing their leaves creating swirls of color, and the staccato clicks of her heels made a feminine contrast to the thud of my boots. The sun was warm, but the wind negated that. Charlotte didn't seem to notice any of it. She walked along with a thoughtful look and half a smile on her face. Every once in a while, she'd look at me as if she had something to say.

I waited until a pair walking the opposite direction passed us and said, "Spit it out already."

She glanced at me then said, "It's just that I'm thinking we have a lot in common, though I don't suppose you would agree."

Was she crazy? I couldn't think of one thing we had in common except where we worked. I shrugged at her.

She chuckled low then added, "I'm looking forward to working with you and getting to know you better. I'm impressed by all you have accomplished so far ... and you so young and new to the business."

I wasn't sure how to answer that. Be flattered? Brush it off? I settled for, "Chief says you're the best."

We crunched our way through a pile of leaves where the path turned to head back toward our starting point. I was ready for this walk to end and get back to the office.

Charlotte cleared her throat, letting me know she had more to say. That time I didn't prompt her to speak. She touched my arm and stopped moving. I took a step back, and she let her arm drop to her side. No one else was near us. She gave me a sad smile and said, "I know you didn't choose this career. But you never complained. You accepted these circumstances and got busy learning. You are good. I mean, really good."

"Thanks," I said looking into the distance.

"Even so," she went on, "I wish we had never met. That you had never gotten mixed up in any of this. I wish I could have protected you from it."

Protect me? What the hell was she talking about? "You didn't even know me before I joined the DSS. How could you have protected me from anything?"

"True. But I know you haven't had it easy."

"How would you know anything about that?"

"I'm good at finding intel. As Chief says, I'm among the best."

"So?" Annoyance crept into my tone, but I didn't care.

"Chief told me to investigate your past while you were in the interrogation room. I traced your life from birth until the day the DSS picked you up. Not too long ago, you were an innocent girl who played field hockey and Lacrosse and sang in the school chorus —with a solo during your senior year spring concert. You took care of your grandfather and sometimes worked two of three part-time jobs to put food on the table. I know that the DSS coerced you into this business—that none of this is by your choice."

I stiffened with all my muscles going tight. Did Charlotte's admission make me angry, sad, scared, or what? My head jumped with scattered thoughts. Just how much did she know about who I was before? It was true, I used to love singing, team sports, and having friends. But that was before. Before Pappy died. Before I found my way to D.C. When she spoke again, she rushed her words and looked right at me. "Raine, I know how important my role is to your success, your survival even, and I promise, I'll do all I can to keep you informed and safe.

"Thanks. I think we should get going." I turned and led the way back to her car feeling vulnerable and exposed. I kept telling myself she was just doing her job, but anger burned in my stomach.

We returned to her car, riding back to the office in silence. The moment the car stopped, I was out and trotting to my motorcycle. A minute later, I exited the garage and raced home where I locked the door and closed the blinds. No one could knock me off my equilibrium there.

In the corner of the main room, I kept a free-standing, heavy punching bag—my two-in-one stress relieving/training toy. A plastic bin on the floor held tape, boxing gloves, and half-mitts. I spent a couple of hours hitting and kicking my punching bag, wondering how the hell was I supposed to work with her going forward? When she knew so much about me, but I knew nothing about her. Alike? We were nothing alike.

CHAPTER TEN

Saturday morning—0700—a phone call from Chief. "Can you be here in an hour? I got a break on a problem. You remember the Chinese gang that hacked the Pentagon computers last year? You got one of the ring leaders for us, but the rest got away?"

I was technically on vacation but did promise him I'd be available if something came up. I swallowed my irritation and replied, "Yeah." The DSS was a 24/7 job. I had no choice in the matter, so I didn't whine about it. Shit happens.

"One of our west coast employees secured a location on the second in command," Chief said. "He's back in the country. We're gonna give our guy a call, so you can share what you know."

"Yeah, okay. On my way." I'd go in and all but hated getting woken up early after a late night of drinking. I was supposed to be sleeping. Yesterday, after dinner, I was restless, so I went to the dojang to work out and ended up leaving with one of the owners, Ricky. I'd known him about seven months and had been having sex with him for the last five. While he wasn't as skilled as Connor, the sex was good. I only got in around 0300.

During the ride in, I remembered how the DSS found where

that one guy hid, but the first two problem solvers Chief sent couldn't get past his security. I had watched for four days. The fucker ordered food from the same Chinese restaurant every evening at 1900 hours. An analysis revealed that I had a similar body outline to the teen boy who delivered the food each time, which kinda irked me. The office gave me a taser that looked like a cheap cell phone. I intercepted the order, tased, and drugged the delivery kid. Then I took his clothes, put on a wig to match the kid's hair with his baseball cap, and delivered the food. I kept my head down and damn if that idiot mark didn't open the door himself saying, 'About time you got here.' I put one in his chest, then one in his head. Now, there was a chance another of the gang would get eliminated.

I rolled into the office five minutes late on purpose—just to let Chief know I wasn't a poodle jumping through hoops. Even though I was. The aroma of coffee and food reached my nose, and though I was a bit hungover, my stomach rumbled for food. I should have hit a drive-thru for breakfast too.

Chief had left his office windows clear, and the door stood ajar. I knocked and walked in. A moment later, Charlotte entered and set out coffees and breakfast sandwiches. Chief got a biscuit with egg, cheese, and bacon like he preferred, and I got a muffin with egg, cheese, and sausage like I preferred. How did Charlotte know that?

"Thanks," I mumbled to her. Of course, she smiled in return. Whatever. Even at 0800 on a Saturday, she wore a suit and heels. Make-up too. All I did was put on yesterday's clothes, brushed my teeth, and the top layer of my hair. They were lucky they got that much out of me.

Chief dialed the west coast agent, and Charlotte retrieved my original report. We helped the guy set a plan of action. Though the three of us had talked for over an hour, I didn't learn the guy's name, nor he, mine. The office was strict about that. Chief had said they only let us get to know one or two other problem solvers for better security. One of us getting caught and interrogated wouldn't compromise the whole office. Can't reveal what you don't know.

Charlotte excused herself, and I stayed to see if Chief needed anything else. We talked for a few minutes then I hit the bathroom before going home. Charlotte was still in there leaning over a sink. I saw blood and froze.

She waved to me without turning her head. "Just a nosebleed. Would you please hand me some paper towels?"

I'd dealt with nosebleeds before for myself and others. At the dojo, sometimes we got carried away and hurt each other. It had happened on the job too. Only once with Connor when my heel connected with his nose. He wasn't upset since it was an accident. It wouldn't have happened if he hadn't twisted me up like a pretzel. My hips can only swivel so far before they spring back.

I pulled a wad of towels from the dispenser and gave them to her. Both her hands and the sink were a bloody mess. I grabbed a few more towels, held them to her nose, and pinched.

"If you have any blood in your mouth, spit, don't swallow."

"Okay," Charlotte said in a voice muffled under the towels. I squeezed her nose for a good two minutes before letting go. The bleeding stopped.

"Thanks, Raine. I—" She cut off when Andrea's voice drifted in from outside the door. "Darn it," Charlotte said. "She's coming in here, and I don't want to answer any questions. Help me clean up." She furiously wiped at her face making an even bigger smear.

What was the big deal about a nosebleed? Then again, Andrea was annoying. She'd make a big deal of it to the whole office.

"Stop," I said. "Too rough. You'll make it start again." Andrea's voice came closer. "Get in a stall. I'll take care of it."

I grabbed the bloody towels, swiped some blood off Charlotte's face and smeared it under my nose, scooped up some more blood from the sink and added it to my upper lip. The outer door pushed open, and Charlotte slammed the stall door shut. I turned to face Andrea who stopped in her tracks when she saw me.

"Is that blood?"

"Yeah. Took a hit yesterday at Tai Kwon Do. It's bleeding again."

"I hate blood. It makes me queasy."

She hated blood and worked in this office? "If you don't like it, go use the fucking men's room." I put as much attitude into those words as I dared. Andrea couldn't get out the door fast enough.

I turned on the water and washed the sink and myself. Charlotte left the stall and washed the blood from her hands and face at another sink. To hide the evidence, I squished the bloody paper towels into a ball, wrapped a bunch of clean ones around them, then stuffed the ball deep into the middle of the trash can. When Charlotte hugged me, I nearly jumped out of my skin.

"Thank you, Raine," she said, pressing her face into my neck and taking in a shuddering breath.

She didn't release me right away even when I kept my arms at my side. Jesus.

"I really appreciate your help," she said finally letting go.

She straightened her clothes and went back to her desk. I went into the stall she used because I still needed to pee, and I wanted to make sure no stray drops of blood were in there. If anyone knew about blood trails and caution, it was me.

When I left the bathroom, I paused at Charlotte's station before leaving. "You staying or headed home?"

"As soon as my hands stop shaking, I'll go home." Her whole body trembled. She looked like a hot mess.

"Want me to drive you home?"

"I don't think I can balance on your bike right now."

"I could drive you in your car."

"How will you get your bike then?"

"I'll take a cab or Uber back."

She thought for a moment. I expected Charlotte to say she was fine; instead, she said, "I'd appreciate it if you'd drive me home, and then you can take my car home with you and just pick me up for work tomorrow. Your bike will be fine here overnight."

That was true. The office was more secure than my apartment lot. I didn't remind her about my plans for a few days off. One more day, no big deal.

"Yeah, okay. Ready?"

Charlotte picked up her purse and coat then followed me to the garage. We didn't talk much on the ride. She mentioned my chapped lips. I told her they got that way in the cold weather, being on the bike and all. It was time to switch to my Jeep Cherokee full-time since motorcycles didn't do so well with the ice and snow. At her door, she gave me a sad but stoic smile, squeezed my arm, and got out.

At home, I jumped into the shower. I never admitted it out loud, but I didn't like having anyone's blood on me. It happened, was part of the job, but I hated it because it reminded me too much of Daniel's blood.

I pushed away the memories and pulled up a parkour route on my phone. A lot of people at the office and dojang practiced it. I had run intermediate parkour routes for the past year and then advanced to higher surfaces. I figured it was only a matter of time before I found myself running for my life. I banked on parkour to give me an edge.

I ran alone. It was easier that way. People were a lot of responsibility. You had to be nice to them, even when you were pissed-off. You had to stay in touch and talk about stuff. Most of the stuff in my head was too dark to share with anyone.

CHAPTER ELEVEN

That evening while I poured a whiskey, my phone chimed. It was a text from Charlotte, asking what time I'd pick her up the next morning. I replied 0730, drank, and poured some more.

During my first months with the office, I had worked hard, studied hard, and did my best to keep busy. When I slowed down, I thought about Daniel's death and about my situation. About how I continually trained to be a better killer, how I was alone in the world, and how I killed people in cold blood. On nights like that, it was hard to fall asleep without the whiskey's help.

The next morning, I pulled up to her Georgetown apartment building, using the shallow half circle her building had in front of it for picking up and dropping off. Charlotte waited on the sidewalk. I stopped in front of her and put the car in park, thinking she would come around to the driver's side and exchange places with me. Before I could move, she opened the passenger door and sat. After putting on her seatbelt, she handed me a small paper bag.

"What's this?" My words came out harsh, which didn't faze Charlotte. The bag looked like a trap. Not the hurt me kind of trap.

More like the 'getting too close to exchanging gifts between friends' kind of trap.

"Open it."

Inside was a bakery cookie wrapped in wax paper. Chocolate-chocolate chip. How the hell did she know my favorite cookie? Next to the cookie were two tubes of lip balm. I scowled into the bag.

"Thank you for the ride home yesterday. I didn't know what scent of lip balm you liked, so I got both a plain and cherry."

Turning my head to her, I raised one eyebrow.

She laughed at me. "You're wondering how I know what food you like, aren't you?"

I held her in my raised eyebrow stare. Over the last couple of weeks, I discovered that Charlotte knew lots of stuff about me, meaning I wasn't half as hidden as I thought. I didn't like that feeling.

She shook her head. "Silly girl, I take care of all your expense reports. I've only ever seen you order an egg, cheese, and sausage sandwich on a muffin when you hit a drive-thru for breakfast. You like turkey and American cheese sandwiches with mayo, almost always get a chocolate-chocolate chip cookie and more often than not, steak for dinner."

The corner of my mouth twitched in what some might say was the start of a smile. "Thanks." I put my hand on the gear shift.

"Raine, a moment please." Her mood shifted. She sighed, looked down, and her hands clasped so tightly her knuckles turned white. Something heavy weighed on her mind. Shit. Now what?

"There is something I want to discuss with you that I'd rather not say anywhere near the office. Something important yet ... delicate."

What the hell?

"I feel I can trust you to be discreet," she said. "To please keep what I am going to tell you in the strictest confidence."

And suddenly the reason for the friendliness, smiles, and gifts became clear. She wouldn't be the first person to think I'd help her out with ex-husband or boyfriend trouble. Anyway, what else could Charlotte want? I kept the car in park and waited for her to speak. When she did, she wouldn't look at me.

"Raine, I have a brain tumor. Large and inoperable. It's killing me. I haven't told anyone at the office yet."

She just blurted that out in a calm and steady voice like she was talking about something ... I don't know ... not deadly. I snapped my head to her then put my eyes back on the steering wheel and said, "Sorry to hear that." I wasn't expecting anything like what she said and didn't know why I needed to know it. We weren't friends. We barely knew each other.

She took a deep breath and added, "It's going to take me a long time to die, and it's going to be difficult. First, I'll begin losing my memory. I'll lose my ability to walk, to care for myself, even the simplest of tasks." She lowered her head. "Loss of memory, loss of physical functions ... loss of self," she said, her voice getting quieter.

"Why are you telling me this? We're not exactly friends."

"I have a favor to ask you."

"Yeah?" No, I didn't want to adopt her cat or sprinkle her ashes. She swallowed hard. I was ready to jump out of her car and bolt.

She turned to me, her face tense and sad at the same time. Her voice thickened when she said, "It won't be long before I begin to lose my ability to function, a few more months, really. When that happens, please, kill me. Quickly. Quietly. No fuss. I'd do it myself, but I won't be able to follow through. I know that. I need you. Please, Raine."

"You're kidding, right? Is this a joke? Is Chief testing me?" I leaned into her personal space, making her lean back. "You know what? You can fuck off." That bitch went and pissed me off but good.

She made a sad, little smile. "No, I'm not kidding. I'm a coward and can't do it myself. I'm asking you because you have integrity. I've heard you debating assignments with Chief. You're not in this game for some thrills or because you don't have a heart." She paused and looked into my eyes. "You're different."

"Oh, you know that, do you?" I didn't try to soften the venom in my voice. No way I'd let her see how much she had shocked and upset me.

She made a sad curve of her lips and said, "I do know that. You have a great deal of heart though you try to hide it."

She had that ... I don't know ... all-knowing look in her eyes. Kind of soft and wise at the same time, like an old, used-up, milking cow that knows the set up better than you but still lets you lead her behind the barn.

"Please, Raine, I need you to help me," she said in a firm voice.

I stared out the windshield lost in thought, not convinced that she was honest. After some seconds ticked by, I asked, "You for real?"

"Yes, I am." She kept her eyes right on mine.

"How do I know you're not setting me up?"

"What? Do you want to see my medical records?"

"Yeah, for starters."

Charlotte frowned. "I've told you something I haven't told anyone else. I'm telling you the truth."

"You know as well as I do, that in our business, truth is a flexible thing."

I strained to hear her next statement—so soft was her voice.

"This is hard enough without my integrity being questioned. I would never lie about a thing like this. If I had any hope at all, I'd fight to stay alive—even a little while longer."

I remembered the photo of a boy on her desk and asked, "What about your son? You just going to leave him behind?"

"I'm divorced and he lives in California with his dad. My son is only fifteen. No matter what, I'm not going to be here to see him become a man."

If she was betting on the kid card to untwist my heart, she was gonna lose. I retained my bad ass attitude. "Nope. Not me. I go after bad guys. Assholes. I don't do charity cases." And I didn't work without sanction either.

She leaned back on her seat and stared at nothing, clasping and unclasping her hands. The woman had a lot of nerve asking me to do that. If caught, the authorities would charge me with murder, and the office wouldn't fix anything on my account. And they'd be right not to. I'd go to jail. Or more likely, they'd look at me as a problem—one they'd solve in a matter of hours. Charlotte didn't move or speak.

"We need to get to the office," I said. "I'll get out and you can drive yourself in. I'll take an Uber there."

She pulled her hands apart. "No. You're right. I shouldn't have asked you. I apologize. Please, would you drive me in?"

A car behind us laid on its horn to get me moving already. I flipped him the bird and peeled off. I wouldn't think about what she just asked. I wouldn't. It never happened. On top of that, Charlotte had given me a cookie and lip balm. What was that about? And the lunch. Did I have to buy something for her? I hated being in someone's debt. Such a pain in the ass. I decided I could leave something on her desk when she wasn't there. Maybe flowers. She liked flowers. No way was I inviting her to lunch. She didn't look like the sandwich on a barstool type, anyway.

The nerve of that woman. She asked me to buck the office. Buck Chief, who gave me a chance when he could have sent me straight to jail. Yeah, the office taught me to kill, but they held me on a very short leash. For the best. I did my job, operated inside the rules, and tried to forget about it when I went to sleep. At fourteen months into a ten-year contract, I wasn't sure I could do that job for the rest of my life, but at that moment, I had made peace with it.

Did she really have cancer, and if she did, why did she choose me? How was I going to work with her going forward? After parking Charlotte's car, I stowed the paper bag inside my jacket and took off on my bike. I had a few days off and didn't want to waste one more minute at the office. I toyed with the idea of asking Connor to hang out with me, maybe hit the Baltimore Inner Harbor or something, but then I'd be stuck with him for two or three days. What if we didn't get along? What if he read too much into it? Never mind.

In the end, I went to the Inner Harbor area myself, saw the National Aquarium, wandered through some shops, and treated myself to an overnight stay at a hotel. In the room, I removed the holster from my belt, stared at it in my hand for a couple of minutes, then put it on the bedside table, laying a towel over it. TV, room service, and a bottle of whiskey. That was all I needed. I ordered three different desserts for dinner, let the whiskey carry me away, and fell asleep in my clothes.

I dreamed of Daniel again. In my alcohol-induced sleep, the dream twisted and spun in weird directions—past and present mixing together as if he had been there with me during training and on my jobs. I woke with a gasp, sitting straight up. My heart pounded, and tears wet my face. The only time I cried anymore was in my sleep. In the moments it took to catch my breath, I relived those first days after he died—when I first vowed to kill the men who murdered him.

Back then, I watched Nick's Bar where his killer had an apartment that served as more of a headquarters than a living space. I counted at least eight men and one slutty woman coming and going at predictable intervals, including the man who pulled the trigger, ending Daniel's life.

Thirteen days after Daniel's murder, I watched for the Russians to leave the apartment for whatever they did each morning. That day, the woman in the heels and big hair threw a hissy on the sidewalk. From my position, I couldn't tell why. It took some time for her to calm down.

When they drove away a few minutes after nine, I moved to the back of the building, climbed on a dumpster, then shimmied my way up the wall to enter through a second-floor bathroom window. My surveillance showed they always left that window open a crack. I hid in the shower behind a filthy, brown curtain and waited. Two hours later, one returned.

I had attached the suppressor to one of Daniel's guns. He taught me a .22 was best to use to kill someone, because the small bullet entered the brain but didn't leave it. It wasn't powerful enough to exit, so it bounced off the other side of the cranium and caused catastrophic damage. Two taps with a .22, and your target was dead ninety-nine percent of the time.

The man came into the bathroom and stood at the toilet. I was two feet away and didn't hesitate. One bullet to the head. I caught him before he fell and eased him to the floor, his dick still dribbling pee. Warm blood splashed my face and stained my hoodie, but I hardly noticed. Second shot to the head. Just like what happened to Daniel. Draw, no hesitation, double tap. One down.

Again, I hid behind the shower curtain and waited. Two more walked into the apartment. I peeked through the crack in the door. They turned on the TV good and loud and watched a soccer game. Two exposed heads, side by side on the sofa, yelled at the TV, their eyes never leaving the screen. Those were the two who dragged Daniel to the sidewalk. I crept from the bathroom. No hesitation. Alternated two shots each. I wrapped their heads in towels then used area rugs to drag them to the bathroom. A blanket over the sofa hid the blood stains. I wiped up the rest from the floor and tossed the mess into the bathtub. Nothing made it to the walls.

I sat on the toilet's tank, my feet on the lid next to those three dead bodies. Since I had left the window open, flies descended into the blood and gore to keep me company. From growing up on a farm, I knew first came the flies then the other insects, mice, rats, and scavenging critters. Nature knew how to clean up.

For a while, I went numb. I don't remember my thoughts during that waiting time. At noon, two more Russian-speaking men came in, snapping me back to the present. I watched them from the door's crack. They looked around and sounded like they were cursing because no one else was there. I watched them sit at the table and look at a bunch of papers. They argued. I was stone-cold calm as I crept behind. One more gone.

The other turned, freaked, and reached for the gun in his waistband. I shot him in the chest. He was still alive and tried to call for help. I put a second bullet in his heart then one in his head. That last man was the piece of shit who had murdered Daniel. More were part of the gang, but five dead, especially the one at my feet, was all I could handle. So much for a woman not being a threat. I turned to go out the bathroom window when the front door burst open.

The whiskey bottle slipped from my hand and hit the floor, spilling some. I jumped off the bed to grab it, shaking my head to push away those memories. It was 0230. On the way to the bathroom, my legs buckled, and I grasped for the doorjamb to steady myself. I splashed cold water on my face then went back to bed in a foul mood with my whiskey bottle. It was after 1100 when I woke. Those damn memories spoiled the visit. I got on my bike and left.

CHAPTER TWELVE

I took a few more days off, worked out, read, and studied. The office required I read analysis reports about the current political climate, surveillance techniques, technology updates, and criminal activity analysis. I got the Washington Post online too and started learning Russian. I didn't so much learn the language as memorize words, phrases, and whole sentences. I was getting better at understanding spoken Russian and was doing pretty good with reading and writing it. I didn't speak it well at all because I had no one to practice with, and my accent sucked.

It wasn't smart to approach the Russian community for lessons seeing how interconnected they were, and I couldn't have them get to know me. Chief once mentioned hooking me up with some folks at the CIA, but nothing came of that. The office wanted to keep me a secret even from the CIA. The translation program at work gave us decent interpretations, but I wanted to be able to take care of myself.

I had a pretty good memory for facts, lists, and faces. In high school, I hardly had to study as long as I paid attention in class.

Chief called it a prodigious memory. The first time he said that I looked up the word to see if I'd been insulted or not.

On the second night at home, I pulled out my study binder but didn't open it. I was sick of reading about the world's problems. Sick of wondering how little, old me was going to make a dent in that mess. I needed a break, so I texted Connor who texted back saying, 'Come on over.'

When I got there, he was on the phone, talking about dosages and side effects of some drug. He signaled one minute and paced, which gave me the chance to watch him—how he walked, held the phone.

He used a different voice. A doctor's voice—one he didn't use with me even when he was doctoring me. His face looked more serious. It was easy to imagine him in a hospital, wearing a white coat, surrounded by other doctors. That view of Connor reinforced the idea that if it weren't for his circumstances, he'd never have anything to do with the likes of me. He'd be with some perfectly educated woman with nice manners and polished nails. They'd go out to fancy restaurants and shows and stuff. She'd fit right in with the other doctor's wives. Not that I'd ever want to fit in with them, pretentious assholes.

To cover my scrutiny, I glanced at the medical journals on the side table. He kept up with things. Good to know. My magazines were about motorcycles, martial arts, and weapons. Stuff you'd expect in a guy's home. It was what interested me though, which is sort of a lie. If I weren't doing that job, I wouldn't have bothered with weapons journals. My hunting rifle would have been all I cared about. I picked up a novel he left open over the sofa arm. Spy thriller with agents and assassins mentioned in the description. I wondered if anything in there mirrored stuff I experienced.

Connor disconnected and turned to me, eliciting that sweet moment of anticipation. A thrill shot through my body with tingles that formed in the places I expected him to touch. I backed up toward the sofa, but Connor grabbed my wrist tight enough to hurt and pulled me straight into the bedroom. We couldn't get undressed fast enough and crashed into each other.

I let him pin me to the bed. He grabbed my wrists and pulled both my arms over my head, and his eyes narrowed. Not in anger, not in frustration, but gleaming with something akin to a beast which triggered a moment of panic in me. Adrenalin raced through my muscles, and I nearly lashed out when Conner held my arms there. I couldn't break his grip, and my mind ran through possible escape solutions. To break free, I'd have to use my knees and legs together in combination with a head butt to the nose.

The realization I could get free if I really wanted to kept me from hurting Connor. I relaxed and let him enjoy his show of power. Because of the DSS, and their training, I was on guard all the time. Why couldn't I let someone else be in charge once in a while? Anybody else, I'd have broken the hold, but it was Connor. I let him take care of me when I had gotten hurt and was unable to defend myself. If I couldn't trust him, then I couldn't trust anyone.

He breathed heavier, and I inhaled more than the usual tang of sweat. A primitive musk enveloped us that drove me crazy. Connor squeezed my wrists until I gasped and lifted my upper lip in pain. Then he loosened his grip a little until it was just right. I wrapped my legs around his waist and bit his shoulder.

It turned out to be a good time—one I wouldn't have minded repeating. After, we stayed in bed eating cookies. Casual as I was able, I asked, "Could a person with a brain tumor have nosebleeds?"

"Sure." He didn't elaborate but gave me a look like he was waiting for me to say something more.

"Oh." Maybe Charlotte was telling the truth. Still, confirmation of one symptom was no guarantee.

"It often happens in the disease's later stages. Are you having nosebleeds?"

"No. Well, I got hit at the dojang, but that's expected."

Connor grabbed my chin and peered at my nose. "Still straight." He gave it a squeeze between his thumb and index finger. "This hurt?"

"It's been weeks since it happened. I was just wondering." He looked as if he would ask another question, which I forestalled by grabbing his cock, scratching his balls, and initiating round two. Damn, he was fun. All too soon though, I had to go home and turn my mind back to my current case.

CHAPTER THIRTEEN

Soon it was Wednesday, noon, the day before Thanksgiving. I had no plans for the holiday other than to sit at home, relax, and hope no emergencies popped up. Chief invited me to dinner, and so did Cathy who was hosting a few people from the building, but I said no to both. Elroy promised to set me up with dinner as long as I went across the street to pick it up. He'd be too busy cooking for his family for deliveries.

My stomach rumbled. A bar called Kramer's was a half-mile down the street from the office. Kinda a dumpy place, which meant my kind of place, but they had decent sandwiches. And it was quiet. I could eat in peace while reading. The bartender knew me and left me alone.

Before I left the office, I stopped at Charlotte's desk to leave her some notes and saw a bagel near her elbow.

"Is that your lunch?" I figured her for the salad type.

"Yes, today it is. I didn't have time to pack, and this was left over from yesterday's meeting."

Damn it. She was sick. Maybe she was sick. I had no proof.

"Do you have your notes about the Zhiglovs recent movements?"

"Yeah. Here." I tapped my tablet and linked it to hers. "The notes are from the cameras at the vacant house. A corporation owns the house hidden behind other corporations, mostly registered in the Cayman Islands. CAIT is still working on a name."

If she did have cancer, she needed a better lunch than a bagel. My head screamed no even as stupid words left my mouth. "I'm going out for a sandwich. Want me to bring you something back?"

"Oh, Raine, you're so thoughtful. That would be nice."

I wasn't thoughtful. Not really. "So, a sandwich? The place I'm going to doesn't do much. Turkey or roast beef, American or pepper jack cheese. Bag of chips."

"Where are you going?"

"This bar called Kramer's."

"I've passed by there—but have never gone in, though. May I come with you?" Charlotte asked.

Crap. I was stuck. No meant I was a shit, and yes meant I was an idiot. Chief would ride my ass if I made Charlotte upset even if he didn't know about her condition. If she really had a condition.

"They don't have tables. Just bar stools."

She picked up her purse. "Is it okay if I drive us? I get a little winded when I walk that far."

"Sure."

Ten minutes later, we had arrived and ordered. The constant drone of the TV and the voices of the regulars meant I didn't have to talk much. At first, the three regulars stared at Charlotte's suit and heels, but because she was with me, they didn't say anything. Charlotte chatted with the bartender and another guy about some TV show like she showed up there every day. She surprised me when she ordered a stout ale.

Both sandwiches came out with sparkly toothpicks holding them together. Never saw that there before. Guess it was for Charlotte. She classed up any place she stepped into. Because it was my turn, I took care of the check, which was a new thing for me, and we left.

Charlotte said, "We still have time. Maybe a little walk to the end of the block to stretch our legs?"

Another walk with Charlotte. I didn't like the first one we took, so I gave her my suspicious look and she added, "Just a walk, no questions or favors."

"Yeah, okay," I said, shrugging.

Cars rushed by, but few people used the sidewalk. I put Charlotte on the inside and walked closer to the curb because I remembered a teacher saying that was a polite way to take care of someone smaller or weaker than you. Lost in thought, I wasn't paying attention to my surroundings as we crossed an alley.

Charlotte shrieked. A man had wrapped his arm around her neck and yanked her into the alley; his other hand put a gun to her head. Adrenalin flooded my body as I pushed aside panic. I followed, pulling my Glock, ready to kill. That asshole picked the wrong person to mess with. He dragged her behind a dumpster with the gun still to her head. I couldn't get a clear shot.

"Drop it, chica," he said. He wrenched her, and she yelped with pain. His voice. I knew it. A flash of cold slithered over my skin. It wasn't about Charlotte. He was Martinez's English-speaking bodyguard—the one called Lamas. His hair and beard were long and filthy, his clothes ragged and stained. "You made me a lot of trouble, puta. Now the jefe's people are trying to kill me for letting him get killed. Wasn't my fault."

I held my ground, didn't lower my gun.

He jabbed Charlotte's head with the end of the pistol. "You want her to die? I don't got nothing to lose, puta. Put down the gun."

Nothing to lose, he said. Worst kind of enemy. I raised the nose of my gun to the sky, both of my palms facing out and slowly set it on the ground. I still had my combat knife under my left arm and my switchblade in my boot. Stupid. Stupid. Stupid. Why hadn't I paid attention? It was my fault Charlotte was in danger.

"Kick it under the dumpster," he said.

I kicked it, never taking my eyes off him.

"They want me dead for what you did. They won't help me get out of the country."

"Let her go. You got me. She's no good to you."

"Run, Raine," Charlotte said. "I don't matter. This takes care of things." She looked right at me when she said that.

Fuck. Shit. Fuck. "Let her go." Other people didn't fight my battles.

Lamas backed deeper into the alley with Charlotte. I followed. His crazy eyes twitched like they were spasming, sweat streamed from his scalp. I believed him when he said his organization cut him loose and he had nothing to lose. He stopped near a pile of black garbage bags stacked against a brick wall. Most of the windows were boarded up.

"I've been trying to find you, and then I get a phone call saying you was in that bar real close to me. Like God put you there for me."

He pointed the gun away from Charlotte and to the sky when he said the word God. At that moment, Charlotte stomped her heel into his instep and headbutted his chin. When his arm pulled away from her neck, she grabbed his wrist and bit it.

While stunned by Charlotte's actions, I still gathered my brains enough to spring forward and tackle him, though not hard enough to knock him to the ground. His gun flew out of his hand and disappeared into the pile of garbage. Charlotte staggered a few steps away. Lamas broke my tenuous hold and pushed me back, making me stumble for footing. We both pulled a knife as I shed my coat, dropping it to the ground.

The office trained me to think fast—ran me through many

simulations. That wasn't my first time facing a man larger and stronger with a knife. He swiped the blade at my chest. Testing me. Testing my reflexes. I swerved away.

"Go, Charlotte. Run!"

I lunged at him and missed. He came at me again, and I made a good kick to his ribs pushing him back some. We circled each other, looking for an opening. I needed to get in closer then give him a target for his attention so I could hurt him. My left arm. Even if he stabbed it, that probably wouldn't be a killing injury.

I repositioned and faked a strike with my left. He didn't take the bait but aimed lower for my abdomen. I twisted, and he got my left pelvic bone, the blade sliding up and into my side. I growl-screamed at the pain, leaned in, and thrust my blade up under his sternum.

Found his heart.

Gave my knife a quarter turn.

Didn't let up until I was sure. Never leave it to chance.

The guy made a guttural noise in his throat and dropped. Pulling my knife out caused a splash of blood over my front. More gushed from his mouth. Yeah, he was dead. I staggered back, desperate to stay on my feet. The slash in my side burned. I clapped my hand over the wound, smearing my own warm, sticky blood over my hand. I hated it just as much when it was my own blood.

Charlotte ran to me. "Oh God, Raine."

"I told you to run."

"I'll call for help."

"No! No police." I put my bloody knife in its sheath and staggered a few steps.

"Are you hurt bad?"

She tried to move my hand. I wouldn't let her. "Not bad," I said through gritted teeth. At least I hoped not bad.

"I'll get the car. Can you wait here?"

I scanned the empty alley. No one seemed to watch from the upper windows. Lamas lay up against the wall in the pile of garbage bags not visible to a casual look. "Yeah. Okay."

Charlotte hurried away. I grabbed my jacket then thought about my gun. Had to get it, since it wore my fingerprints—and it was my favorite. I half dropped, half sat next to the dumpster and retrieved it. At least it hadn't slid too far under the bin. Blood seeped between my fingers. I needed a compress, so one-handed, I took off my boot to get my sock and pressed it to the gash. It turned red. I pressed harder while jamming the boot back on my foot.

Tires squealed, a horn from a cut-off driver blared, and Charlotte made a U-turn in the street. She pulled up to the alley and came to a stop, blocking the opening. Rushing over, she helped me up, carried my coat, and put me into the car. Almost flooring the gas pedal, she took off. Turned out she was a damn good getaway driver.

"I need to get you to a hospital, Raine."

"No hospital. They ask too many questions."

"Chief would fix anything."

"No. Take me home. I'm fine." The coat over my lap hid the bloody sock from her view.

"Where do you live?"

"Head west on I-66. I'll let you know the turnoff."

Damn it, she was going to find out where I lived. And shit, she probably already knew. A pothole bounced the car, and I suppressed a wince then shifted on the seat, trying to minimize the blood staining the upholstery.

"Don't worry about that," Charlotte said. She pressed harder on the accelerator.

CHAPTER FOURTEEN

Charlotte parked in the lot next to my building and wrapped her arms around me to help me inside. Thank God Cathy didn't hear us, come out of her apartment, and start asking questions. I gave Charlotte my keys to open the door, and once inside, I fell to my sofa. She kneeled and reached for the hand over my wound. Snatching the bloody sock out of the way, she then pushed back the tear in my jeans to look.

Charlotte gasped then pressed the sock back over the slice. "You've got to get to a hospital. I'll call 911," she said as she picked up her cell phone. I gathered strength and knocked the phone from her hand. She made a high-pitched squeak.

"No hospital." My voice was more growl than words.

Charlotte had two red spots on her cheeks but retained her composure. "Raine," she said, her voice taking with authority, "you need a doctor. This wound must be checked and stitched. It's much worse than I thought."

"I know a doctor. He'll come. You can leave, and I'll call him."

"I'm not leaving." We glared at each other. Expelling air, Charlotte retrieved her phone and said, "Fine. What's his number?"

Dizziness overcame me, and I fell back on the sofa. Damn it. Blood stains everywhere meant I would have to buy a new couch. "It's in my phone." My jacket lay next to me on the floor. I fumbled in the pocket.

Charlotte snatched up my blood-stained jacket not balking at holding it. She grabbed my phone, then took a step back just out of my reach. "I'm not leaving, young lady," she said. "How do I unlock your phone?"

I was in no shape to chase her. "Damn it, woman. Give me my fucking phone."

"In a reverse situation, you wouldn't leave me, and I won't leave you. Here's your choice, Missy—"

Missy? Fuck that.

"—let me help you, or I'll call 911. Then I'll call Chief."

She held her ground. Even through my anger and pain, I respected that. "Fine." I really meant the other f-word. For a moment, my anger made me forget the pain. "Open the phone with eight, two, zero, two, one." The month and year I met Daniel. "Go to my contacts and scroll to Connor."

She found him and pressed call. I put out my hand for my cell, hoping he'd answer. He did, but Charlotte wouldn't give me the phone.

"Is this Connor?" she asked.

I couldn't hear his response, though I knew he wouldn't give himself away to a stranger even if the call came from my phone. "Give me the fucking phone, or he'll hang up." I tried to shout loud enough to carry my voice to Connor's ears.

"I'm Charlotte, a friend of Raine's. Raine's been stabbed." She listened a moment then said to me, "He's pretending he's not Connor, and he doesn't know you."

Well, of course. He was careful. "Give me the fucking phone." When I got hold of it, I asked, "Are you there?"

"Raine? You okay?"

"Stab wound. Slice along the pelvic bone. Some penetration just above the top of the bone into my side. Maybe an inch. Can't get to you." My strength failed, and the phone slipped from my hand.

Charlotte snatched it and asked Connor, "What do I do until you get here?"

Connor must have answered because Charlotte nodded her head a few times and asked me, "What's your address?" She repeated my address into the phone—someone else would know where I lived—listened some more and hung up.

"He said to keep pressure on the wound, and he'll be here in twenty." She grabbed a towel from the kitchen. "Here, let me do it." She moved the sock. Blood covered her hands, and she even had my bloody handprint on her suit jacket's shoulder. "Who is this man?" she asked.

"Doesn't matter." I forced the words out through gritted teeth. "He's on his way. You can leave now."

"I know how to keep a secret, Raine. I work at the same place you do. You've kept my secret, and I'll keep yours. And his. I hope this guy knows what he's doing. Now, lay still and save your strength."

Since I couldn't make Charlotte go away, I had to trust her. Connor wouldn't be happy about it. He might walk in, decide I wasn't worth it, and walk back out again. Maybe I drifted close to unconscious because a pounding on the door took me by surprise. Charlotte put my hand back on the towel and went to open it.

Connor slid in, wearing a backpack and towing a suitcase. He locked the door behind him then his eyes narrowed when they darted toward Charlotte.

"She's okay. We work together. She's cool," I said, feeling a ridiculous amount of relief upon seeing him.

Connor didn't look convinced, but he didn't leave either.

Pulling his case behind him, he came to the sofa, glanced at my eyes, then moved my hand to look at the wound.

"Good one," he said in a sardonic tone and gave his head a shake. To Charlotte, he ordered, "Cover the kitchen table with a sheet. Get me lots of towels and a bowl of water." He opened the suitcase to put on a disposable surgical gown and gloves.

"C'mon," he said as he lifted me. Charlotte had already put a sheet on the table and was filling a pot with water. She set it on the counter near Connor and brought a sofa pillow for my head while Connor cut my jeans and underwear off. I was in no position to protest my modesty.

Charlotte stood on the other side of the table. "What can I do to help?"

"I'll tell you in a minute," Connor said.

Connor poked, pushed, and got that razor-sharp focus he always did when he took care of a wound. Under his care, I let myself drift until he brought me back with some instructions. "I'm going to clean it up and stitch you. It'll hurt. You have no choice but to take it. You know I don't have any kind of anesthesia."

"Yeah, okay."

"Charlotte. Don't hold her hands. She'll break your fingers. Roll a towel and let her squeeze that."

Connor got to work. I grunted each time the needle pierced my skin but didn't cry out. After, Connor dressed the site, cleaned me up, and made me swallow some antibiotic and a Percocet then carried me to my bed.

Connor said to Charlotte, "You can go now. I got this."

"I see you do," Charlotte answered. "Beautiful sutures. However, Raine has no food or other supplies in the house. I'll go get some and be back to look after you looking after Raine."

The dying woman was going to look after us. Then it occurred to me at that moment, I was closer to death than she was. I didn't hear the rest of their conversation because I fell asleep.

. . .

Sunlight stabbed my eyes. My mouth tasted bad, and a thick scum coated my teeth. I never had a hangover like that before. Then I moved. Pain raced from my side to the rest of my body. Somebody groaned. It was me. Memories flitted through my mind. A man's angry face, blood on my hand, a scream. Before I could sort out the images, a chair scraped the floor, and Connor came in my room.

"Easy there. Don't wreck my sutures."

"I have to pee." My voice came out hoarse and scratchy.

"I have a pee pad under you. Go ahead."

"Hell no. Help me up."

"Hang on then. Charlotte got a bedpan when she went out for supplies the other day."

Bedpan? Fuck no. Turned out I didn't have the strength to argue. Connor had the good sense to look at the ceiling while I went.

"What time is it?"

"Two p.m."

"What day is it?"

"Friday. You got hurt on Wednesday and have been out of it with a fever. You hungry?"

"Yeah." Shit. I lost two days?

Charlotte came in with a cup of broth, which she handed to Connor. They seemed comfortable together. Time to put an end to that. I kept the parts of my life segmented. First, the broth. I finished the cup and said, "Thank you both for helping. I'm good now. You can go back to your lives. Tell Chief I'll call him later." I gave them my goodbye stare.

They looked at each other and shook their heads. "Told you," Connor said.

"You didn't have to tell me," Charlotte replied. "I know this girl well enough."

Inside, I panicked. There were two too many people in my apartment. I tried again. "I'm fine—" A knock on the door interrupted me. Connor motioned shush to Charlotte and went to the door.

"Yeah?" he called.

"Raine, you in there?"

Elroy. Who called him? Why was he at my door? "It's Elroy," I said. "From the diner across the street. Open the door and tell him I'm fine, or he'll have a hissy."

Connor opened the door a crack. Elroy must have put his weight on it because Connor stumbled back.

"Raine, girl! Where are you?"

Shit. Shit. Shit. "Bedroom, Elroy. Why are you here?"

Elroy marched into my room and looked at me in bed with the covers up to my armpits. His eyes popped. "Checking on you. You've been in your apartment three days and ain't once called for food. You didn't come get your Thanksgiving mashed potatoes and gravy yesterday. I got concerned."

Thanksgiving? I'd forgotten. And Elroy kept tabs on me? On top of that, I made Charlotte and Connor miss Thanksgiving.

Charlotte said, "Oh, aren't you sweet. Raine's a little injured, but we've been taking care of her."

"Injured? Like what?" Elroy asked.

I jumped in before anyone else could. "Took a spill on my bike. Slid a little. An abrasion. I'm fine."

"Told you that bike was dangerous," Elroy said. "Glad you're okay, then. You need anything?"

"No." My stomach rumbled. All three heard it.

"I'll just run back across the street and get you a steak. I got some left-over potatoes and gravy too." Elroy made to move.

"No steak," Connor said. "Her stomach isn't ready for it yet. How about some scrambled eggs?"

Charlotte jumped in. "I brought eggs the other day and bread and butter too. I'll whip it up in a jiff."

"Just so's you all know," Elroy said, "I been making eggs and toast since I became a cook at fourteen. Does this girl even have a frying pan?"

Charlotte and Elroy left the room as they talked about eggs and pans. Three too many people were in my business. How was I going to get rid of them?

Connor sat on the bed. "Raine, honey, you can't move yet. You can't take care of yourself." He put his hand to my face. "I know you don't take help well, but if you don't this time, I'll have to send you to the hospital. Do you want that?"

I let my glare do my talking. Connor dropped his hand and shook his head. "Tell you what. You eat their eggs, and I'll get rid of them. It'll be you, me, and the TV. Deal?"

I tensed my leg and abdomen muscles to see how hurt I was. Black appeared at the edge of my vision leaving me no choice but concession. "Yeah. Okay. I only need one more day."

"I don't think you realize how bad you're hurt."

Damn it all. And what about Chief? My face must have shown my thoughts.

"Don't worry. Charlotte fixed it with your boss," Connor said.

Two days had gone by, and other people had been in charge of my life. That terrified me more than a bullet. I forced myself to calm down. If I reinjured myself, it'd take longer to heal and longer to get rid of everybody. I lowered my head. "Deal."

I ate the eggs, allowed Charlotte to change the bed sheets, and told Elroy it was okay to come back later with dessert. He promised a double helping of butterscotch pudding, which sounded worth the trouble of having him in my apartment. Connor kept his promise, used his doctor voice, and sent everyone on their way.

I called Chief. He said by the time Charlotte phoned him, the local PD was all over the site. He was monitoring the situation, but so far, the cops had no clue about who took the dude out. They did get a sample of my blood and therefore had my DNA. Also, I left a partial bloody handprint on the dumpster. Those were worries. Chief said he'd handle it. Disconnecting, I did my best to stifle a yawn.

"Nap time," Connor said. "Lord knows, I need one too."

He settled me on one side of the bed and got in the other side. I suppressed a protest. He was giving up days of his life to doctor me. Who was I to tell him he couldn't sleep in my bed?

As I drifted off, he said, "So, this is how I get breakfast with you."

The next day, I could move some, and Connor gave me a cane. I made my way into the living room and scanned it. Everything was in place other than some dishes in the drying rack. My phone was attached to its charger, and my coat hung on its hook. I reached for my coat and took it to the table.

"What'cha doing?" Connor asked.

"Where's my gun? My knife?"

"Your gun is in your bedside drawer. I removed the magazine. Charlotte washed your knife and sheath, and they're in the drying rack."

"Thanks." I pictured Charlotte, in a skirt and heels at the sink with a sponge, cleaning blood off my knife. That must have been a sight. I checked my coat to see how bad the bloodstains were. To my surprise, I saw only the edges of where they'd been.

"Charlotte cleaned your jacket and sofa too. We threw away your jeans and T-shirt—you know—because I cut them off you."

"That's okay." Under other circumstances, that explanation would have gotten my libido going. I rummaged through one of my coat's zipper pockets, looking for my things. They weren't there. Panic rose in my gut.

"They're over on the kitchen counter, Raine."

I hobbled my way to where Connor pointed and relaxed when I found my talismans sitting on a saucer to one side. Charlotte treated my silly, little good luck charms as if they were important. I wasn't really a superstitious person, but those two items meant a lot to me. The first was a squashed shotgun shell. Pappy dug it out of a tree the first time I hit the bullseye with the shotgun he bought me when I was twelve. The gun was second-hand but was a real good one. He was proud of me that day. The second item was his Christmas present to me when I was fourteen. Soon after, my daddy died. It was a small, heart-shaped river stone worn smooth by the current. He etched 'Pappy loves Sarah' into the surface. To anyone else, it was trivial, but to me, it was proof someone had loved me.

Connor looked from over my shoulder. "Who's Sarah?"

Damn it. I never meant for anyone to see my stone. I could have lied but chose to trust Connor with the truth. "Sarah is my given name. I never use it."

"Was it your dad or granddad you called pappy?" he asked, continuing with questions I didn't want to answer.

"My granddad. He raised me. Died of a heart attack a while ago."

"He must have been a good man."

"To me, he was." We weren't the most popular family in the area. No church, no steady work, no pretty house. Pappy was kinda surly to anyone from town and didn't like people getting up into his business. Maybe because he couldn't read much. His voice was rough—his hands were gentle. Gentle when he helped me dress as a child, gentle when he bandaged a hurt, gentle when he put his arms around me to help hold my first shotgun. His absence still hurt. I picked up my talismans and walked them to my nightstand, so I could hold them when I needed to. I returned to the kitchen and lowered myself into a chair.

"Thank you for taking care of me and staying here." I looked at Connor sideways, suddenly shy to face him head on. I hadn't spent that much time with any one person in a long time. He came and gently hugged me to his chest.

"When Charlotte phoned, I got worried. Then when I arrived here and saw how bad the wound was, I almost called the paramedics."

"I'm glad you didn't."

"I know how tough you are. I'm glad you're okay. I wouldn't want to lose you." He stroked my hair. I weakened and leaned into him. After a minute, Connor let go and pulled the other chair to me. He sat and took my hands. "How did this happen? Charlotte wouldn't tell me. She just looked at the floor and then went and cleaned something."

I froze my face. By orders, I couldn't tell him. Besides, if he knew what I really did for a living, he'd run for the hills. "I'm not allowed to say."

"Is it your job?"

"Yeah."

"And Charlotte's too?"

"Charlotte works in the office. I work in the field. She got caught up by accident."

Connor nodded, but his face looked puzzled. "You can trust me."

"And I do. But I'm under orders."

He didn't look happy about my refusal. Instead of pushing, he changed my dressings. The next day, he checked me over and started saying something about two more days. When I insisted that I was fine, Connor packed up his stuff and went home.

That same afternoon, Chief showed up at my door. His eyes took in the whole of my apartment in one sweep, though he was the only one who didn't comment on its sparse furnishings. He held up two coffees and a bag that I suspected held donuts. With a bubble of excitement over the unexpected treat, I hobbled to the kitchen table where we took seats.

"Checking up on me?" I asked.

Chief unfolded the bag, offered me the open end, and invited me to choose a donut. "I'm seeing for myself you're okay and on the mend. Plus, we got one other thing to hash out."

I furrowed my brow and tried to guess what pitfall was in front of me. "Is there fallout from my kill because it wasn't sanctioned?"

"No, not that. Lamas was scum. He's no loss. I mean, who's the doctor who took care of you? And don't say nobody."

I already figured I wouldn't get away with a none of your business attitude, but how to deal with Chief and still protect Connor? Too much time stretched out while I raced for something to say. I found nothing but the truth in front of me.

"He's my ..." Not boyfriend. Not acquaintance either. "He's my friend. He doesn't know who I work for. And he's discreet."

Chief did the squinty-eyed, nose pinch thing. "You mean Connor Desjardins, formerly, M.D., stripped of his license, who now provides medical care to the wealthy underbelly of the city?"

Silence built until I said, "I guess you know all about him?"

"Of course. Didn't know you knew him until now."

Damn, Chief was good. "Is my knowing him going to be a problem?"

"Who introduced you to Desjardins?"

"Walters back when I took that bullet graze to my shoulder."

"You know, the DSS has agreements with two or three other doctors."

"Yeah, I know."

Chief made a heavy sigh. "Whatever. You need anything? Food, prescription?"

"No, I'm fine."

"I'll see you in the office in a few days then." He left without saying goodbye or looking back.

CHAPTER FIFTEEN

Two weeks went by fast. Elroy kept me fed. I ate a lot of suppers at the diner just to get out of my apartment. Elroy ate his whole meal with me, not just dessert, sharing funny stories from his days as a Navy cook and making me laugh. Some of the building tenants brought me cookies and soups. Turned out, Charlotte met Cathy and told her about my "motorcycle accident", damn it. All the food gifts meant I had to say hi to everyone whenever I saw them.

I had healed well, and after two weeks, I didn't need the cane anymore and drove myself to the office in my Jeep Cherokee. I loved my motorcycle, but the SUV had heated seats and cup holders.

When walking the tunnel on my way to the office elevator, the warning signal sounded. I ducked into one of the hiding spots along the smooth wall that was just big enough for two. A ten-inch screen built into the wall let me see what was going on outside. I assumed CAIT also could see me with a camera, though I didn't bother to look for one just then. Instead, I reached for my gun.

The elevator doors opened. Chief and three suits, one not from our office, stood inside. They entered the tunnel, and Chief brought up the rear. The outsider suit was FBI Deputy Director Wayne. Why was he here? Although we worked closely with the FBI, often pretending to be them, the two agencies tried to maintain a healthy distance.

As Chief passed my position, he gave me a jerk of his thumb gesture. Eyes on the cameras must have told him which hidey hole I had chosen. After they cleared the tunnel, I continued into the office.

The elevator came to a bumpy stop at Chief's floor, making me wince. I limped my way toward my usual chair then stopped short. Jack Miller, or Janky Jack Miller as I called him, sat in my waiting chair, smirking at me. That smug, condescending dick was with the company as a problem solver for twenty some years.

Janky Jack and I mixed it up more than once over the past year. He told me he knew more ways to kill me with his bare hands than I had years on earth. I did one job with him back in my early days. He grabbed my tits. I kicked his balls. We almost botched the job because the mark noticed us and bolted. I chased the target around the back of the warehouse, shot him, and gathered Jack off the ground, then we took off.

Although he cut me some slack for not abandoning Jack, Chief declared he'd never put us together again before he gave me a long-ass lecture and docked my pay. I didn't know if Jack got the same treatment and that irked me.

Chief should have warned me Jack was there. At least a text? I was always on guard when dealing with Janky Jack Miller. My body stiffened and took on a defensive posture.

He had cut his gray-shot hair so it stood in spikes all over his head. The shit grinned at me with his tiny, square teeth. "Good morning to you, little Raindrop. And how is our girl-wonder of the DSS?"

Without answering, I slid my eyes to Andrea's desk where she fussed over a vase of flowers. Jack was always sucking up, bringing

Andrea flowers or chocolates or some cheap-ass piece of shit. Apparently, he had once been Andrea's father's protégé before her father and mother got killed on the job.

"Heard about your slip-up—getting yourself stabbed," he said. "If you ask nice, I'll give you some pointers."

Behind her desk, Andrea nodded and said, "You should take Jack up on his offer. He's the best we've got around here."

I maintained my bitch face and didn't speak.

Jack made a nasty smile. "Now don't be that way, sweetheart. Give us a big rainbow smile."

My hand curled into a fist. I had already played the alley fight over in my mind more than a hundred times trying to understand what I could have done better, quicker. I came up with nothing except having positioned myself closer to the alley while keeping Charlotte closer to the street. Then he would have grabbed me. Then it would have ended much differently.

I didn't need Jack in my face and opened my mouth to let him know. Before I spoke, the forensics expert from upstairs, Shepherd, took my arm in a grip that was tight enough to let me know he was schooling me. "Raine, Charlotte has some new intel for you. Go see her." Though he spoke mildly, I knew a command when I heard one.

I hadn't worked much with Shepherd before, though he seemed a decent sort. He was a former military guy who seemed to be a younger version of Chief. I broke eye contact with Jack and turned to limp toward Charlotte's station. She seemed engrossed with something on her computer screen. Shaking off the tension, I tried a joke.

"Is that Amazon?" Not much of a joke.

She looked up and gave me a smile. Guess I was getting used to that. I didn't smile back but didn't flinch either.

"Raine. Good to see you looking so well. I've been worried about you."

Why would she worry about me? "I got your texts. I answered them." One-or two-word answers. She's lucky she got that much.

"That's not the same as seeing you up and walking around." She peered hard at me. "Your coloring looks good. Here. For you." She handed me a wrapper with a chocolate-chocolate chip cookie. "Welcome back."

"Thanks." Another gift cookie. It was like Charlotte didn't understand about boundaries or didn't care about my boundaries. I didn't know how to go about reminding her that all I wanted was a professional relationship. Considering the way I lived my life, I didn't really deserve a friend. I took the cookie with one hand and reached into my pocket with the other for an envelope. "Here. Paying you back for the food and stuff you bought when I was hurt." The food, medical supplies, bedpan (now in the dumpster), a cane, some pots, and cooking tools, among the items. The cleaning up of blood from my jacket, the sofa, and her car seat.

"Raine, you don't have to."

"I can't owe a debt. I can't." I thrust the envelope of cash at her. "Here." Just like my pappy, I preferred using cash.

"All right, Raine. I understand." She took the envelope and tucked it into her purse. I turned to go. "Raine, a moment, please." Charlotte leaned toward me and lowered her voice. "Chief asked you and me to wait for him in the conference room."

I looked to Chief's darkened office with narrowed eyes then at Janky Jack again. He watched me with that smug, leering expression of his. I fumed but didn't engage the shit. As Chief once told me, live to fight another day. How did he come up with that stuff?

"Yeah. Okay." I bet Charlotte was relieved I agreed so easily.

"You go on ahead, and I'll bring along some coffee for us."

Charlotte wanted me out of the way fast; I didn't blame her. Cookie in hand, I limped to the conference room. She arrived a few minutes later, carrying a tray with two coffees, a cookie for herself, and her tablet. Was Charlotte born sweet and efficient or did she study to be that way? I had no idea.

Both my feet were up on another chair as it eased the pull on my side. She didn't seem to care and maybe she never did. Maybe she stared at me the first day I spoke with her because she knew we'd work more closely and not because my feet were on the furniture.

"Are you okay?" I asked. It hit me that I was a jerk because Lamas held onto her for a few minutes and roughed her up. I had never asked.

"I'm fine, Raine. After you fell asleep, I told Connor a little of what happened, and he checked me over. Just a few bruises. No worries." She looked at her cup, and then asked, "Is it often like that for you out there?"

Yes. No. Not exactly. "First time that's ever happened. He was a witness to the Martinez job even though I don't like to have witnesses. Orders said to leave them alone if I could, so I mostly did."

I was sorry I didn't take them all out that day in the hotel. I could have. Chief informed me that the office didn't know where the other one hid or if he was out to get me either. I hadn't forgotten that shit Lamas said he'd gotten a phone call about where to find me. Who the hell phoned him with my location? Did those jerks know where I lived or hung out? What if they spotted me before I spotted them? I had more questions than answers. Chief told me to lie low until he sorted stuff out.

"Did you tell anyone where we were going for lunch that day?" I asked.

"Only Chief and Andrea. I didn't speak to anyone else about anything."

Somehow, information had leaked out. I set those thoughts aside for the moment and shifted my focus. "Charlotte, you were pretty awesome stomping and headbutting Lamas. Really badass." I grinned at her and didn't try to hide it.

"That's me. Badass." She laughed, then with her voice almost a whisper she said, "There was my big chance to let Lamas take care of my problem, and instead of accepting it, I fought back."

Our grins faded away. She said, "It's not that I want to die. But since I have no say, I want to go my own way. That one thing will be in my control. That, and I couldn't bear to see you get hurt. Speaking of which, you were pretty badass yourself."

I looked away. Badass in a job that made me feel guilty for each life I took.

Out of nowhere, Charlotte said, "Your boyfriend is really handsome. And a good doctor. Have you two been together long?"

Huh? Where did she get that idea? "He's not my boyfriend. I don't have those."

"But you do have a close relationship."

I took my feet off the other chair and pulled my limbs closer to my center, crossing my arms in front of my chest. Why was she all up in my business? The best defense was a good offense. I heard that somewhere and decided to mess with Charlotte a little.

"He's just a doctor who takes care of stuff without questions or alerting the authorities. And he's a fuck buddy. That's all." I anticipated she'd choke on her cookie.

Instead, she said, "I had one of those once. Right after my divorce. Mmm. Connor's a good choice for that."

Her words almost made me choke on *my* cookie. I covered by taking a gulp of coffee.

"What?" she said with sass in her tone. "Am I too much of a priss to have a fuck buddy?"

My world turned upside down. Charlotte said the word fuck in an ordinary conversation and told me she liked to fuck. I looked to the door hoping Chief would appear and derail the conversation.

Nope. Leaning back in my chair all casual like I said, "I have two or three, depending on the season."

Charlotte didn't take the bait. "I think Connor is less casual about you than you know. He was terribly worried, especially when you developed a fever. He stayed next to you for twenty-four hours. Wouldn't even let me sit with you to take a nap."

My arrogance deflating, I looked at my cookie crumbs. "He's a good doctor."

Charlotte chuckled to herself and let the subject drop.

A moment later, Chief came through the door, carrying a heavy banker box. "Ladies," he said, placing the box to one side of the table and seating himself. "I saw Jack to the elevator and watched the door close, so drop your scowl, Raine."

Scowl? I wasn't making my mean face, was I? Didn't think I was. Rather than dwell on that, I said, "What's my next job?"

Chief leaned back in his chair and gave me a hard stare. "No problem-solving or field jobs for the next two weeks at least."

"I'm fine. Just need a few days—"

"Don't argue, Raine. Made the call myself. You need time to heal. To rest. I know you want to work, so I'm apprenticing you to the analysts, two or three of them. Learn how they do their jobs. You'll sit with our CAIT people too. Pick up a few more hacking skills—learn to navigate the dark web."

The dark web, where so much of the illegal stuff happened. Unhappy about getting pushed to the side when the Zhiglovs were so active, I realized learning techniques to navigate the dark web more effectively would be useful. Still, I felt compelled to protest. "What about Martinez's other bodyguard? He's still out there, y'know."

"And we're working on it," Chief said. "In fact, I'm giving you and Charlotte the task of finding him—from the inside. When you do, you'll prep another employee to deal with them."

Guess he meant Tony or Jack. "It should be me. I should take care of it." I gave him my mean face.

"We're a team here. None of us works alone, even though some might pretend they do."

Was that a crack at me? It was. I chose to ignore it. "And if I happen to come across him while going about my life?"

"You're under orders. You do not go looking for him. If attacked, defend. If in public, retreat. Remember that. Do not engage if you don't have to. No one would believe it was an accident or your finger slipped. Not you. Report the sighting and leave it to me. I mean that, Raine." He leaned forward to stab my eyes with his 'I'm the boss' look.

It got through my head Chief was serious, and I was pushing on his last nerve. "Yeah, whatever."

"It'd be nice to take him alive and get some questions answered." With that, Chief relaxed in his chair. "If you behave, I'll give you something else to work on that might hold your interest."

"Like what?"

"More intel on the Zhiglov gang."

I sat up straight in the chair, ignoring the pull of pain on my side. That alone told Chief I was interested. Daniel again. His ghost kept calling my attention. I couldn't stop myself—my mind took over, and I replayed those memories.

Fifteen months ago, after I killed five gang members on the second floor of that bar and turned to leave, the door burst open. I froze for a moment and watched tear gas fill the room. When eight armed and armored men wearing gas masks stormed the place, I turned and tried to run for the bathroom window. I didn't make it far. My eyes streamed tears, and I bent over, struggling to breathe.

They yelled orders, tossed furniture, and pointed rifles at the two bodies next to the table. Others found the bodies in the bathroom. Some guy disarmed and held me, twisting my arms behind my back. Even so, I kept trying to crawl across the floor to get away, like I ever had a chance of that. They cuffed and dragged me out of the apartment—half carried me down the stairs—and out to the street, throwing me into the back of a van. I could barely see but felt someone secure me to the van's floor with shackles. That same person then poured water into my eyes to clear the gas. I recognized his face as one from the second group who had entered Daniel's condo after the Zhiglovs murdered him.

Lonnie Capshaw, the man who would become my boss, led the team who interrogated me for three days and nights. He gave me water but almost no food. Kept me blindfolded, covered in the blood of the men I had murdered, and soaked in my own pee. They beat me, denied me sleep, and overwhelmed my senses with loud sirens, drums, and then absolute silence. They flashed strobe lights at me for ... maybe hours. When I passed out, they revived me with a bucket of icy water. After a while, I hardly remembered my own name.

I told them nothing or just said whatever came into my mind. Nonsense, lies, truth, all mixed together. Five murders. How would I save myself from jail? From those guys killing me? I wanted to live. I didn't know how to make that happen, so I retreated into my own mind and gave them nothing concrete. No confession.

Sometime on the third day, Chief broke me. I still don't know how that happened. I told him everything about me and Daniel. Every job I helped with. Every detail of our relationship. Chief believed me. Believed I was nobody and didn't know about the office or Daniel's role as an employee of the DSS. Chief was ape-shit crazy about his agent's death. It turned out, Daniel was Chief's direct report and protégé and not a criminal like he had led me to believe. But he broke every rule, having me along on his assignments.

In the end, a week and a half after they captured me, Chief and I struck a deal. If I agreed to join the DSS, they'd train me, teach me to be useful to my country. Or I could go to jail on multiple murder charges for the rest of my life. If that wasn't enticing enough, Chief let me know about the salary and benefits. The likes of me was never gonna get a better deal. The hitch? It was a ten-year indenture. I had to serve as an 'exemplary employee' for ten years, or I'd become a problem they'd solve real quick.

"Raine." Chief's voice came from far away. "Raine! You with me?"

Both he and Charlotte stared intently at my face. I snapped my head to him. "Yeah. I'm in. Where'd the intel come from?"

"Deputy Director Wayne."

"Why's he sharing?"

"Not sharing. He's under orders from high up."

"How high up?"

"Never mind that. Just know he was told to back off both the Zhiglovs and Ovechkins."

I lifted my chin at the box. "Is that it?"

"It is. God damn paper when it should be electronic. First thing, you and Charlotte move this shit to e-files then destroy the paper. Work in a vacuum. No other eyes. Got it?" We nodded. "You'll start now and cannot leave the building until everything is scanned and the paper is destroyed. Any problems with that?"

Fine. His call. Charlotte and I set up at her station and went to work. We scanned, sorted, and loaded files. After, we took all the paper to the big, confetti shredder and destroyed the records. It took eleven and a half hours with Andrea ordering food in. Exhausted, we both went home for some sleep, then returned at 0800 to start in on the intel.

The next day, I set myself up in the conference room because Charlotte was working on someone else's urgent situation. She gave me several tasks and said she would check in with me when she could.

The tech in that room impressed me, and it was always getting an upgrade. The table's entire surface was a tablet. Each seat could have its own screen, or an operator could create between one and four screens, depending on how they wanted to disseminate information. The walls were screens too, and we could write on them over top the intel, making connections and drawing out scenarios. We could film ourselves, tap into other parts of the office, or call up our remote cameras. It'd be cool to watch an epic movie in that room, put it on all four walls, sit in the center of the table, and surround myself with it. Maybe someday I'd do just that.

The first thing I looked at was the most recent footage from Victor and Sonia's house. Absolutely nothing new. Same people, same cars. Next, I sifted through hundreds of pages of monotonous reports with only tiny nuggets of useful stuff. Photos. We had the same, but I plowed through it all, looking for a diamond among the shit. Six hours later, I couldn't ignore my stomach anymore. I phoned Andrea. "I need food."

"Sure, Raine, I can get—"

"Don't care. Bring me anything." I disconnected.

Forty, stupid, long minutes later, she brought a bag to the conference room. "Thanks," I said, barely looking up from the screens. She stared at my mess with wide eyes. I had set up four different workstations and switched between them as something caught my attention. I taped stuff to the walls—photos, descriptions, some in English, some in Russian. I wrote over most of the open spaces. Aerosmith blasted from my phone because some days a body just needed the classics to stay focused.

"Ummm," Andrea said. "I'm supposed to set up this room for a meeting tomorrow morning. I'll have to move your stuff before then."

I took a sniff at the food bag. Steak, so I decided to be nice. "I'll clean it up before I leave."

"Okay. Thanks."

I was kinda pissed I'd have to move everything, but it wasn't her fault. "Thanks for the food," I called to her as she left.

I ate while continuing to study the files. Time was passing, and I was no closer to getting the evidence needed to take down the Zhiglovs.

CHAPTER SIXTEEN

From the FBI files, Charlotte and I discovered a few ideas for moving the case forward. I asked permission to stake out another business, a warehouse just over the Maryland line at the docks. Ownership on the books listed a Russian export business. Sonia's new boy toy, Alexander, was in the habit of visiting the site at least once a week—I wanted to know why. It took Chief three days to answer, and it was no.

"Why?" I was ready with data and reasons for yes.

"The DHS already has surveillance in place, and we'd just be tripping over each other. Besides, so far the place is mostly empty."

"Can't we kick out the DHS and take over?"

"A lot of work for very little gain. We'll get hold of their data."

"They gonna share?"

"Sure."

"You don't think they'll hold stuff back?"

"They might. Gotta see it first."

"Sounds like it's a race to see who's gonna take these assholes down first."

"It's gonna be us, Raine. Us. Besides, I'm not totally relying on the DHS or the FBI." Chief didn't say anything more, and I knew better than to ask. Mostly, I was glad someone else took that case as seriously as I did.

Charlotte and I spent time every day going through the material we scanned, working around my scheduled times with the CAIT team. Chief gave us an empty office, and we decorated the walls with photos, charts, maps, anything that caught our eye.

One day, Chief appeared in the doorway. "A citizen reported another body. Ovechkin. We got there before the cops and took charge. Shepherd's running the show. Why don't you head over?" Chief gave me the address, and I was out the door.

It took me a half hour to get to the alley in the Brentwood neighborhood—one of the more dangerous places in the city. It would have been more like twenty minutes on my motorcycle since I wouldn't have cared much about traffic rules.

I parked my Cherokee with the vans marked Crime Scene Investigation, blew past the vulture-like reporters, and stepped into the alley. It was a disgusting mess like any other one, reeking of garbage, piss, and littered with drug paraphernalia. Cold wind gusts blew dry leaves straight down the dim and grubby passage while broken glass crunched under my foot. I grabbed a knit cap from my pocket, pulled it on to keep my hair out of my eyes, and walked forward.

A tech stopped me, her arm outstretched and palm facing me. "Leave immediately."

"Looking for Shepherd. Chief Capshaw sent me."

The tech looked me over then said, "Wait here." She walked over to a guy in a black overcoat. Shepherd turned then waved me over.

"Hey, Raine," he said as he stuck out his hand.

"Hey," I said, shaking his hand. "Chief sent me. What do you have?"

"Yeah, I heard. C'mon over." Shepherd walked me to a corpse

inside an open body bag. I skirted an oily puddle to squat next to it. The face was gone. Large caliber bullets again.

"What's on his chest?" I asked.

Shepherd put on gloves and lifted the guy's shirt. There, we viewed the Prince of Thieves Cross and the old Russian flag with only the vague outline of a gun. The gun would have been filled in to be more visible as the guy moved up the ranks. "A lower-level Ovechkin. And no hands again," I said.

"Yup."

"Chances of getting an ID, slim to none. Fresh import, I'm guessing?"

"That's the direction I'm thinking right now. We'll know more once everything is processed."

"Any witnesses?"

"A woman who said she saw two big guys enter the alley, one of them carrying a lumpy carpet on his shoulder. She said he had arms like a young Arnold Schwarzenegger. When we got specific with our questions, the woman took off. She didn't have any ID on her, but we have her photo. We'll try to track her down."

"Is the rug still here?"

"Nope. Took it with them."

"Did they enter from this end?"

"No." Shepherd jutted his chin toward the other end. "From the south, then they turned into the alley." I went off in that direction. Shepherd called after me, "Don't touch anything."

I fucking knew not to touch anything. Nothing jumped out at me during my sweep of the alley or the street to either side. I stood just outside the opening and let my gaze roam. Across the street, a man stood on the sidewalk, both his hands in his back pockets, watching three men install a new awning over the storefront. A skinny dude, pale, balding with long wisps of hair combed over his head. His upper lip sported a mustache that was way too big for his face.

It looked like a brand-new business was moving in, seeing how ladders and painting stuff cluttered the interior of the otherwise empty store. When the man turned his back to me, I sauntered across the street, ever so casual. I didn't want to spook him, and I didn't know how I would open my conversation. There were two tens and a twenty on me. Not much of a bribe to talk.

When I got about ten feet from him, he turned and looked me up and down. His clothes had paint splatters and dark rings drooped under his eyes. The man shifted to face me, already twitching with nerves and narrowed eyes. I hadn't even spoken yet.

"Don't know nothing," he said.

Oh yeah. He knew something. "How do you even know what I'm gonna ask?"

"I watched you come out of the alley where them police is." Instead of squaring up before me like most men would, he shrank back and turned himself sideways. Above us, the three workers installing the awning seemed oblivious to our conversation.

"I'm not a cop, but I want to know what you saw." I gestured to the alley. "Were you working here all night? What happened?"

"Nothing." His voice went up an octave.

I approached close enough to smell fresh paint on his clothing. I persisted with, "You were here all night, painting. You looked out your window. What did you see?"

"I told you. Nothing."

He turned to go into the store. I ran forward, and he only got the door open an inch before I pushed it closed again. If I had better manners or more finesse, I could have charmed the information out of him. Not me. I fell back on grit.

"I see you have a new awning there," I said, jerking my head toward it. "And you're fixing up your new place real nice." He looked sideways at me, trying to edge away. I wouldn't let him. I lowered my voice and made it mean. "You tell me what you saw, and I don't throw a firebomb in your window. You tell me what you saw, and I don't ruin your pretty, new awning. Right?"

He swallowed hard, darted his eyes about, and then he spilled. "I didn't see two gorillas go in that alley, one of them carrying something big. I didn't see the other one throw something small away in that dumpster."

"The dumpster just inside?"

"Yeah."

"All right. Your place is safe. What else didn't you see?"

"Saw nothing else. Swear."

The awning guys went to their truck. I pulled out my switchblade. Not to brandish it. Just to up my cred by holding it and slapping into my palm like a nervous tick. "Don't talk to anyone else. You hear?"

"Yeah."

I got out of his way, and he hustled himself into the store. Sometimes, I was a real bitch.

At the dumpster, I climbed its side to peer in even as Shepherd walked toward me. Once again, I noticed his peculiar gait. Not exactly a limp, but something was off with the way he moved. I turned back to scan the black bags of trash, then there between two bags, a small white something. I waved Shepherd closer.

"What'cha got, Raine?"

"Don't know. Need gloves and a longer reach."

Shepherd spoke into his headset, summoning a beanpole of a man who jogged to us. He snapped on gloves and asked what I needed. I directed him to the crumpled, white thing. Marlboro wrapper. Russian label.

"Bag that and run prints. Maybe it'll match the other one I found at the overpass dead Ovechkin scene," I said.

"Yeah," Beanpole said. "I pulled the prints from the first one. I'll let you know later today."

"Raine, your new friend is waving to you," Shepherd said.

The store owner across the street gestured me over. When I got there, he said, "You really won't hurt my place? I put all my savings into it. It's all I got."

Mean face. "Are you holding back on me?"

He shifted his eyes back and forth before saying in almost a whisper, "I'll tell you one thing more. Those gorillas came back out, walked over there," he pointed about twenty-five feet away, "and got in a black sedan. Mercedes, I think. There was a pretty lady driving it. She waited in the car the whole time."

I took out my phone and scrolled to a picture of Sonia. "This her?"

"Yeah. That's the lady."

"Thanks. I won't bother you. Don't talk to anyone else, either." I returned to the other end of the alley and left.

CHAPTER SEVENTEEN

I got Christmas invitations from Chief and Elroy. Declined both. Charlotte was going to California for a few days to see her son, and Connor mentioned something about going home to see his parents in New Orleans. Cathy brought over a little plastic tree with sparkly lights. I smiled pretty for her over it, and after she left, I unplugged it and put it in the closet. Pappy used to bring in a little tree for Christmas when I was young. The year my daddy went to jail, he stopped doing that, and I hadn't had a tree since.

Chief kept me busy, training on tech equipment, and I learned from Charlotte how an analyst did their job. It wasn't as easy as I thought—sifting for clues, following ideas that led to dead ends. Sometimes, it got frustrating. I found a new respect for the education and skills of the analysts during that time. It also forced me to spend my whole day with people, something I had done my best to avoid for a very long time. It was like I had to revive a skill set I thought I had abandoned. And, while hard, it wasn't too bad. We spent most of our time on the Zhiglov situation and so far, our pitifully small dossier—even with the extra stuff from the FBI—didn't impress Chief.

He unloaded his irritations at us. "I need better than this if we want to move on these guys," he yelled. "Where are they setting up? What's their game?"

Those were the big questions we tried to answer but came up with nothing.

"I put two of you on this so we could move quick. Two brains, double the results, for Christ's sake." He slammed his coffee cup on the desk, slopping the liquid over the sides.

Chief didn't need to chastise me since I was already doing a better job on myself. Just like him, for me it was personal. Trouble was, he taught me there was no such thing as personal in our job. It was business. Take care of business, go home, start over the next day. When it got personal, employees got sloppy. Personal got us dead.

For a day and a half, I'd researched small businesses owned by Russians or Russian descendants in a fifty-mile radius of the original bar they used as a headquarters. I found a Russian freighter tied up in the Baltimore harbor at the South Locust Point Marine Terminal. Named Papa's Max, its registration belonged to a Russian conglomerate. Tracing back its true ownership had turned out to be a bitch. I mapped the connections between the businesses and tried to tie them back to the gang leadership. I didn't find much on our case but found intel the CIA, Homeland Security, or the FBI could use. Chief passed it on. That afternoon, instead of concentrating, I wondered about Connor and his strange behavior back when I was hurt.

I had let Connor stay for two days after Charlotte left, but once I could move around on a cane, I got antsy for him to leave. I mean, we slept in the same bed, shared a bathroom, started to do couple things. I refused to let myself get dragged into that. On the third day, I woke first and went to the kitchen where I made breakfast. Toaster waffles with syrup, cups of yogurt, and coffee. Charlotte had stocked me well. The smell of coffee woke Connor, and he shuffled into the kitchen with tousled hair and sleepy eyes.

"You made breakfast?" he asked, looking at the table.

"I did," I said and eased myself into a seat. "Eat while it's warm." About halfway through, I said, "I bet you're glad I'm healing so you can get out of here."

"You're hardly healed."

"I'm doing well enough. No more infection, and I can move around on my own. You don't have to hang here anymore. I know you have places to be."

"I don't mind. You need me, and I like hanging with you."

The last thing I needed was Connor getting all weird on me. He seemed like he was getting ideas, and I needed to put a stop to that. Besides, anyone I got close to died on me. Maybe I was a bad luck charm or something. "Anyway, I have some cash here, but I'll have to owe you the rest. Get me a total, and I'll have it by tomorrow."

"Raine, you don't have to pay me anymore. We've moved past that, don't you think?"

Connor was taking our relationship in an uncomfortable direction. I never gave him encouragement and always paid him in cash for his doctoring. He always had been happy to collect. I went to my secret hiding place, a fake vent in the bathroom that opened with a hidden pressure lock, and retrieved some money. I had squirreled cash away like that all over the place. I even had several thousand buried in a jar in a local cemetery. You know—for just in case. I put it behind a grave marker with the name McDonald on it. Made it easy to remember since it was my former surname.

"Here's two thousand. Like I said, I'll get to the bank in a day or two and give you a call."

Connor pushed his plate away. He didn't reach for the envelope, so I put it on the table. He looked depressed or something.

He said, "Yeah, I'll get dressed."

A few minutes later, he packed his medical suitcase. I picked up the envelope again and walked him to the door, shoving the money in his backpack. Pappy taught me to never leave a debt hanging.

I leaned on the cane and hugged him with one arm. "Thank you, Connor. Thanks for taking care of me again. I owe you one."

He sighed. "No, you don't owe me anything. You paid? Right?"

"Uhh, yeah."

He kissed the top of my head. "I'll call you tomorrow. Will you pick up the phone?"

"Yeah, I will." Strange question. Connor kissed my head again and left.

I let out a relieved breath to finally have my apartment to myself. Quiet though. Still hungry, I ate both mine and the remains of Connor's waffles, annoyed by his behavior.

People packing up to go home drew me back to the present. Four o'clock had rolled around, and the day shift left as the second shift arrived. It was December thirtieth. A lot of non-essentials scheduled off for the next day in anticipation of the holiday—another one I ignored. I'd be working.

Charlotte, one day back from California, sat back in her chair with half-lidded eyes. "Raine, I'm headed home. It's been a long day for me. The trip wore me out."

"Yeah, I hear you. Have a good night."

Because I daydreamed the last hour away, obsessing over Connor's behavior, I pulled my chair closer to the computer screen and set to work for real. The next time I looked up, it was seven-thirty. Time to hit a drive-thru and go home.

The new player in the Zhiglov picture was Alexander Boychenko. He had a juvenile rap sheet for theft and assault and no known affiliations before becoming part of the Zhiglov cartel.

The office knew next to nothing about him, which hampered our investigation. We needed to know what made him tick—who he answered to. During the first week of January, I came up with an idea.

The tech lab issued me a few of the new toys they showed me when I was in the lab with Tony. One was a biodegradable listening device which stuck to most anything like skin, fabric, plastic, or metal, and would disintegrate within three hours. Perfect. If I planted it on Alexander at the right time, we'd hear his conversations, but the bug would disappear before his next sweep, leaving no evidence behind.

Our surveillance said he and Sonia left their house at eleven and headed for the city to keep a lunch reservation at Antonio's. Something about a buyer being nervous about the product. What product? Drugs? Explosives?

With Miss Chickie's help, I had dressed as a harried executive complete with a gray-shot wig in a top knot. Gray suit, overcoat, conservative heels, and clever make-up gave me some age wrinkles on my face and hands.

The tail let me know when they were about to pull up to the restaurant. I got out of a Honda Accord, fussed with my suit until I saw them, and marched forward. Sonia walked to Alexander's right and an unknown Middle Eastern looking man to his left. My face was in my phone, and I ran into the man flanking Alexander, danced around him, and tripped into Alexander.

"Watch where you're going!" I shouted in a New York accent. "You men think you own the sidewalk!" I got that little bug stuck under his jacket lapel.

I extricated myself from their midst and continued marching down the sidewalk. They said, Американская сука—American bitch—and entered the restaurant. An office van waited just around the corner. When I approached, Shepherd popped the lock for me to get in. His tablet was already playing their conversation, and

Anderson began transcribing it for us. I had no idea Anderson knew Russian. How come nobody told me that?

We listened to Alexander speak to Sonia in Russian, angry that the buyer sent a representative instead of coming himself. To the representative though, he spoke English smoothly and calmly. The first part of the conversation was mundane. Then talk about why Alexander had delayed the meeting ... complications ... CIA and DHS interference ... worries ... soothing words. Nothing concrete. They used no names, spoke no locations. They never said what the product was. It was all just more pieces of the puzzle.

Our person inside the restaurant took photos of the representative, and the CAIT team ran facial recognition scans. All through the lunch, they called for more vodka. Always more vodka. For once, Sonia remained silent and didn't interrupt Alexander with her usual whining. Maybe he let her know ahead of time she better be quiet. I'd have to check the transcripts from earlier that day at the house to know for sure.

"We expected the government interference," Alexander said to the buyer. "Nothing to worry about. We have already set a false trail for them to follow, and they are doing just that."

"We are trusting you with a lot of money," the buyer's rep said.

"I assure you, we are taking every precaution," Alexander promised.

That was when Sonia broke in and announced she was going to the ladies' room, and the buyer excused himself to have a cigarette on the sidewalk. Alexander's phone rang. We heard only his side of the conversation, all in Russian, but it was obvious he spoke to his boss by the deferential tone he took and the half-defensive, half-assuring words he chose. Damn, but we needed to know who he answered to. The rep approached the table and Alexander hung up.

When Sonia returned from the bathroom, she joined the conversation. "All this talk of business; it is too stressful. Tonight, we go out—dancing, drinking." She pitched her voice lower and sort of seductive when she said, "We have fun and get to know one another better. No?"

Alexander broke in. "I don't think that's a good idea—"

"Where?" the rep asked.

"We go to Club Dekadent. Alexander, send a car to bring them."

"Sounds good," the client replied.

With that, Alexander had to give in to Sonia's wish without further fuss.

Me too. I'd be at Club Dekadent with them, plant a bug and tracker on the rep, and maybe discover the buyer or find out what the Zhiglovs were selling. On the way back to the office, I phoned Miss Chickie to prepare a club outfit then contacted Chief to tell him about Alexander's conversation with the stranger.

"He keeps deferring to the boss," I said. "He has to ask the boss, get okay from the boss."

"Is he calling to Russia, or are the calls coming in from Russia?"

"Not sure. We'd have to hack their cell account or get a bug on his phone."

"Then your question is who and where. Also, how to get a sensor on his phone."

I let my mind wander a bit then offered, "Maybe he's not really getting approval. Maybe he's pretending to have a boss to keep the heat off himself?"

"Always a possibility."

Great. Another possibility. That's all I needed.

Club Dekadent was a newer, high-end place located near Dupont Circle. I arrived in a black, leather bustier and sleek black stretch pants with sexy, black heels. I wore a conduction mike/receiver in my mouth, and a button on my bustier was a camera. The tech people had removed the shoe's original heels and replaced them with leather-covered titanium. In the practice gym, I had put one of those heels through the eye of a ballistics dummy, broken through the ocular bone surface behind the eye, and pushed the heel into the brain. The idea of doing that for real left me a little sick, but then again, if it came to a choice of me or them, it would always be them.

The bartender requested ID before he served me, so I showed him one of my office fakes. I only got groped twice on the ass while I sipped whiskey with water. I had arrived just in time to watch Sonia and her entourage settle themselves in a circular, red leather booth reserved for VIP's who wanted to be seen. One of the men was the person Alexander ate lunch with that afternoon. The other face, also Middle Eastern looking, was new to me. Both wore dark, conservative suits, with short, conservative hairstyles. Only the rep seemed comfortable in the club setting—the other guy, the actual buyer, not so much.

Pitching my voice low and hardly moving my lips, I asked the office, "Can I have confirmation my camera and transmitter are working?"

"Affirmative, Raine," came a reply from a voice I couldn't place.

"I need a name on the stranger to Alexander's right."

"Already running a facial recognition program," said the same voice. "Stand by."

Maybe I needed to learn who all those office people were.

2200 on a wintry Friday night, and the young and wealthy of D.C.'s elite with their bodyguards packed the place. The music was loud and crappy while enough pot fumes drifted through the air to give everyone a contact high. I planned to gravitate closer to the table and see what I could learn from their conversations and actions. Sonia jumped up after a few minutes and headed for the bathroom. I followed.

The spaghetti strap on her dress had broken. She stood in front of the mirror, picking it up and dropping it, giving everyone a good view of her right breast and its tattoo. It was like she hoped everyone would take a look. Snickering sounds filled my head because the guys in the office saw all that through my camera. What was it about a boob that turned grown men into idiots?

It was the tattoo that interested me, so I wiggled past a woman doing a line of coke and gave it a closer inspection. A Russian bear, similar to the rest of the gang. Sonia's, however, was 3-D with beautiful shading. It was one bear positioned as if it hugged her nipple. Really artistic and striking. Even though not really a part of the gang, leave it to the beauty queen not only to have one of those but to make sure hers outdid everyone else's.

She turned to me. "What am I to do?"

Too late for me to feign indifference and move away. One of the voices in my head said, "Shit. Work it, Thompson."

Maybe Sonia was so wrapped up in herself she wouldn't remember my face—not that I'd ever count on it. "I have a safety pin." I reached into my handbag and held it out to her.

"You pin." She dropped her hand and expected me to wait on her. More laughing in my head. It only took a moment to fasten the strap. She inspected the repair and decided it warranted a reward.

"You come sit at my table with me. My family. You'll drink vodka with us. No?"

Might as well. She had my face. Sitting with them meant I didn't have to eavesdrop or try to look like I wasn't looking. "Yeah, okay. But I need a minute, first."

"I'll see you there." Queen Sonia swept out of the bathroom, leaving her overwhelming perfume in her wake. I went into a stall, and though the bathroom was noisy, I lowered my voice to speak to the home team. "Hey, you heard, right?"

A voice snickered and said, "Sure did."

"Gonna hang with them awhile. I'll plant some bugs and stuff as I can."

I got an *Affirmative* back.

All eyes watched me when I approached Sonia's table. She stood, kissed my cheeks, and introduced me as her rescuer. "What is your name?" she asked.

"Katie. It's so nice of you to ask me to sit with y'all. What's your name?" I plastered a beaming smile on my face.

"I am Sonia." She kicked at one of the henchmen with her four-inch platform heels. The hulk grunted, shifted his bulk, and made room for me to sit next to her. She rattled off a few names, Grigor, Luca, and Georgi, which I already knew from audio files, but pretended otherwise. I repeated the names back so the office would hear them clearly to match faces to the names. Neither of the stranger's names were ones I recognized. One of the men pressed a shot of vodka into my hand, Sonia made the toast, *vashe zdorov'ye,* or to our health, and we tossed it back. You'd think a whiskey shooter like me could handle vodka, and on the surface, I did. Going down though, vodka was a whole 'nother animal. Right away, I felt a buzz forming.

I stuck a bug to the underside of the table, though I wasn't sure how well it would work with all the background noise, but it seemed worth the effort. They all smoked non-stop. Marlboro, the Russian label. When they offered me one, I declined, never having picked up the habit. We drank another shot, and I tried to figure out how to avoid more, needing a clear head to listen and understand their Russian conversations.

The one named Georgi asked me, "How old are you?"

That nasty fool was wondering if I was legal, I bet. I giggled. "Why, I'm twenty-one, of course. I wouldn't be allowed in here if I wasn't."

He smiled at me but shifted his eyes to the one called Grigor and said in Russian, "She's lying. I bet she's eighteen or nineteen."

They asked me a few more things. I said I worked as a receptionist at a hairdresser and made it seem like I was sharp as a bowl of Jell-O.

The group shifted seats. I found myself squeezed between one of the muscles and the buyer who put his arm over the back of the booth, not quite daring to put it on my shoulders yet. A GPS tracker and a listening bug hid in the waistband of my slacks. I planted the tracker first in the buyer's coat pocket then waited for the chance to transfer the listening device. I didn't know if or how often he checked himself for bugs. If or when he found them, I hoped he blamed Alexander.

The next shot put into my hand got spilled under the table before I raised the glass to my lips. The men switched the conversation from sports and sex to something about a shipment coming in. The buyer, Mohammad al Bari, kept asking if the 'something' was ready. If it was good enough. I thought maybe the word referred to transportation. The office would let me know. My gut told me it was important. How big was the thing if they needed to arrange special transportation? Was it a bomb?

Sonia kept hitting or poking at Alexander, sometimes whispering in his ear. So annoying. I wanted to hear what he said to the buyers, but that bitch made everything about her. She leaned across another person to speak to the buyer. When he settled back, he leaned into me and put his arm on my shoulder, allowing his fingers to graze my skin. While giving him a smile, I got the damn bug placed in his suit breast pocket. I'd rather he wasn't touching me but letting him made enough of a distraction to do my work.

Just when the conversation became interesting, when the men started narrowing down the date for the shipment, Sonia announced it was time to dance.

"The men, they talk business, we go."

She took my hand and pulled me to the dance floor. It wasn't smart to resist, so I went and decided to enjoy it. One of the bodyguards joined us, and for all his bulk, he moved well.

I got closer to Sonia to dance at her side. "Is Alexander your boyfriend? He's really hot."

Sonia gave me a weird smile. Like condescending. "Boyfriend. Yes. You could say that. I am a woman of big passions. I need a strong man."

"Alexander seems strong."

"He is not strong like my husband, Victor. Victor was strong. Very strong man. Very passionate man."

"Oh, are you divorced?"

Sonia's face clouded over. "No. He was killed. Murdered. Cut down like a dog." For a moment, she had rage in her eyes before she regained control. "We dance. No talking."

It was unsettling to hear her speak of Victor. I'd never stood before one of my target's family before. From Sonia's point of view, she was a victim, and just for a moment, I allowed myself to acknowledge that I knew how she felt. I knew her pain because she and I both lost men we loved. Then my anger surged again. If Victor hadn't killed Daniel, I wouldn't have killed Victor. Sonia and I would have never stood face to face.

I pushed aside those thoughts and fell into the rhythm of the music, letting it calm me so I could refocus on my mission. Sonia and I stayed on the dance floor for a half hour which didn't get me any closer to solving the case. I moved to her side. "I'm thirsty."

"Yes, I'm thirsty too. We sit now."

She led me back to the group. They gave me more vodka, and I listened to talk about soccer, the merits of one type of weapon over another, and investments. I guess even bad guys knew the value of a strong investment portfolio.

Since I wasn't supposed to understand Russian, I sat there trying not to look bored, unable to steer the conversation. Was it worth staying? Every minute I remained gave them more time to memorize my face—or for me to make a mistake.

Sonia started making out with Alexander. It got all sloppy. The buyer didn't look happy about it either. One of the bodyguards looked at me like I was a big bowl of borscht prepared just for him. Yeah. Time to exit before it became too awkward.

"I'm going to the ladies' room," I said and moved off in that direction, circled the dance floor, and went out the door. On the street, on my way to my car, my cell phone rang.

"Hey Chief."

"Anderson just sent me the video from the club. Good work getting those bugs planted."

How'd Chief know it was safe to call me just then? Oh, right. Body camera. I forgot to shut it off. "Thanks. Hope it pays off. They've all got my face," I said, turning off the tech.

"So, how'd you get there?"

I gave him the rundown of my day and how I got cornered in the bathroom. I told him about the tattoo on Sonia's tit, which he saw on camera, and what I heard. We both agreed the group was sure to remember me, and I couldn't ever let them see my real face again.

CHAPTER EIGHTEEN

The next morning, I parked in the office garage and moved toward the tunnel when Charlotte's car turned the corner and went to her space. I ducked behind a pillar because I didn't feel like walking the tunnel or riding the elevator with her. She was getting too close for comfort, and I needed to reestablish some space before she got the idea we were friends. Her stupid request to die hung in the air between us every time we had a conversation.

I listened to her car door open and paid attention to the clack of her heels on the cement. When I guessed she was twenty feet ahead of my pillar, I peeked around it to confirm. Yep, twenty feet, facing away. Charlotte was almost to the tunnel entrance when her left foot walked into her right foot, and she tripped, pitching forward, purse flying, falling hard on her hands, and crying out in pain.

I hesitated behind the pillar, grimaced, and in frustration, banged my head against it once, sending a spike of pain shooting through my head before moving to her aid. If I were more detached, I wouldn't have. Damn it. She helped me when I was hurt.

"Charlotte, you okay?"

She pushed herself back to sit on the concrete when I squatted next to her. Charlotte smiled through her pain and blinked fast to clear away a few tears. Always that damn smile.

"Raine. I tripped over my own feet." She had scraped one of her knees and ruined her pantyhose. Who wore pantyhose anymore?

"Can you stand? I'll help you up." I got behind her, put my hands under her arms, and hauled her up. She wobbled and winced, lifting her right foot and leaning on me.

"I've sprained my ankle."

What the hell was I supposed to do? "Can you walk at all?" I listened in case someone else in the garage could take over. Nope.

"Maybe if you support me, I can make it to the elevator," she said.

Well, what could I say? No? Couldn't do that. Chief would be spitting angry if I left Charlotte stranded in the garage. Besides, the place had cameras and speakers all over it. Upstairs had already seen everything.

"Maybe you need to go home and put it up," I suggested.

"No. I have too much to do today. I'll put it up at my desk. Perhaps if I take your arm?"

I readjusted my backpack then shouldered her purse and satchel. I put my right arm around her waist and crossed my left arm over my body for her to hold. She limped through the tunnel to where the elevator waited in the open position. Yup. Eyes upstairs saw everything.

I propped Charlotte in the corner. She must have been in pain because she held her foot in the air and didn't talk during the ride. At our floor, I gave her my arms again to walk her to her station. Andrea saw us and hurried over.

"Oh my God, Charlotte. What happened?"

Andrea took over the nursing duties. Before I made my escape, Charlotte turned to me and said, "Thank you, Raine. I really appreciate your help." Tears filled her eyes. I assumed they didn't come from the pain of her injuries.

I mumbled, "Yeah," and walked away. Part of me felt like a bitch for not fussing over her, and part of me was relieved to get away.

Anderson waved me to his station. "I have intel from the bug you placed on the buyer. He went to a house just west of Baltimore. We didn't get much because he found the bug within ten minutes of getting there."

"Who does he think planted it?"

"Before he destroyed it, he said something about a guy bumping into him in the men's room."

He wasn't looking for me. "Did he find the tracker?"

"Not yet."

"Good." I sat to listen to the whole recording, trying to fit him into the story I was building. Engrossed in my work, I forgot about Charlotte.

Later, she limped into the bathroom while I washed my hands. I thought I might have to start using the bathroom at the other end of the floor.

"Thank you for coming to my rescue again. I don't know what I would have done without you."

"CAIT would have seen you on camera, and they would have sent someone down to help you."

"Clever Raine. Always thinking so quick on your feet."

I dismissed the comment and thought about what I was supposed to say. "So, you're okay now?"

"A little sprain. Nothing serious. It's just that ... well, it's starting to get a little harder each day. I'll have to let the office know soon. They'll put me on medical leave and send me home to die. Can't have someone with a deteriorating brain making critical decisions."

I nodded because I didn't trust myself not to say something stupid.

She opened her mouth, but it took a few seconds for words to leave it. "Are you sure you wouldn't reconsider?" She met my eyes in the mirror, then looked away. "No. Never mind. Just a momentary weakness on my part. Sorry." Charlotte smoothed her skirt.

Her question made that cold, prickly feeling run over my skin. Why me? Why'd she have to go and ask me? "Are you still thinking it's a good idea?" I couldn't believe she still thought she wanted to die that way.

"It would make things easier on me and my family. My son. Long, drawn-out affairs bring even healthy members of a family to their knees."

I let out a burst of air and closed my eyes. I'd been around enough to know that was true.

She read my mind and pounced. "You're reconsidering, aren't you?"

Her voice held hope, damn it. She'd gotten under my skin. Part of me hated her, except I didn't really. I stared into space and after some time said, "I'm gonna need proof before I even think about this." I hardly believed the words that came out of my mouth.

"Fine," she said. "I'll show you my medical records."

"Not good enough. Records can be faked." She opened her mouth to protest, but I stopped her. "You're an analyst. You deal in fake records. You create them. Your paycheck is based on fake records."

She didn't have a retort for that.

"Then what would it take?" she asked.

"Who's your doctor?"

"Dr. Richard Mueller. Why?"

"I'll speak with him first. Introduce me as your concerned cousin. If he can convince me you're legit ..."

"If I pass this test, will you do it?"

"Maybe." I shook my head. "Probably not. I'll think about it."

Charlotte texted me two days later just after I finished working out. "I set up a consultation appointment with my doctor next Monday at three. Can you join me?"

I texted back, "Yes. Address?" I didn't want to go but had made a promise.

The third week of January brought a dusting of snow followed by sleet to D.C. Sitting inside the office each day was frustrating. I wanted a direction. I wanted to move. Since shit ramped up on the Zhiglov case, I'd been jumpy and cranky, feeling like justice would never happen.

Most nights, I tossed and turned, pictures of good times with Daniel and blood mixing together. Last night, the final vision before I woke with a gasp was of me leaning over him, my hands covered in blood. In the dream, he opened his eyes and said, "Help me." Coming fully awake, I felt the guilt crushing me. I wanted to kill them all. I wanted to avenge Daniel. I wanted it over. It would never be over.

It was 0420. I couldn't get back to sleep, so I went for a long run, trying and failing to outpace my thoughts, my demons. I returned home a little calmer and more focused.

At the office, I gave myself an attitude adjustment telling myself I needed to act more professional. Less emotional. And though tired, and still somewhat shook, I was ready to do whatever I needed to do. Chief called me into his office and blackened the glass while I sat with my foot on the chair. The messed-up Rubik's Cube made me scowl.

Chief snatched the cube and put it in a drawer before I could grab it. "Need your full attention."

"What's up?"

"How'd you like to shake a Russian tree and see what falls

out?" I raised one eyebrow at him. Chief opened a file on his tablet and turned the screen so we could both see it. It showed a photo of two men I recognized as lower level Zhiglovs. They were the bear muscle probably responsible for nearly a dozen murders, including the three recently dead Ovechkins. "You know where these two hang out?"

"That nasty strip club way up there on Thirteenth Street near Columbia Heights? The one the health inspectors fined last year?"

Chief grunted. "Prints off both those cigarette packs match the one on the left." He indicated the taller of the two, maybe six-two and a jaw like a cement block. "I want you to take both out. Better if it's together. We need it done in the next few days though. How do you want to play it?"

"Does it need to look like an accident?"

"It needs to look on purpose."

That made it easier. "As if the Ovechkins are retaliating? They keep things simple. Shots to the head or chest."

"You know your Ovechkins."

I couldn't figure out what Chief had in mind. "What's this supposed to do for finding our buyers?"

"It's supposed to divert the Zhiglovs and keep them worried about threats. Maybe they'll move faster and make a mistake."

"Really?"

"A long shot, I know," he said. "But it can't hurt anything. Maybe it'll help."

I sat in that dumpy neighborhood and watched the club for two days. No street cleaners swept the cracked and pot-holed streets. No one bothered to clean up the graffiti or power wash the bricks. Tourists didn't go to that part of town—no need to waste money making that neighborhood look nice. A dull coating of grime covered everything, even turning the dusting of snow black within a couple of hours.

I watched Dumb and Dumber, as I called them, go into the strip club a little before 1100 each morning and come out just after 1300. For a price, the door guy told me how much they drank. A shit ton. Even so, when they came out, they walked just as steady as when they went in.

The two walked one block to where they always left their car as if that spot was reserved just for them, and maybe it was. I decided the job should be there, where they were the only two bears around. Broad daylight should show the Ovechkin's had some balls. It made more of a statement—demonstrated more anger.

How to do it without witnesses and how to leave the bodies in plain sight? Also, I needed to use an Ovechkin caliber of choice—either a .38 or a .45. I had selected a Colt Cobra snub-nose.38 from the weapons locker and practiced with it in the office's two lane, lower level, gun range. It was a fun little weapon.

Dumb and Dumber had to cross an alley to get to their car. They always peered into it before proceeding, so they weren't completely stupid. If I stood there, I'd have to appear helpless and give them a reason to come closer.

The next day, I again watched them enter the club. Earlier, I had put a camera on a street sign to show me the door on my tablet feed, so I'd have a heads up when they left. At 1245, I entered the alley from the other end, wearing a blond wig and a denim duster over thigh-high stockings and flats. Maybe I should have worn heels but couldn't run in those. Damn, but that was another way guys had it easier.

Thirty-something degrees and no socks or boots. Under the duster, not much. A white nighty, mostly sheer, nothing underneath. A few people passed along the alley, but by cleaning my nails with a knife, I kept everyone moving. It's the little details that make or break a set up. To reinforce my cover, I put a little white dish soap inside a couple of condoms and placed those at the edge of the building as if I used that alley for business. My pockets held a half dozen more condom packets as props. The job had to happen fast. Really fast, and I couldn't let them get too close.

At 1300, they left the club a couple minutes later than usual, making me antsy. I almost didn't lift my eyes from my tablet screen except to confirm the alley remained empty, which it did thank God. I tamped down my anxiety and put away the tablet. When they checked the alley, I called to them.

"Hey, honey. Looking for a date?"

They both stopped walking to check me out. I opened the duster, letting them get a good look. I held the right side of the duster back behind my waist and discreetly put my hand on the gun. Dumb and Dumber grinned.

"I got a special today for handsome men only." The lip gloss I slathered on felt sticky with each word. I made myself smile. "Thirty each."

They walked a few steps closer but didn't approach. They'd been in too many fights not to be wary. I pinched my nipple with my other hand. Their eyes fixated on that.

"We'll pay you twenty each," one said.

"How about twenty-five?"

"We don't pay at all, usually," the other said. "As you say, we're handsome men." They both laughed.

"Yeah, okay. Twenty." They smirked like they knew they weren't going to pay me anything anyway.

Step by step, I backed into the alley some more, glad they took their time following—sauntering really—their eyes on my tits. I grabbed the hem of the nighty and slowly pulled it up. When their eyes shifted to my crotch, I pulled the revolver with the suppressor, shot the closest in the lung, re-cocked and shot the other in the heart just as he sighted me with his pistol. The first guy moved and reached for his weapon. I ran forward and shot him in the head.

Second dude was still breathing, but one more bullet, and he was dead.

Some blood splattered me, but I buttoned my coat to hide the stains while I checked for witnesses—damn it was cold—then grabbed their weapons and the stuff in their pockets. Back to my car, blonde wig off after the first block, and out of there. The usual message to Chief didn't seem to fit, so I texted, "Successful bear hunt."

At the office, I changed clothes in the locker room before meeting with Chief. The nighty went into the trash.

"Any word yet?" I didn't want to think about what I just did—ending two lives. Those thoughts got shoved deep down where I didn't have to face them. Besides, they killed plenty of people. Not like they were innocent of anything.

"Yup. The local PD is all over the site. Lots of activity at Nick's Bar. Lots of phone calls and pissed-off cussing. Sonia's wailing up a storm. It turns out they were brothers and her cousins. She's screaming for retribution. Alexander said he'd take care of it."

"And they're blaming ...?"

"The Ovechkins, of course."

"And now?"

"We have tails waiting to follow the higher ups. We wait and see where they lead us."

"Do you have one for me to follow?"

"Nope. You've seen too much. I want your face hidden. Don't worry, there's plenty of work for you to do."

CHAPTER NINETEEN

Five days flew by, and I had to make good on my promise to attend Charlotte's doctor appointment. I sat in the waiting room with her and a bunch of sick, old people. The place smelled funny, and I couldn't sit still. I bounced one leg while I messed with my phone, and after twenty minutes, I was ready to jump out the window. Charlotte read her ebook as if that was exactly where she wanted to be.

When a nurse called for us, she looked me up and down, passed judgment on my leather and boots, and curled her lip a little. I gave it back to her while leaning into her space.

Charlotte held out her hand and said, "Raine, may I lean on your arm?" Good distraction technique. I gave Charlotte my arm as the nurse stiffened and led us to Dr. Mueller's office.

He looked like a TV doctor. Not the handsome, sexy type. More like the competent, really smart type. Hair whiter than gray, fiftyish, sharp, intelligent eyes. It wouldn't be easy to fool that one. Dr. Mueller looked me over and glanced at Charlotte. He seemed unconvinced we were relations. So what? Our word against his doubt. Charlotte and I signed the HIPAA forms, me using one of my aliases.

Charlotte opened the meeting saying, "My cousin has been good to me; very helpful over the last few weeks, but she's concerned maybe we've overlooked something. I set up this appointment, so she could hear about my condition and set her mind at ease."

Dr. Mueller nodded and steepled his fingers in front of his mouth. Why did doctors do that? I had already researched his background. Back at the office, I had cornered Anderson. He knew he owed me because of the dog bite—I had shown him a photo of the bruise—and without knowing why, he investigated the doctor. Our little secret. The doctor's background was clean as a nun's starched white habit.

Charlotte babbled on. "Would you please explain my condition to my cousin and let her know my path?" She cleared her throat and added, "Let her know what to expect from my deterioration."

I flicked my eyes to her. Deterioration? Shit. That was a heavy word.

Dr. Mueller showed me the MRI's and other test results while explaining about intracranial tumors. Hers was inoperable. He answered my questions and didn't dumb things down for the leather-wearing degenerate sitting in front of him. That made me respect him, and I controlled my asshole attitude.

I took notes during the consultation, studied the MRIs, and listened to a bunch of medical jargon. The brain cancer was real. A big, dark blotch on the MRI sat deep inside Charlotte's brain. I felt something almost like panic, like I was hearing the information for the first time. It was for real that Charlotte was sick and dying. I didn't understand how she could sit there so calm, so accepting. While talking, I had started bouncing my leg, so I pushed down on my thigh with my palm. Ten minutes later, we left. Before parting ways, I told Charlotte I still had things to check out and left it at that. She drove out of the lot, and I sat in my car and called Connor.

"Hey, you busy?"

"Never too busy for you. You okay? Any problems with your injury?"

"I'm fine. Want to hang out?"

"C'mon over."

A half hour later, I knocked on his apartment door. When he opened it, he said, "You're looking good."

"I'm feeling much better."

"Are you now?" He gave me the look.

I planned on having a talk about Charlotte's case when I got to Connor's condo, but things didn't work out that way. He looked so sexy in his blue sweatpants, white T-shirt, and bare feet that I forgot about medical questions.

I stepped into his arms, kissed him, then bit his lower lip drawing a little blood. He grabbed me by the hair, forced my head back, and kissed my throat. The next hour was another good time. Not as physical as usual—I still had some pain in my side—not the right kind—still, the sex was great.

After, I lay on my stomach next to Connor and relaxed. He knew how to pull my hair just right. My scalp still stung, but it'd subside in an hour or so.

His fingers rubbed the bruises on my upper arms. "You still okay with this?"

"I'm back, aren't I?" I fingered the new bite mark I put on his chest. "You upset about this?"

"Do I sound upset?"

Two of a kind. Ten minutes later, I had enough of lazing in bed. "How about a shower?"

Connor yawned. "Just as I was falling asleep."

"Meet me in there if you like."

The shower led to another round of sex—and a new

thumbprint bruise on my breast. After the shower, I got around to asking him questions about an acquaintance's diagnosis. He gestured for us to sit at his kitchen table.

"Well, I can't be one hundred percent sure since I wasn't there, but yes. It does sound true. Everything you've told me adds up."

"So, she really is facing a messy end? She'll have to endure a slow death?"

"Yeah. First, she'll lose control of her body and finally her mind. She'll have to have someone do everything for her near the end. She'll have a catheter and a feeding tube. It's a sucky way to go."

"And there's no hope? No weird experimental treatment in some foreign country?"

"Nope. That's the hard part of medicine. Some things we can do a lot to help. Other things, almost nothing at all." I got silent for a few minutes. Connor asked, "Who are we talking about? A relative of yours?"

"No, not a relative. Just somebody I know."

"Is it Charlotte?"

I snapped my head at him, giving it away like some kind of ignorant amateur, damn it. "How did you know? Did she say something while I was out of it?"

"No, but I noticed she had some coordination problems and frequent headaches. She had a nosebleed while you were unconscious. I remembered you asked me about tumors and nosebleeds a few weeks ago."

He got quiet and stared at the wall, and his lips became a thin, white line. "Something happened the other day. It's got me acting like a self-pitying pussy."

I kept quiet, inviting him to speak.

Connor looked at his clasped hands. "I went to the gaming store at the mall and decided to have lunch at the food court. A boy, about twelve, fell off his chair with an epileptic seizure. A violent one. His head hit the corner of a garbage can, and he started to bleed."

"What did you do?"

"Nothing."

I raised my eyebrow at him.

Connor dropped his eyes from my stare and said, "I may have been able to help, but because I lost my license and because of the plea deal, I couldn't do anything. I watched him seize. Even though I have all kinds of knowledge and skills, I'm not allowed to use them. I'm not even protected by the Good Samaritan law. I watched him bleed, and his mom had to wait for the EMT's to arrive."

Connor pounded the table making a plate jump. "There's nothing anyone can do for your friend and that sucks. I'm not allowed to do anything for anyone, except in secret, and that sucks. I'm a good doctor, damn it. The whole world sucks."

He was wrong. She wasn't my friend. Although it wasn't my usual style, I went to him and held Connor's head to my chest, kissed his hair, and rubbed his shoulders.

My pappy died of a heart attack, and I hadn't been able to help him. When he fell over at the dinner table, I attempted CPR and screamed at him to stop it—to get up—to not die. I sat on the kitchen floor all night and stared at his body. He was my only family. The only one on Earth who loved me. Everyone else was already gone, and there I was...left alone. Each breath I drew that night ached, and I wondered where I found the strength to take the next breath.

Early that terrible morning, a thin, weak ribbon of sunlight had come through the window and sliced across his face from temple to jaw. The tears finally came, the keening, and the outright anger. Full light showed before I calmed enough to think. Not wanting to shame Pappy, I gathered my courage to deal with his death. Our house had an empty fifty or more acres behind it. Using our old tractor, I buried him, in secret, within sight of the house.

My daddy had died three years before when another inmate stabbed him. My momma had died when I was two, and I had no idea about my brother's whereabouts.—All Pappy and I had was each other, and it had been enough.

A heavy sigh from Connor brought me back to the present. His muscles relaxed, and he put his arms around my waist, still resting his head on my breasts. He asked, "How about I order dinner in, open a bottle of wine, and we watch a movie?"

Shit. That sounded like a date. A cozy date. I already spent too much time there and stepped out of my comfort zone. I lied. "Can't. I told Charlotte I'd come over and check on her."

He nodded and walked me to the door. "Give me a call," he said.

"I will."

Another door closed behind me. For the best. I mean, I let the man I loved die right in front of me—just like Pappy. I was no good at taking care of anybody.

CHAPTER TWENTY

I racked my brains about how to get more intel on the Zhiglovs. Chief said the upstairs suits tried to get the DHS to share, but they claimed they had nothing. What hope was there for the world when the same side couldn't get along?

Charlotte and I sat in the conference room and ate Chinese takeout. Like Elroy, she was another one who pushed vegetables on me.

"Try the broccoli. The glaze makes it sweet."

"If I eat one, will you get off my ass about it?"

"Deal."

I chose the smallest piece. Wasn't the worst thing in the world. My mind kept returning to Nick's Bar where I killed five of the gang. Was that because it was familiar to me or because my brain was trying to process something? "It may be an exercise in futility, but I'm gonna ask Chief to let me stake out the bar with a full complement of tech. Got a feeling about it."

"You've watched it for two years. Nothing."

"Alexander is new, and Sonia is back. I have to give it a try."

Charlotte took another bite but looked at me out of the corner of her eye like she had something to say.

"What?" I asked.

"I ... well, maybe not ... I ..."

"You think it's a bad idea? Just say it."

"I was thinking I could join you." Her face went red.

"Why? Besides, you're not trained."

"How hard is it to sit in a van, watch, and take notes?"

She had a point. I mean we made it out to be hard, but if you weren't noticed, it wasn't hard. The trick was not getting noticed or being able to do something about it if you were. "Chief won't approve it."

"So, we'd have to go through Chief?"

I was tempted to say yeah to Charlotte and have her along for some of the time. Then again, I'd have to listen to her chatter, so maybe not. Anyway, I wouldn't without Chief's approval. He was good to me, and I wouldn't lie to him like that. I grunted and took another forkful, hoping Charlotte would drop the idea.

"You see, it's kinda something on my bucket list. You know—to do something more than sit in an office and watch other people do all the real work. The work that counts."

Bucket list. Yeah, like she could use that on me. I cocked my head. "You don't think your work counts? That it isn't real?"

"I sit at my station perfectly safe and watch you do all sorts of incredibly difficult fieldwork. I've watched your body camera and have seen punches coming at you, seen you dodge bullets. You do the hard work."

"Without you and the other analysts, I couldn't do my part of the job. I never realized how much you did or how difficult it was until now." Words left my mouth before I could stop them. "If you can get Chief to agree, okay."

I was such a fucking idiot.

Charlotte sat straighter and widened her eyes. "Really?"

"Not really, but ... I don't see how you'd get Chief to agree anyway."

Charlotte and I sat across from Chief's desk. She had just finished making her request.

"Sorry, Charlotte. Denied. It takes a lot of training, even if it doesn't look like it."

Charlotte dropped her eyes and didn't argue. "Okay. Was worth a shot."

I kept my expression even but was glad Chief hadn't gone soft and approved the request. Aside from Charlotte's chatter, if anything went wrong, I'd spend energy defending her rather than going after those shits. Chief used to be in the field. He knew about that.

"Tell you what though ..." Chief said.

What the hell?

"You'll head Raine's support team and keep in touch with her while on surveillance."

Charlotte grinned. "Yes. I'd like that."

"It would mean remaining at the office for the length of the operation. I'll put Shepherd on this, and you'll both report to him."

"Yes, Chief." She saw it as a good compromise.

"Raine, Shepherd will take the lead on the surveillance. Don't give me that face. You don't have enough experience with this or the tech. Use it as a learning session."

That he didn't think I was good enough to run a surveillance pissed me off, but rather than mouth-off and ruin the chance, I swallowed my irritation. I was playing for a bigger prize than my ego. One way or another, I would take down every one of those Zhiglov shits.

Two days later, I sat in a UPS style box truck with Shepherd half a block away and across the street from Nick's Bar. The truck had Maryland plates, appeared trashed on the outside, but was tricked out on the inside. It held surveillance equipment, a claustrophobic cot next to the ceiling, and even a portable toilet. The building closest to us was vacant. The office put a sign in the window that read *Heinz's Meat Market—Coming Soon!* and placed magnetic signs on the van's doors to match. Chief gave us forty-eight hours. I chose Thursday and Friday because, in the past, that's when I saw the most activity.

At 0600, Shepherd and I pulled up, parked, and moved to the back, shutting the divider to the front seats. Shepherd wore tactical gear and looked so comfortable in it that it was as if he'd been born wearing it. I wore my usual jeans, T-shirt, and leather jacket, the better to blend on the street. Shepherd began flipping switches and brought the computers online.

"What do you want me to do?" I asked.

"Get the audio working."

After we set up, I settled onto the side bench in my favorite watching position. Sitting up, legs stretched in front of me, ankles crossed, camera controls at my side. My tablet with the video feed sat in a swing arm hovering over my lap. Shepherd stayed in a chair at the bank of computers. Set up only took fifteen minutes, another five for the communications check, and the waiting began.

Charlotte didn't last ten minutes before opening the mike to our earpieces, which wasn't surprising. "I found most of the supplies on your provisions list, Raine. None of it was very healthy, and I couldn't find homemade venison jerky."

"It's hard to find around here. No problem. I took care of that." Having grown up making my own venison jerky, I couldn't stand the massed-produced stuff.

Shepherd looked into the bags and gave me a shake of his head. "Girl, how do you survive on this stuff?"

I liked to have certain foods with me on surveillance. Venison jerky for protein, jar of peanut butter and Ritz crackers, M&M's,

and bottles of water. For all my unhealthy ways, I mostly drank water because I didn't much like soda. We didn't have the money for it when I was a kid, so I never got used to it.

"Oh, good then," Charlotte said. "A variety of MREs are in the provisions cabinet. I put some fruit, cut up vegetables, ranch dressing, and yogurt in the cooler."

"Thanks," Shepherd said. "That'll save my stomach."

I answered, "Thanks. Out."

Shepherd wasn't a talker either, so we got on well during the first few hours of being crammed in the van. About 0900, things got interesting when a black Lincoln, a newer model than they used five years ago, pulled up. Five people got out. Two large men first—the muscle. Then came Alexander in a suit carrying a briefcase, Sonia in her usual short skirt and heels and little dog in her arms, and one skinny guy with scruffy facial hair.

"You got this on video, right?" I asked.

"Got it," Shepherd answered, never taking his eyes from the screen. Two men came out of the bar and greeted the five on the sidewalk. Russian style kissing all around. Sonia's little dog squirmed and barked incessantly in her arms.

"Has Sonia put on weight?" I asked. "Her ass looks weird."

Shepherd looked harder at the screen. "I don't know. Maybe."

By that time, the party on the sidewalk was over, and the group moved inside. "I'm getting a closer look." I shucked my leather jacket but kept my zippered hoodie and pulled the hood over my hair.

"Our orders are to observe."

"And that's all I'm going to do."

"From here," Shepherd said, but I had already opened the door and ignored him. Supposed I would pay for that later.

I left the van on the cracked and weed-choked sidewalk, crossed the street, ducked into the alley, and followed it to the back of the bar. If my hunch was right, I only had a few moments to get into place. My breathing hitched when I stood below the second-floor bathroom window. It wasn't my first time shinnying up the building to that window. Emotions had no place on the job, so I took a breath and scanned the empty alley.

A dumpster sat under the window and several pipes ran from the ground to the roof right past the window. Those, along with the narrow brick ledge, running along the building marking the floors, made the climb easy. The bathroom window stood open a crack. Those people hadn't learned anything in the year and some since I'd last been there.

I got myself eye-level with the window, toes on the ledge, hand gripping the pipes, but stayed to the side. The mirror over the sink gave me a sliver of sight to the interior. Someone entered the bathroom. I swung toward the window a bit, caught a glimpse of him in the mirror, then pulled back. The smaller guy. A zipper, then peeing. I swung forward again and glanced at the mirror. I could just make out the top of his head, facing forward. The dude sat to pee. Either he was a dude sitting like a girl or he was a girl. I used the noise of the flush to climb down, jumped the last few feet to the asphalt, and made my way back to the van.

"Anyone see you?" Shepherd asked.

"Of course not. By the way, I'm almost positive the new, skinny dude is female."

"Then she's in disguise? Wonder why?"

"Me too. Did you get good footage of her face?"

"Not really. The others blocked him. Her."

I opened the mike. "Charlotte, do you have that last bit of film? With the group on the sidewalk?"

"Yes, Raine."

"Need analysis on it A.S.A.P. The little guy. He's female—maybe—or really effeminate. See if you can get an ID."

We settled in for the rest of our surveillance. The longer I sat there, the more my bad memories pressed forward. I regretted the lack of whiskey even though there was no place for that stuff when working. Guess I must have started brooding hard.

"You okay, Raine?" Shepherd asked.

I shook my head to clear it. "Yeah, fine. You hungry?" I held out some venison jerky.

"You looked out of it just now." He had spun his chair away from the console to face me.

I grunted and rested my chin on my knees. Shepherd had concerns, and to continue working together, he needed to know I'd have his back if things went wrong. "I guess you know I've been here before? To this building?"

"Yeah, I was part of the mission." His gaze increased in intensity when he asked, "Is it hard being here again?"

Hard? Being at the place where I killed the man who murdered Daniel and four more of his gang? Shepherd waited for an answer. I tried to tell him no, it's okay, but my voice broke. Tears stung my eyes, and I swallowed hard. God damn it. "It doesn't matter anymore." I reached for the bag of M&M's and repositioned myself.

Shepherd stared a moment longer, then turned back to the console and said, "If you want to talk about it, I'll listen."

I ignored that last bit.

The rest of the day went by with nothing more of interest. Same ol' people going in, same ol' people coming out. Shepherd left me alone with my thoughts for about an hour before striking up an innocuous conversation. Turned out, he possessed an encyclopedic knowledge of handguns. I let him hold my Glock, and he admired the custom grip. He told me I could try his Sig Sauer P226 at the firing range sometime. If Chief held the company socials at the firing range, I might show up for a while.

I got up my courage and asked, "Did you know Daniel?"

Shepherd hesitated with his answer long enough to make me uncomfortable. He was a guy who always kept himself controlled and calm, but I saw his hands tighten. "Yeah. We were buddies."

"Then this is important to you too."

His face fell into solemn lines, and he met my eyes. "It is."

"You were part of the raid that captured me?"

"Yeah. I was one of the guys who dragged you to the van."

Wow. I never realized that. Showed how out of it I was. I shrugged and shifted back to my screen. Shepherd gave me my space.

About 1800 that night, Anderson told us he and Charlotte couldn't figure out the woman/man.

"I'll get on it when I get back in the office," I said.

"Don't worry. We'll get this done."

At 2300, our four people of interest left in the same car. Both Sonia and the woman/man hid behind the bodyguards, so we didn't get good video on them. After that, it was numbingly boring until 0600 rolled around. We slept in shifts, and the next day, more of the same.

Chief denied me permission to enter the bar or the apartment to leave bugs. Shepherd and I returned to the office to analyze the intel and hopefully make progress on the case. The bears didn't say anything that gave us clues about what they were up to. Except for the skinny guy on the sidewalk, I didn't think the surveillance was useful, and I wasn't feeling confident about our progress.

CHAPTER TWENTY-ONE

I sat working at Charlotte's station because she phoned in sick. About 1000 my cell rang.

"Raine, please I need a favor," Charlotte said.

"Yeah?" Now what?

"Is anyone near to hear you?"

"No. Why?"

"I'm at the hospital. I had another nosebleed, and it wouldn't stop, so I went to the emergency room. They cauterized it then called Dr. Mueller on me. He said I can't go home by myself and won't release me until I have help. I told him and the hospital I'd call my cousin, who lives with me, to come pick me up."

I found myself doing Chief's squinty-eye, nose pinch move. Why me? Then again, from her perspective, I had already played the part of her cousin. Stupid me had gotten sucked right into her mess. "Yeah, okay. Which hospital?"

"George Washington University Hospital."

I packed my stuff and went to Chief's office. Closed door, darkened windows. Andrea stared at me with her hands hovering over her keyboard. "Tell Chief I went to work from home. He'll get his report later." I walked away without waiting for a reply. After all, I had a reputation for bitchiness to maintain.

When I arrived at the ER, I flashed a fake federal marshal's badge to get past the metal detector with my Glock. The badge was useful for things like that. Forty-two people sat in the waiting area. The admissions desk directed me inside where the stink of people shifted to the smell of antiseptic and something sour. There, past a moaning woman, I found Charlotte pale and lethargic on a bed. I adjusted the curtains to better shield us from the rest of the room.

"You okay? Any pain?"

She turned a puffy face to me. "No. No pain. Just tired from the ordeal."

Connor once explained how he judged pain beyond what the patient told him. He looked for the tightness around the eyes and the corners of the mouth and said if you read them right, they'd let you know when a patient was lying. I had asked if he used that with me during sex. He smiled and answered, "Of course," like it was the most obvious thing in the world. Since that conversation, I also tried to develop that skill. Charlotte had both indicators of pain.

A resident came and asked me a few questions. He explained how to care for Charlotte at home and said she needed someone with her for the next twenty-four hours.

Fuck. What was I supposed to do about that?

I shifted my face from either neutral or concerned as expected and repeated his instructions back to him. A nurse came over, Charlotte signed some forms, and we left.

She lived in Georgetown, about four blocks from Connor, in a ritzy building on the eighth floor. The building had a guard and working cameras in the lobby, but the ones in the elevator and the hallways were fake. Management gave the tenants only the illusion of security.

Once inside her apartment, Charlotte said thanks, she was fine, and I could go. I would have. I turned toward the door, but she sank to her knees. I ran to Charlotte and put her on the sofa. It was then I remembered how she stayed with me when I was hurt.

"I'll stay a few hours until you feel better." After all, I did owe her a debt for her time.

I settled Charlotte in her ultra-feminine bedroom with peach tones on the frilly drapes and floral duvet. It had the same cream-colored carpeting as the rest of the apartment, silk flowers, and a make-up vanity that looked like it came out of a magazine. After I pulled the blankets over her, I returned to my car for my pack and went back to work. Chief got his report, and later, I had dinner delivered. Charlotte was still pale, weak, and ate only a small portion of the pasta dish she chose.

She pushed her plate away and said, "I'm feeling much better. Thank you for staying. I'll be fine now, so you can go home."

A quick assessment of her condition and a smidgen of guilt kept me from accepting her offer. "I'll stay the night on your sofa. You probably won't be able to go to work tomorrow, so you better think of a stomach flu or something to call in with." I didn't have a change of clothes with me, but that was nothing new.

She lowered her head. "Thank you, Raine. I'm sorry to be such a bother."

"You're no more bother to me than I was to you."

Damn it. That wasn't exactly what I was supposed to say. It sounded like I was keeping score. It would have been nicer if I said, it's no bother at all, though she'd know it was a lie if I said that.

We watched TV before I sent Charlotte to her room. I eased her into bed and pulled up the covers. She seemed to be running a fever, so I stuffed a thermometer in her mouth. When it beeped, it confirmed she had one. I didn't know what to make of that, so I went back to the living room and called Connor since he already knew her and her condition.

"Raine! You coming over?"

"Can't. I'm here with Charlotte, and there's a problem." I explained to Connor what happened and asked if a fever was normal or if I should take her back to the hospital.

"Low grade?"

"One oh one-ish."

"Give her some Tylenol and keep an eye on her. If the fever spikes, go back to the hospital, otherwise she should be better by morning."

I followed Connor's instructions and watched TV a while longer. I couldn't get comfortable on Charlotte's sofa and lay awake. Her apartment smelled weird with a floral scent that soaked the air. A candle? That potpourri stuff? Then a low-pitched sound. Crying. Charlotte was crying.

I pressed the sofa pillows over my ears. Damn it all. She wouldn't ignore me. I punched a pillow a few times before I stood and moved to her doorway. I didn't knock, just entered her room. She lay with her back to me, sobbing into a pillow, unaware I stood next to the bed. My pappy wasn't the most demonstrative man, but I remembered him soothing some nightmares when I was young. He sat on the edge of my bed, stroked my hair, and told me bad dreams weren't real. Trouble was that her problems were real. I sat on her bed and reached for her head.

She startled. "Raine. I'm sorry, I didn't mean to disturb you."

Of course, she apologized. "It's okay." I didn't need to ask why she was crying. She struggled to stop but then let the tears flow again. Maybe some primitive instinct took over because I lay on the bed next to her, put my arm around her, and let her cry. I didn't realize I was crying too until I felt her stroke my hair. Once, twice. She shifted to put her arms around me. Charlotte had a faint, lemony smell, and her fever sent heat seeping through my clothes to warm my skin. My first instinct was to push her away. Instead, I froze, held my breath and squeezed my eyes until my own tears subsided. A moment more, and I drew a clearing breath.

"You can let go now."

"Raine, it's okay if you want to cry or—"

"No."

"There's no shame in—"

"I'm fine," I said, copying Chief's military sternness. I wouldn't allow my memories or anything else to control me like that. Not like when I was Sarah McDonald. I was Raine Thompson now, and Raine Thompson didn't cry. I squirmed out of her embrace and sat up.

"Okay," she said, reaching for the tissue box on her bedside table. "You know, we all have a story, a sadness in our life."

What would she know about that? Oh, right. The brain tumor that was killing her. "Sure," I said. She got me thinking though.

If Pappy hadn't died, I would have stayed in Grundy, working the farm, taking shifts at the feed mill or someplace, doing odd jobs for extra cash, and still hunting our supper. Never having expected or known anything else, I probably would have been fine with that. Even if the DSS let me go right then, how would I fit back into Grundy? I found out the world was a big place, and Grundy had become so small.

Charlotte pulled me from my thoughts saying, "Do you know why I'm divorced?"

"You don't have to tell me anything." I hoped she wouldn't.

"It was my fault. I won't get into details, but I had an affair and got caught."

"You don't seem the type."

"What's the type?" Charlotte rolled onto her back. "Anyway, my husband and I had hit a rough patch, and I ... strayed. I lost my husband, and my son chose to live with him. I ruined my family. It eats away at me every minute of every day. I think that's where the tumor came from. My own sorrow and guilt massing in my brain."

Charlotte put her hands to her face and wept again. "I wasn't a good mother anyway. I worked long hours, let the office come first too often. I suppose I'm addicted to the adrenalin and chose to be there instead of at home. It's no wonder he chose to go with his dad."

Addicted to the adrenalin. I understood that. I felt it too, and sometimes it scared me how much I liked it.

Charlotte shifted on the bed. "Thank you, Raine. I didn't mean to break down like that. It's just ... the cancer is spreading faster now. Faster than Dr. Mueller expected."

I put my hand on her shoulder but controlled myself. She only cried a minute more before she stopped. "You're okay now, right?" I was bouncing back—finding my control. So what she knew all about me? It didn't mean anything.

"Yes, I'm okay."

I got off the bed and fixed the sheets before I went back to the sofa but didn't sleep right away. I pulled out the heart-shaped stone Pappy etched for me and rubbed my thumb over the smooth side until my eyes felt heavy. The next morning, Charlotte's fever faded, and she was stronger. She stayed home while I went to work.

The morning dragged with nothing much to hold my attention. I hated being in the office and wanted to be wherever the Zhiglovs were—hunting them. After lunch, Chief called me to his office.

"Good news," he said.

"What's that?"

"Local PD picked up Martinez's loose bodyguard. Cortez. He was hiding out in a suburb of Baltimore with a cousin. Anderson discovered that."

A sense of relief and satisfaction surged through me. One less gunman on the streets looking for me. "Where is he now?"

"Been turned over to immigration. They'll delay his paperwork until we get a chance to question him."

"Who's going to do that? I want in on it. Had he and Lamas been watching the office? Who made that phone call to Lamas about finding me in that bar?"

"I've got someone else on it. You have other stuff to think about."

"Am I going to take care of the problem?"

"No."

"Why not?" I didn't like the idea of him beating the system and getting loose again. Over the past few weeks, I'd been looking over my shoulder far too often, and it had been exhausting. The sooner he was out of the picture, the better for me.

"We have reason to believe Lamas was acting on his own, and this guy's not worth the effort. Too low on the food chain and deportation terrifies him. I've a feeling someone on his home end will take care of the problem. He seriously messed up, letting his boss get killed."

I shrugged at that. "Then who called Lamas to say I was in that bar?"

"Best guess, someone from the embassy who was sympathetic to him. They must have watched the office. I believe now that he's dead, and this one is in custody. You're in the clear."

"How did someone from the embassy know who I was and where to find me?"

"Look, Raine, as hard as we try to keep the DSS a secret, other organizations know we exist. It's possible the embassy harbored a mole and gave Lamas and Cortez a clue. With Lamas dead, it's a non-issue. He was a loose cannon, and even his own people didn't like him." Chief leaned back and swiveled his chair. "It happens. It's part of the job. Let it fade for now. We have more important things to occupy our time."

I didn't think so but let it go for the moment and said, "Got a clearer picture on the Zhiglovs. I'm convinced Alexander is a figurehead, but I still don't know who's calling the shots or who they're calling them to."

"Keep at it, Raine. Do your homework. Don't rush things. You'll get your chance."

"Yeah," I said and went to a workstation.

I turned cranky over the next couple of days, snapping at everyone in the office. I told Andrea she was annoying and almost made her cry. I kept it up until Chief called me into his office.

"What the hell is wrong with you?" He eyed me slouched in the chair. I made my mean face. "That doesn't work on me," he said.

Chief was out of patience. I needed to say something but couldn't talk about Charlotte and how it unnerved me to admit her request ate at me. He'd spot a lie if I tried one of those. There was no option except to give him a truth.

I kicked his desk and said, "I'm getting nowhere with the Zhiglovs, and I'm letting Daniel down."

In the days immediately after Daniel's death while I stalked his murderers, I lived in the cellar of an abandoned building. When not watching the gang, I scurried out to get food, peed over a drain, and plotted. Over a year had gone by, and I was still plotting. I vowed to kill not only the shooter but anyone associated with him.

More than a year went by, and though I killed the shooter and four others, the gang still existed. I wounded them, but they were recovering and picking up speed. Soon, they'd operate with impunity again. They'd kill innocent people. I turned my face to the floor. I'd be damned if I cried in front of Chief. Never once after my interrogation with him had I cried in his presence for any reason.

He put both forearms on his desk, and when he spoke, his voice came softly. "You're not letting anyone down. Least of all Daniel."

Hunched over, I shrugged and wouldn't look at Chief. I spoke to hide my anger over Charlotte, but those words were too true to be comfortable or detached. I was letting Daniel down.

"I feel impotent about our progress too." Chief kicked his own desk and ran his hand over his hair. "I cared about Daniel, and like you, I vowed to get them. I'm where you are."

I believed Chief wasn't just saying words to placate me. "I don't know where to turn next." Was I speaking about the Russians or Charlotte? Both?

"I never told you, but I found some notes Daniel took about you."

My head shot up. Chief never mentioned those until just now? Shit.

"He had it in his head you'd be a great employee for the DSS. He thought he'd give you a bit of training, then introduce you to me. He wanted you two to work as a team."

It was oddly satisfying to hear my assumption confirmed. I didn't know how to respond, so I kept my eyes on my hands.

"He was in love with you, and I think you with him?"

It took me a long time to answer, "Yeah."

"In this business, you can't think with your heart. It might be your motivation, but it can't take over your brain."

"Yeah."

"Listen to me. I've got something that needs saying. I tried to talk to you about this before, but you weren't ready to hear it."

I crinkled my brow. "What are you getting at?"

"When I first started training you, I tried to talk to you about Daniel. About who he was, and what he did to you."

"Daniel? He didn't do anything but love me."

"He brought you into the business without your knowledge or

consent. He put you in danger without proper training. He risked your life repeatedly. Daniel was wrong."

"He took care of me. I'm the one who messed up that night."

"Listen, girl. I've spent fifteen months teaching you, bringing you up to speed. It takes a long time to train in this job. Years. Daniel gave you weeks before you were backing him up. Had I known what was going on, I would have put an end to it. He didn't report his actions or his intel. He didn't allow the office to back him up. I don't know why. He knew better."

I kept silent. Chief made too much sense and began to override my emotions.

"Now that you've been doing this awhile, would you bring someone as green as you were to a job?"

That got my attention. Damn it. No, I wouldn't have. I'd spend too much precious energy protecting them and wouldn't concentrate on ... Oh, fuck. Chief was right, and accepting his truths felt like a knife in my heart. I hadn't even let Charlotte sit surveillance with me out of fear she would get hurt. For a moment, I forgot to breathe, and when I did draw breath, it happened in a ragged gasp. I remained in a protective hunch even when Chief sat back in his chair.

"You're a good investigator and problem solver. Good instincts and willing to learn. Stop blaming yourself for Daniel's mistakes. You're doing a good job, but we've got a ways to go on this case. Can you find a way to clear your head?"

"I'll go downstairs to the gym and get it together."

"Do that." Chief swiveled his chair a couple of times then said, "This is what else we're going to do. We're going to let the problem sit a week."

"But ..."

"But it's what we need to do. Sometimes, you let something sit and stew. You rest your brain. You come back to it, and things you didn't–couldn't–see before jump right out at you. I've seen it a hundred times. We're going to let it sit."

"That doesn't feel right, Chief."

"We're going to give it a try. You and me. I'm gonna give you some other work to keep you busy."

That week, the office sent me to Camden, New Jersey where I worked as the second-shift cleaning woman in an import/export office. I let my hair get matted, wore nasty prosthetic teeth, and decorated my face with a bunch of silicone peel and stick acne. There, I took dozens of photos of documents, shipping containers, trucks coming in and out, and behaved myself. Got four bugs and two cameras planted.

When Charlotte texted that she had enough intel, I ditched the rest of my shift. I rode my motorcycle to Philadelphia and checked into a hotel under my Jade Winters alias. After a shower and unknotting my hair, I took a taxi to South Street where lots of clubs lined up in a tight little area. There, I was anonymous in a black, suede miniskirt, and a black satin bra under a cropped, lace top. I added black, fishnet tights, and cleaned up my Doc Martens. Then I put on lots of eyeliner, and dark wine lipstick edged in black. I finished the look off with several silver hoops and cuffs in each ear and an armful of cheap, silver bangles.

I made my way along South Street and chose a club at random. First thing, two shots of whiskey, then I hit the dance floor, at first by myself, then moving from person to person, men, women, whoever, releasing tension to the music's beat. Arms over my head, my hips swayed, gyrated, invited. I had left my hair loose, and its movement matched my body's motions.

Men bought me drinks, though I had the bartender put them in my hand rather than let someone have the chance to sneak something into my glass. It was nothing to slip a roofie. Still, I tasted for

Rohypnol's salty flavor whenever I took a sip. You never knew, and that was why I always kept charcoal capsules on me.

I stuck to beer while I sized up the guys, planning to hook up with one of them. Why not? Two hours in, I chose a guy in his mid-twenties—the hot, brooding type. Long, dark, wavy hair, full lips, slight sneer. Said his name was Travis Harper and that he was an actor. Never heard of him. Whatever. We danced with my hands around his neck and his groin grinding into mine. We kissed. He had good technique. He told me about his car and the other famous actors he knew, and I thought about cutting him loose, then didn't. So what if he was stupid? I wasn't gonna screw him for his brains.

"Come on, baby. Let's go make the earth move," he said into my ear.

I had drunk enough to make my head spin and my walk wobble. "You have an apartment here or what?" I asked.

"Staying at the Hyatt Regency Penn's Landing."

Same hotel as me. Convenient, though he didn't need to know that. "Let's go."

He was all over me in the elevator and the hall. Once in the room, after I insisted on a condom, the sex was pretty vanilla—as was everything about him. I thought I'd give him a second chance for round two, but he went and opened his stupid mouth.

"Bet you can't wait to tell all your friends you fucked Travis Harper, can't you?"

God damn it. Why was he talking?

"Promise you, baby, you'll never have anyone else as good as me."

Yeah, I'd heard that before and had mostly been disappointed. Except for Conn— Hell. Why'd he pop in my mind? Travis Harper, piece of shit. I pushed him off my body and grabbed my clothes.

"Where you going?" His voice took on an edge.

I didn't bother to answer, just dressed and stuffed my tights into my purse. When my hand reached for the door handle, he grabbed my left. I pulled the switchblade from my boot, hit the button, and held it to his face. "I'm not in the mood for this shit." Yeah, pretty boy dropped my wrist and backed off. When I opened the door, he bitched at me about the money he spent on drinks. How stupid was he?

I raised my knife again, twisted my wrist to flip him off, and spent the rest of the night alone in my room where I had the mini bar at my disposal. The ride back to D.C. the next morning was a bitch with the hangover throbbing in my head.

CHAPTER TWENTY-TWO

A skill Chief taught me back in the beginning was how to follow someone in a crowd, in empty spaces, day, night, every sort of situation. At first, I thought it was easy. Then Chief gave me a test without telling me it was a test.

I followed a guy who was supposed to be leading me to where his boss hid so another agent could deal with the problem. I followed him four blocks through the city and into an office building. I used all Chief's rules. All the rules in the manual. The guy went to the third-floor mezzanine, and when I got there, he was gone. I continued forward and passed by a thick pillar. He got me—grabbed, subdued, and hung me over the mezzanine—the lobby's marble floor the only thing on my mind at that moment. I didn't know what to do to save myself, and I couldn't bring myself to beg. Staring into his eyes, I made my face hostile.

He laughed. "Stupid, little puppy." He gave me a shake then flipped me back onto the mezzanine, locking me in a tight grip. I fumed at not being able to move my arms an inch. "Go home to Chief and tell him you failed, puppy."

He threw me, and I rolled about six feet before I scrambled to my feet. The guy disappeared behind a heavy security door; I tried the door, but it was locked. My phone vibrated with a text from Chief.

Come back in.

Shit. Shit. Shit. I'd been played. I never saw that guy again. Chief worked me hard on surveillance skills for weeks.

I wasn't supposed to be near Sonia, but I couldn't sit home and wait for the techs or other investigators to tell me what was going on. The analyst on duty that evening said Sonia was at her home, so once again, I was outside Nick's Bar. My gut told me the answers would come from there. It was quiet until 0100 when three men left in a van. Amazing how the Zhiglovs found all those extra-big dudes. I guess they bred them big in their family.

That night, I drove a souped-up Honda Civic from the motor pool and allowed a bit of a gap to form between me and the van. They entered the city, and twenty minutes later, near L Street NE and Louisiana Avenue, they pulled to the curb. From almost a block away, I slipped my car in behind a box truck, scrambled over the gear shift, and watched from the passenger side. All three men got out then entered an alley. With so much crime happening in alleys, why didn't the police monitor them better? Jeez.

I exited the car and crept across the street to their van where I stuck a tracker under the bumper and activated it. Next, I slunk to the sidewalk against the building with my shoulders hunched using short, quick steps. A car drove by and blasted rap, but when the music faded, I heard voices from the alley. Was it them or someone else? I squatted behind some concrete steps and peered out. Two men exited the alley, got back in the van, and took off. What happened to the third? Hurry to my vehicle or enter the alley? I chose the alley.

Gun in hand, I walked five paces past the opening then paused. I hadn't seen anyone or anything when I went by. No one seemed to pay attention to me. Retracing my steps, I entered the alley and used the lights over a few of the doors for visibility. I kept to the middle and swept my eyes for anything suspicious.

Up ahead, the shimmer of something leaked from a pile of garbage. I hurried forward, shined my penlight, and found the third guy shot in the eye and chest, lying in the trash pile. He groaned. The dude was still alive—no weapon in sight.

"Hey, can you talk?" I asked.

He opened his good eye to me. "Take to police," he said.

"Yeah, I'll call the cops."

"Take to police. Jump in pocket." He moved his left hand some. "Take to pol ..."

The guy never finished. Blood leaked from his mouth, and his body sighed. I rooted in his left jacket pocket. Empty. I pulled his coat open and checked the inside pocket. Found a jump drive then grabbed his phone, wallet, and a set of keys. Nothing else on him. Sloppy of those guys, leaving anything behind. I placed the jump into one of my inner zipper pockets and stowed the other stuff.

I stood to leave the way I came when a van pulled in. The shits had circled back, I supposed to dispose of the body. Damn it. I should have checked the tracker app on my phone to make sure they left the area. There were three in the van from what I saw. Guess they went to pick up the third guy.

The headlights caught me, and the van accelerated. The tires screeched to a stop, and one bear jumped out and came at me. He started to pull a gun. I was quicker. One shot to the chest and several shots at the windshield. Bullet-proof glass. No suppressor meant loud blasts, which led to shouts from the windows above us.

The others got out firing at me. Bullets hit the brick walls and sent shards and grit flying. I darted deeper into the darker part of the alley, took a left around the corner into the cross alley, and almost ran into some fire escape stairs. Dead end in both directions —angry bears at my back. Up the ladder.

One shot came at me, but it was deflected by the metal ladder.

The whole structure shuddered as two of those assholes ran up the fire escape after me. At the top, I found an area of rooftops, some sloped, separated with low firewalls of three to four feet high. The city's light pollution and a moon shining in a cloudless sky gave me enough to see, letting me run across the expanse, and I headed southeast toward a more populated neighborhood.

My parkour training came into play. Flying past equipment, I ran up the first slope and slid down then cleared the first wall without sacrificing speed, cleared the second and kept going. Shouts and one gunshot whizzed by me. After maybe five buildings, I came to the final roof before a gap across another alley. Critical error. I spun, looking for a direction. No place to go, no way down. That building was sleek concrete—no footholds. Eight fucking feet across and the other building maybe two feet lower. Another gunshot whizzed past me, and I twisted to look behind. Two bears, three buildings away. Eight feet to safety, six stories up. No options, no choice.

In training, I had easily cleared ten-foot jumps on the ground. I could make it. Another bullet missed me. I returned three shots, all misses, backed up, ran forward, and jumped. No looking down. Sighted my target—the flat roof of the next building. I sailed through the air for a second or an hour—landed and shoulder rolled on the next roof, bruising my elbow and arm on the rough surface. Oh shit, I was alive. I would have celebrated but for two more gunshots.

A six by four-foot corrugated metal structure sat on the roof. I scrambled on my hands and feet to get behind it and lay flat, hoping anything inside would keep me safe as the thin walls wouldn't stop bullets. My breath came in ragged gasps, and I fought to calm down and think. More shots fired, but only one came through the metal at the top of the structure. I went to the side and fired back. Hit one. Chest. Maybe a lung shot, leaving two.

Two? When did that other dude show up? How many damn

Zhiglovs were running around the neighborhood that night? Letting one eye peek out, I saw they had stopped at the roof's edge. It didn't seem like those shits with more muscle than brain could make the jump too. For a moment, I was safe, so I yanked my jacket off my shoulder and peeked at my arm. Bleeding—not too bad. More sting than wound. For just a moment, I let myself breathe and regroup.

It was then the fear hit me. Real bullets fired at me. Real men trying their best to kill me. Chief once said some fear was a good thing. It'd keep me from getting too complacent, or too cocky. The main thing was to recognize and use it to propel me into action. With that in mind, I took one last deep breath and turned my attention to escape. The roof shed had a door. With any luck, it wouldn't just house machinery—there'd be a staircase or ladder. Locked. The two bears shouted at me, at each other, whatever. Probably calling for reinforcements.

I fired off four more shots shouting, "Медвежье дерьмо." Bear shit. "Сосут член дерьмо." Cock-sucking shits. Yeah, I didn't just learn the grammar. I learned the bad words too.

Gun in waistband, lockpicking kit in hand. A simple cylinder lockset. I opened the door and looked in. More bullets came my way, trying to keep me pinned and scared, and it was working. Inside, I found HVAC machinery and a beautiful ladder. No way off that roof but the way I came or down the ladder. Crawling inside, I locked the door behind me, descended, and came out in a mechanical room. When I peeked out that door, I saw an expensive-looking executive office level with carpeting and offices—some with open doors. Safety lights made intervals of glowing circles. I slipped out of the mechanical room and located the fire exit signs and stairwell. As I passed an admin's desk, I snatched her ID to use on the electronic door locks.

Descending, I found the fifth and fourth floors dark. At the third floor, I heard shouts from the bottom. Russian shouts. How'd they get down there so fast? Unless there were more? Now what would I do? They entered the building without setting off the alarm. How?

Looking through the small window into the third floor, I saw it was active with forty or fifty people. The space was wide open, and workers sat at cubicles answering phones. Maybe an all-night fulfillment or help desk operation. Most of the employees faced away from the door, so I used the keycard I stole, entered, and looked for a place to hide while moving away from the stairs. Not the elevator. The bears would be watching that. Maybe take the elevator to the second floor and see about going out a window? A glance at the windows showed they didn't open. Everyone around me wore jeans and casual shirts, so I didn't stick out too much. I grabbed a stack of files, opened the top one, and pretended I was completing some important task. A few people looked my way though no one challenged me. People rarely confronted anyone who looked like they belonged.

My mind raced as fast as my heartbeat, and I scrambled for a plan. Never mind the lavatories. That'd be the first place I'd look if I were on the hunt instead of the hunted. A door marked supplies appeared in front of me. That would be a good place to hide and plan. I entered, flipped on the light, and found an office-sized room with metal shelving crammed with crap. I closed the door behind me. I studied the metal shelves. Maybe I could push one across the door or wedge it between the door and the wall. Each unit was bolted to the wall or floor. Shit. I jammed some plastic bins between the door and the closest shelving unit to prevent anyone from entering.

All those gunshots on the roof and alley. Someone was sure to call the police, and in that neighborhood, they'd respond and maybe search the building. I needed an exit strategy fast. I checked my Glock's magazine. Six bullets in the clip, so I switched it out for a full magazine. Better than later when someone was firing at me.

By that time, it was 0139. From the closet, I couldn't hear sirens, nor did I hear any excitement among the workers. Maybe the police stayed in the alley a block away and wouldn't go any further. That left only the bears to deal with. Who knew how long they'd wait around looking for me?

I didn't want to squat in that closet all night. Call in the cavalry? No. That would tip off the bear's that they were under investigation. Anyway, I needed to learn to do things on my own. Neither Jack nor Tony would have called for help. It was best to get myself out of that mess.

How? Fire alarm? That would clear the building ... I could walk out with everyone else, hide in the crowd, melt away? The fire department and police would show up. Shit. All those gunshots. Bet the cops were already searching.

I scanned the shelves for inspiration. An empty backpack. I stuffed my jacket into it. Next, I found a company logoed golf shirt and put it on over my T-shirt. My hair went into a bun held in place with a pencil. I snatched another black company T-shirt off the shelf, too, stuffing it in my backpack. The office taught me how to use a T-shirt to cover my face ninja-style. It might come in handy.

Time to ease myself out of the closet and blend with the others. Maybe the bears wouldn't even dare enter that floor with all the workers. I opened the door and found most people either at the windows or huddled in groups. One desk near me looked unoccupied that night. I grabbed the pink, floral cardigan off the back of the chair, put it on, then sauntered to the window to stand next to two mid-twenties looking guys. They watched three police cars with flashing lights directly below.

"What's going on?" They looked at me with puzzled faces. "Oh, hi," I said, sticking out my hand. "I'm Lily. Brand new tonight," I said, making my friendliest smile. I'd heard places like that had a high rate of turnover, so my sudden appearance should have been plausible.

"Hi. I'm Tyler, and this is Owen."

"What's going on out there?" I asked again with big, innocent eyes.

"We don't know," Tyler said. "I was showing Owen my new car when all these police showed up."

"You have a new car?" I said letting my face light up with interest. "Which one?" Again, he got one of my best smiles.

Tyler grinned back and pointed to a 2025 Monte Carlo parked across the street.

"My favorite. And it's all yours?"

"Yup." He jingled the keys at me then tossed them to a desk. "Hey Owen, let's go to the lobby and see what's up. You coming?" he asked me.

"No thanks. I'll wait here." I watched them get on the elevator then snatched the keys from Tyler's desk. At least I'd have a way out of there—if I could avoid the bears. Then my mind went and said something stupid to me. What if they shot any woman that looked like me? I couldn't count on the police to take them out, and I couldn't leave wondering if they'd kill someone innocent in my place. Another thought grabbed me. They saw my face. That meant they had a chance of finding out who I was. No. Just no.

I grabbed the T-shirt from the backpack, stuffing some of it into my back pocket for easy access, then resettled the pack over both shoulders. Glock in hand, I eased into the stairwell.

CHAPTER TWENTY-THREE

In the stairwell, I crouched below the door's window and listened. Quiet voices above me. Feet ascending the stairs echoing in soft waves in the dark, vertical space. Taking a moment to let my eyes adjust to the dimness, I caught a whiff of cigarettes lingering in the still air. Bears on the fourth floor moving to the fifth. They had bypassed the third floor—at least for the moment. I kept my ear pointed in their direction while I took off the golf shirt then reached for the T-shirt and tied it over my head and face with the neck hole around my eyes. Still focused on any noises in the stairwell, I reached into the backpack, fished out then attached the suppressor to my Glock, and crept up the stairs on silent feet.

Two voices speaking low. I made out individual phrases. "You go left ... I go first ... Kill that bitch."

Yeah, we'd see about that. I passed the fourth floor and made for the fifth, edgy that I had no idea about the fifth-floor layout. I took a gamble they'd reenter the stairwell from the fifth and make for the sixth. I knew that floor plan. Still on the stairs, I kept my head below sight level and waited for them to leave the fifth. It didn't take long.

They came out, still talking too loudly, the dumb shits. "This floor was a waste of time. I bet she bolted right for the bottom floor." The two went up to the sixth floor. They broke their conversation when we heard noise below us. The police had entered the building shouting about a floor-to-floor search. Great. Like I needed them in my way.

One bear said, *"Спешите."* Hurry.

When I heard the sixth-floor door open then close, I moved behind them on silent feet, pausing at the door to look in the window. They moved along the straight corridor, trying the locked office doors. Their silhouettes showed guns in their hands. Right-handed. Both disappeared into a room to the left. Fear and adrenaline gripped me. Knowing that could cause me to make a mistake, I drew a deep breath and reminded myself I was the hunter and not the hunted. They had no idea I was behind them. Easing the door open quietly as I could, I got low, slipped in, then eased the door closed. Both men were at least twenty-five yards ahead. I'd have a hard time making kill shots in the dark and with a suppressor at that range. My 9mm would make entry and exit wounds too. It'd be a big mess. No way around that.

A recessed admin's station allowed me to fade into the shadows and wait for them to return to the stairwell. I'd have to get them from behind. In the back, like a coward. Not that those two were innocent. They'd just shot one of their own in that alley, and they were on the hunt to kill me. It was me or them. I was on the good side. The right side. That's what I told myself every time.

I cleared my mind and descended to my dark place. There, I focused on their footsteps and their voices—still talking to each other. How stupid were they? Tactical hand-signals were invented for a reason. They seemed to be returning to the stairwell. I pushed deeper into the recess and watched the aisle carpet, waiting for shadows to cross the dim night lights.

Footsteps. Soft bass voices. Breaths. A sigh. Finally, a damn shadow. One bear passed. Just one. Sweat prickled my scalp. Concentrate.

The first one called back from the door. "Yury, *поторопись*." Hurry up.

Yury didn't answer. The first guy returned down the hall, strolling casually, his gun loose at his side. He thought the floor was clear, and he was safe, yet he never thought to recheck the cranny I hid in. I stuck my head around the corner just enough to see. He stood outside an office.

"Yury, put that down."

"It's a nice laptop."

"We are not thieves. Put it down and come on. We must find that woman."

He entered the office, and I drew back, wanting them to come out of the office so I could shoot them in the hallway. Thing was the cops were already searching the building. I was out of waiting time.

I snuck along the hall. Should I make a noise, let them come out, and shoot them? Should I creep up to the door and get them? I came to the last door in the hall, straining to hear movement.

One grabbed me from behind. Wrapped his arms around me like steel bands. He squeezed and yelled for his partner. Yury ran out of the last office. All I could move was my elbow and lower arm. I got my gun pointed at Yury and squeezed off three shots. Torso. Abdomen. Not the heart or lungs. Yury dropped, clutching his middle and moaning.

The bear holding me howled. He threw me across the hall, slamming me into the wall hard enough to disorient me, and I slid to the floor. A foot came at me, and I rolled away, got into a squat, then raised my gun to shoot him. He swatted my hand, and my gun flew.

New plan. I raced to the other end of the hall toward the

admin's station while pulling my switchblade out of my boot. He raced after me and grabbed me by the T-shirt mask, pulling me backward. I hooked my thumb under my chin and yanked it off.

Free to move, I bent forward—stabbed backward—got him in the thigh. He roared at the pain. I twisted and slashed his face, getting him down his left side. It was enough distraction to let me grab his gun from his waistband. In almost one motion, I wrapped the T-shirt around the muzzle and shot him point blank in the heart, the asshole stiffening, then falling straight back like a cartoon character. The T-shirt kept most of the blood from splashing on me but did nothing for the noise. I ran for my Glock with its suppressor and put two bullets in his skull.

Yury was still alive, moaning and writhing on the floor. I put a double tap in his skull.

How close were the cops in the stairwell? Were they on their way yet? I ran to the door, opened it a crack, and listened. No shouts or movement on the stairs. Back to work.

I took a photo of each man's face, rifled their pockets, and checked their bodies. No cameras. No wires or audio. I smashed one dude's glasses just in case, then grabbed the pieces as well as their wallets and phones. Kneeling, I took a moment to remove the batteries from the phones right then, so they couldn't use them to track me back to the DSS. The CAIT team would find out if they sent my photo or other info back to whoever they reported to. I might not be made. I didn't have time to photograph their tattoos. Anyway, with the cops in the building, those two would go to the morgue, and the medical examiner would take photos that CAIT would get hold of.

Again, I looked at Yury. I'd rather finish a person quick with the first bullet. Not that that made me a good person—just not a sadistic one. I hoped the bullet I might take one day was quick. Not stabbed, not strangled. Maybe tranquilizer, then fall asleep—nice and easy. I shook my head to clear it. Now wasn't the time for those thoughts.

How to get out of there? I couldn't go up, I wasn't making that jump again, which meant going down and getting past the police. Back in the stairwell, I made it to the fourth floor and by the noise of officers on the stairs, figured they'd catch me moving to the third. Out of options, I pulled the fire alarm.

When the third floor evacuated, I joined them, happy for the panic, and that in the dark, the black shirt I wore didn't show much in the way of blood splatters. Most people hurried, some yelling. The police officers tried to hold us back and keep order, but we ignored them, pushing out the door to the street. I made it, fingering the stolen car keys in my pocket.

And there was Tyler—leaning against his own car. I had lost my easy ride out of there. The cops directed us to go stand across the street. I shuffled to the back of the crowd, slipped into the alley, and ran. I went two blocks and came up against a guy who probably wanted to rob me—good luck with that. I kicked his knee, jumped a little to hook my fist into his jaw, and kept moving. Ran at least three more zigzagging blocks. At a main artery, I lucked out, flagged a taxi, and gave the driver an address within a block of the office, arriving there at nearly 0230.

On the taxi ride, I had phoned and woke Chief. When I arrived on the fifth floor, Anderson had him on a video call shown on his station monitor. Chief was dressing, meaning I ruined his night's sleep. While emptying my pockets and backpack, I gave Chief and Anderson a rundown of what happened. I showed Chief the items I collected.

"The dead guy in the alley offered you the jump?" he asked like he didn't believe me the first time.

"Yeah. He gave it to me. Told me to take it to the police. I grabbed the rest off him and the other two bears."

"Anderson, call upstairs to forensics and have them pick up that stuff. Tell them it's A.S.A.P. And Raine, give them your shirt. They can get DNA off the blood."

"Okay. Do you think CAIT can check for surveillance footage from the sites?"

"They're already on it."

"Thanks. After they pick up the evidence, I'm gonna hit the shower and change."

"I'll be there in about thirty minutes. Come to my office when you're done."

Thirty minutes later, my hair still wet, I returned to Chief's office still buzzing with adrenaline. A shootout. I had been in an actual shootout and survived.

"Did any of the bears make me, or send my picture back? Am I outed?"

"Yeah, somewhat. A photo from one of their phones shows they got a picture of you from a distance on the rooftops, which they texted to Alexander. It's fuzzy and dark. Just your silhouette really, so they know you're female. They keep referring to you as 'that bitch'. Good news is, they don't know your name or have a clear description."

"Have you heard if there's anything good on that jump and other stuff I got off the dead alley bear?"

"Yeah. The jump had a shitload of stuff. He wasn't a Zhiglov."

"Then who was he?"

"CIA. Just confirmed it."

I paused. "They got someone inside?"

"They thought so. They were going after them for stealing intelligence. Looks like the agent was made from almost the first day. We were on site first, but I shared some of what we found with the DHS."

"So, what did we find?"

"Can't let you know yet."

"Why not?"

"Got things to confirm. Now shut it."

Chief didn't say shut it often, but when he did, he meant it. Even so, I couldn't resist one more question.

"Does the DHS know anything about our case?"

"My contact claims he doesn't. Give our analysts some time to go over the intel."

Chief sent me to catch some sleep in an empty office while the techs and analysts processed the evidence I found. When I woke, I found a breakfast bar in the kitchen cabinet, ate it, and went back to work. It was 1100 hours, and Andrea had the morning off. Chief was in his office with the door closed, his windows darkened. I placed photos from the Zhiglov file on the floor in front of Andrea's desk, the biggest open space that wasn't the conference room, and sat crisscrossed in front of them. The pictures formed a semi-circle in front of me. I grasped for anything, any clue, however unlikely.

Front and center was a still of Sonia outside Nick's Bar with the woman in disguise. Then I studied another photo of Sonia, standing in the same position. She had put on weight. Getting fat? Pregnant? I stared some more. And got shorter? I compared earlier photos with the latest, concentrating on those at the same spot on the sidewalk.

For a moment, my brain didn't process what my eyes saw. The person in the later photos wasn't Sonia. Just someone pretending to be Sonia. Why? Because she was missing? No. Because she feared for her life. I studied who I thought was the woman disguised as a man and compared his or her butt to Sonia's. Seemed like more of a match. The dude was Sonia. And there it was. Obvious. Stupid, stupid, stupid. Me of all people. Stupid.

One person showed up in most photos. A person we vetted and dismissed as a bit player. Victor's trophy wife, beauty queen Sonia. Always the center of attention. Always dressed in some slutty outfit, that is, until I killed a bunch of her men, and she feared for her life. We believed she was just decoration. What if she was the one calling the shots? I ran that scenario through my mind. It worked.

She was in front of us the whole time. Just because she was sexy and dressed like a hooker didn't mean she wasn't smart. Didn't mean she couldn't run a criminal organization. But Russian males didn't take orders from females which explained Victor and Alexander's role. In that restaurant with the buyer's rep, she went to the ladies' room to phone Alexander so no one would hear her giving orders.

It had to be her. She was in charge before and was in charge again. My mind raced, making connections and aligning opportunities with actions. It was Sonia who ordered Daniel's death, not Victor. Stupid me. I'd underestimated what a woman could do.

I ran to Charlotte's station. "Drop everything."

She widened her eyes. "What is it, Raine?"

I wrote Sonia's full name on a pad. "Victor's wife. Get me her background. Family back three or four generations. Acquaintances, connections. Arrest records, medical records, education. Everything. Today."

"I'll get as much as I can. I don't think I'll get it all today, but I'll try."

"You get to work, and at noon, I'll go get you a good lunch. And pie." Charlotte's sweet tooth rivaled mine.

"Deal," she said, making room at her station to work on my hunch.

I returned to the photos and files, hoping my gut feeling would pan out. In case it didn't, I scoured the photos and made notes on anything else. At 1200, I cleaned up my piles and went to get us some food. When I stepped off the elevator at 1230, I found Charlotte bursting with excitement.

"I got lucky," she said, putting a hand on my arm. I stiffened but resisted brushing it away. "I got something good." Charlotte took me by the wrist and pulled me to her screen. "Sonia Zhiglova. Maiden name Sonia Helena Anna Razina. Do you know who her father is?"

My heart fell. "Yeah, I do. Anton Razin. Civil Engineer. We checked that avenue already. Keep digging."

"Wrong!" Charlotte's eyes twinkled over her huge smile. I raised an eyebrow at her. "Razin is her stepfather. Anatoly Yegor Dvornikov is her birth father. Recognize that name?" Charlotte's voice took on a smug tone. And rightly so.

"Anatoly Dvornikov is her birth father? The man every other mob boss—even the Colombian cartels—are afraid of?" I didn't drop my jaw. I had trained myself not to do that, but the urge was there.

"Yup. And guess who talks to her daddy every day? Multiple times. Our bugs picked up her conversations in the background, but we never focused on them." It took me a moment to digest Charlotte's information. "I'll keep digging," she said.

That meant the Dvornikovs had a presence in D.C. all along. No one figured that out, and the implications of that oversight were overwhelming. Too much for my mind. I stared into space, trying to remember something someone said to me about the Dvornikovs.

Shit, what was it?

I squeezed my head with both hands as if that would push the memory to the front of my brain. It worked. Tony. Weeks ago, Tony told me he was working on a case involving the Dvornikovs. Some nasty shit involving biologics. I met Charlotte's eyes. "We need to tell Chief. Right now." I dropped our lunches on her desk and ran up the steps to the mezzanine with my head spinning. Chief's dark windows and closed door meant he was working with someone else, and in the past, he'd made it clear that busting in, no matter what, wasn't acceptable.

Andrea had come in from her morning off and asked, "Is it an emergency?"

I twisted my head to her. Was it? No one's life was on the line at that very minute, yet ... biologics ... could kill thousands, millions. "Yeah. An emergency."

Andrea looked me up and down. She had to see I buzzed with energy. "Stay in the area. I'll check."

I stepped away but kept my eye on Andrea. She never went to the door or picked up the phone, didn't tap her keyboard or seem to do anything specific, yet a minute later, Chief's door opened, and an analyst hustled out. A secret button or something. She had a secret way of alerting Chief. Someday, I'd find it. Andrea met my eyes and jerked her head to the door. I hurried in closing it behind me.

Putting both hands on his desk, I leaned forward. "Chief, the boss we're looking for. I found him. I mean, her. I think. Victor's wife, Sonia. Then and now."

Victor, who shot Daniel, who I then shot dead. After his death, Sonia returned to Russia. She was back, and the gang grew stronger every day. I gave Chief my theory and let him know what Charlotte had found. Chief drew his brows together and said nothing as he ran through the possibilities like a chess master studying a board. I knew better than to interrupt with my second revelation even though it threatened to burst out of me.

All Chief said was, "You may be on to something." His face went neutral. No emotion, no clues. He'd already made the connection to Tony's case but didn't know I had too.

"There's more." I shifted my weight twitching to release tension.

"Go on."

It occurred to me that I might get Tony in trouble, but then again Tony told me to go to Chief if I heard anything. These cases were too important to hold anything back. "Weeks ago, Tony let me know he was working a Dvornikov case in California with another investigator. No details, just that Homeland Security and the CIA were involved, and he told me to keep my ears open for any chatter about biologics. Tony said I needed to let you know the minute I heard anything. Dvornikov is involved in something biologic. And now Sonia is looking for a buyer for some unknown item. It doesn't take a rocket scientist to make a connection."

Chief nodded and closed his eyes in a long blink. "What else do you know?"

"That's it. I don't know what the biologic is, and I don't have solid evidence that's what Sonia's trying to broker."

"Who else knows of this?"

"I don't know. I never told anyone what Tony said to me. Charlotte found the connection between Dvornikov and Sonia, but she doesn't know the whole story."

Chief sat, thinking some more before sitting military straight, punching the intercom and saying, "Charlotte, my office."

It seemed Charlotte and I were about to get a whole 'nother level of intel.

Chief started before Charlotte sat. "We received information months ago about missing, live-virus smallpox vials from Russian version of the CDC," Chief said. "That lab in Siberia and the CDC in Atlanta are the only two locations in the world housing live smallpox."

That conversation headed in a scary direction real fast. I didn't know much about smallpox, but the anxious expressions on Chief and Charlotte's faces set my stomach to rolling.

"Four vials were stolen. The CIA has a list of eighteen possible suspects. So far, they've narrowed it down to four, with the

Dvornikovs at the top of the list. The Russian FSB, Federal Security Bureau, is investigating, but not openly. They aren't cooperating with our side. Complete denial."

"And Tony and the others are already working this case?"

"Yeah, from the Dvornikov side. That jump drive you took off the DHS agent in the alley? It had all kinds of intel that confirms the Dvornikovs have the virus."

"So, we're on the right track."

"Yeah. Good work, Raine. You'll keep on Sonia. Best guess is the vials are either still in Russia or maybe in California with Sonia's father. Sonia might give us a clue about exactly where they are and who's interested in buying them."

I nodded, my brain racing through possibilities among the world's terrorist's groups.

"The CDC's aware live virus could get loose here on US soil. Army Intelligence and the CDC are quietly working to make as much vaccine as they can. Those closest to the case have already received vaccinations, and the CDC is making plans to vaccinate as many people as they can. Problem is, they'll never make enough. Millions will contract the disease, and many will die. Raine, you and all the other DSS employees had the smallpox vaccine, so no worries there."

"Yeah, I know. You forced me to get all kinds of vaccines when I started here."

"This one is different. Hardly anyone in the US under the age of forty-seven is inoculated. We thought the disease was eradicated."

How many millions of people was that?

While speaking with Charlotte and me, Chief shot off texts and messages. He didn't like the replies he received. "News that Sonia is Dvornikov's daughter seems to be a surprise to everyone."

"Who's everyone?" I asked.

"CIA, though who can really tell with them? They'd lie about who their mother was even as they were being born. They don't like to confirm anything." He sat back in his chair, holding his chin, thinking hard. "I've got to take this intel up the food chain. You two," he said, pointing to Charlotte and me. "Keep digging. Neither of you leaves until you clear it with me first. Do not share this intel with anyone."

"Yeah."

"We need to know what Sonia's up to. Ideally, we need to bug her cell phone," Charlotte said.

"She's on her phone all day long," I said. "Even when she's not talking on it, she holds it. If we found a way to get it for a couple of minutes, I could put one of those tiny bugs on her phone." We had an amazing listening device, thin as a human hair, about half an inch long. Stick it on the phone, and we'd hear most everything she said.

"Phones are tricky," Chief said. "The Zhiglovs tend to change them out every few weeks. Does she have jewelry or something she wears all day long, every day? A wedding ring?"

"Her? No. She changes outfits and jewelry all day long, and she doesn't wear a wedding ring anymore. Her phone is the one thing I see her with the most."

Chief paced, thinking some more. "Go down to the tech lab. Tell them you want to bug her phone, but you want to hear both sides of the conversation. We may have to do this more than once, so you'll have to figure out a way to get to her without her knowing."

Oh, yeah. That would be easy. I sat lost in thought for a few moments, then my scrambled notions congealed. "Chief, Charlotte said we have Sonia on audio in the background. Has anyone listened to her?"

"I don't think so. We weren't targeting her."

"Do you think it's worth checking?"

"Maybe." Chief drew out the word and his eyes went unfocused. I assumed he was thinking what I was thinking.

Charlotte jumped in. "I could check our files to confirm we hear Sonia's voice in the background. If we do, I'll have the techs see what they can do to isolate and enhance her words. Maybe we'll get lucky."

"Yeah, do that," Chief said. "Good thinking, Raine. Now, figure out a way to get her phone tapped."

CHAPTER TWENTY-FOUR

The tech people gave me a thin, square-shaped sensor about the size of the circle of paper from a hole punch. It sat in its own small, plastic box, smaller than my palm, with a stylus inside. "Don't touch it with your fingers," the tech guy said. "It's too fragile. Pick it up and place it with the stylus." Great. Another step when I needed to get it done in a hurry. They also gave me two of the hair-like listening devices in the same little box.

All I had to do was get hold of Sonia's phone for a few minutes, open it, and place the sensor on a certain internal part. We'd pick up both sides of the conversation as well as numbers and locations. I'd also use the tool to place the more conventional hair-thin listening device up against the edge of the camera lens where it would be hard to spot, and we'd hear anything else in her vicinity. Easy peasy, right?

We began following Sonia around the clock. She didn't always wear her disguise, and when she didn't, she had lots of protection around her and didn't linger outdoors. Whenever someone saw her in the open, it was her double. Wonder how much she was paying that woman to be her doppelganger? Wonder if that woman really knew what was at stake? Neither bitch had much to fear right then. We weren't going to do anything about Sonia until we knew what their shipment and buyer were all about. With both her own guards and us watching her ass, Sonia was safer than she'd ever been.

Since she'd seen me as me in the club, I'd have to be in disguise when it was time for me to get close to her. Chief put a team in her neighborhood posing as electrical workers. They used external listening devices to hear her conversations but heard nothing related to business. That morning's transcript reported Sonia made a massage appointment at a sleek, private spa in Georgetown for three that afternoon. That was our best chance at her phone. We hustled to get me in.

Miss Chickie put together a uniform to match the ones the employees wore. Charlotte worked with the CAIT team to hack into the salon's computers to learn which massage therapist Sonia would see and in which room. Charlotte also got me a floor plan, and I watched videos about how to give a massage. Yeah, that was going to be the thing that would trip me up. I'd have to avoid that.

Shepherd and Flynn would pose as local Washington D.C. police detectives. I'd find a way to send the real massage therapist to Shepherd who'd keep her busy for a few minutes with questions about a fake case, then I'd deal with Sonia's phone.

At 1415, the surveillance team let me know she left the house as herself in a black van with no side or back windows. At 1445 I was in place at the back door to the spa. When CAIT alerted me Sonia's van was three blocks away, I made my move. The back door had an electronic lock, but CAIT made me an e-card with a magnetic strip, so getting in was easy. I'd tell whoever I met that I was a new employee, the owner's cousin, here to learn. The DSS already had intel on the place and knew that the owner was hardly ever on site and was known for being flighty. We hoped that ruse would work.

The back door led into a receiving/storage area. The next

room was the employee break room. I paused at the partially open door and listened to three employees gossiping about their clients. Who cheated on their spouse, who did what drugs. One of the women mentioned a senator's wife. The name was familiar, but I pushed it aside and focused. When they left the break room, I moved into the main hallway and grabbed a stack of towels.

I wore a light brown wig styled in the French twist all the employees wore, had a fake nose with a huge bump, wore carefully contoured make-up and an elongated chin. My pants and tunic hid extra padding, giving me a chubby shape. Most clients in a place like that didn't bother really looking at the people who worked there, but for an extra layer of disguise, I'd use a British accent.

It was a simple floor plan and from the far end where I stood, I saw a worker lead Sonia into a room. She never looked around. Never registered I stood there. The worker came out a moment later, leaving Sonia to remove her robe and lay on the table.

I'd seen a photo of the massage therapist assigned to Sonia and fussed with the towels until I saw her come out of another room. Before she could knock on Sonia's door, I intercepted her.

"Excuse me, I have a message," I said.

"Who are you?" the therapist asked.

"Louise. I'm new. There are two detectives from the police out on the sidewalk asking for you."

She looked puzzled, then angry. "I swear, if that shit brother of mine—"

"You'd best hurry as they don't look patient. I'll stall your client, luv."

The woman huffed then walked toward the reception area. I spoke to Shepherd through my conduction mike. "She's on her way." Next, I knocked on Sonia's door and was granted admittance.

Sonia lay face down and naked on the table, not even bothering with the sheet. Pretty toned. No cellulite. "Hello, luv," I said. "I'm afraid your regular therapist has been detained a moment. May I get you started?"

"You have experience?" Sonia asked as I edged to where she set her phone.

"I am rather new, but—"

"We wait," Sonia ordered. She kept her eyes closed and her head turned from her phone. I moved to the counter and extended my hand toward it.

"Girl," Sonia said. I froze my hand. "I'm cold. Sheet."

"Yes, mum. Straight away." I found the sheet and covered Sonia. She settled again, and I extended my hand for the phone.

"Girl," she said again.

Damn it. "Yes, mum?"

"My wine. I want it now. Make sure it's not too chilled."

"Yes, mum." I looked around the room. No wine or glass. Sonia's phone rang, and she put her hand out for it like she didn't even have to ask me, which with her money, she didn't. I put the phone in her hand and stepped back, listening while refolding towels. I heard only her side of the conversation, and though it was in Russian, I understood.

"A third bidder? How much? Good. Set up a meeting." Sonia ended the call and tucked the phone against her body. Without opening her eyes, she said in English, "Stupid girl. My wine."

"Yes, mum," I said. "I'll go get your wine." Outside the door, I said to Shepherd, "I need more time."

Flynn replied. "Out of time. Abort."

"Just need five minutes."

Shepherd came on the line. "The woman refused to answer any questions and is right now entering the front door. Abort."

Shit. I went out the back door, unfolded a white rain poncho stashed in my pocket, and wore it to cover the uniform. A block away, I slid into the back seat of Shepherd's car completely pissed, and my voice showed it. "Now what?"

Shepherd stretched and rubbed the back of his neck instead of returning my attitude. "I'm thinking. Get changed. Your bag is back there."

I scrunched down and put on my own clothes. Shepherd, Flynn, and I brainstormed all the way back to the office, and they came up with the idea of trying again at a manicure appointment. I wouldn't be able to go back into that spa, so I nixed that idea. Sonia was always with bodyguards or inside an alarmed and secure building. Maybe run her car off the road and arrive as paramedics? I wasn't crazy about that idea. Simple plans worked better. When we debriefed with Chief, he counseled patience and said the right plan would present itself.

That night, I ate at the diner, and Elroy had dessert with me. "Things good?" I asked.

"Yeah. Business is steady. Got no complaints."

I nodded, and we ate his homemade chocolate cake while I listened to him talk about some new heart-healthy recipes he planned on trying. For a few minutes, I was a normal girl having a conversation with another person about mundane things. Though it felt nice pretending I was just a regular person with regular worries, that afternoon's failure ate at me. I couldn't suspend the hunt even for a few more hours. When I left, I went to stake out Nick's Bar again.

Sitting across and down the street in a Toyota Camry, I watched the same crew of people gathered on the second floor, but then something was different. Both Sonia, in her disguise, and her decoy came to the sidewalk with everyone else. A bear drove around the corner in a hot, white Mercedes convertible with D.C. plates. The bodyguard got out, and Alexander and the real Sonia got in. The rest of their posse got in a Suburban and followed.

No way would I go unnoticed by two cars. I called the office and let the analyst on duty know what I was doing and that I was going to the Alexandria house by a different route. I sped, breaking so many laws I was lucky there wasn't a line of cops behind me, but I got there before them and parked around the corner.

The front of the house had low, thick bushes. I wriggled myself into them to watch the front door and the security keypad. Maybe I could film Alexander hitting the code. That would let me get inside while they slept and take care of the phone that way.

Not a minute after I was set, Alexander and Sonia pulled up. They got out of their car, but their bodyguards stayed in theirs. Sonia was all over Alexander, groping and squeezing. She blocked my view of Alexander's hands at the keypad, damn the bitch, and they entered the house. On the street, the bodyguards took off.

Easing out of the bushes, I crept to the marble pad in front of the door. I looked at the door and wished I could kick it in frustration. A thin outline of light shone through it. No freakin' way. It was amazing how much my job relied on stupid luck. It wasn't completely closed, which meant they hadn't engaged the security system. I squat-walked closer and listened. Lots of moaning and grunting. I dared to push the door open an inch to peek. The door opened to a wide central foyer with a staircase at the back of it and two wide doorways to either side. The noise came from the room on the left. And guess what was on the foyer floor? Among the shoes, a tie, and jacket was Sonia's phone.

Hot damn.

Heart pounding in my ears, I pushed the door open enough to slide in, touching it back to the door jamb again, so the cold or street sounds wouldn't reach them. Like that could happen over Sonia's sex noise.

Problem was that the phone sat on Alexander's jacket right in front of the entrance to the living room. Would they notice if I moved it? I swiveled my neck to the front door, planning my escape if shit went wrong. Then I inched forward to the edge of the living room entrance and let one eye look in. There they were, half undressed on the sofa, Sonia's eyes squeezed closed. Hoping they stayed that way, I eased back, pinched the jacket's fabric between my thumb and index finger, and pulled. A moment later, I had hold of her phone.

They were really at it then. Hopefully, Alexander would hold out long enough for me to get it done. A click clicking noise, then a ball of fluff, and a sneeze. Sweet damn, Sonia's little dog. I had forgotten about it. Stupid.

Don't bark, dog, don't bark.

The puppy sneezed again then wagged its tail at me, so I extended my fingers to it in a friendly way. The dog licked and nipped at my fingertips, making happy little puppy noises. Maybe it could still work. I pulled off the phone's case and opened the back. The puppy, who was dying for attention, kept licking my wrist. To keep him happy and not barking, I paused to pet it. In the background, Sonia screamed, "Faster." I willed Alexander to go slower but to keep Sonia screaming and moaning, or whatever.

A minute later, while the puppy wagged its whole butt and snuffed my ear, I got both bugs planted and put the phone back on Alexander's jacket. The dog made a little growl, grabbed the jacket, and pulled it. Great. Let them think the puppy moved it.

Another idea hit me. After confirming that Sonia and Alexander were still going at it, I wiggled my fingers at the puppy who came to me. I put the third listening device on its collar tag. Hopefully, they didn't sweep the dog for bugs regularly.

I retreated to the door then back to the bushes with my last sight—the puppy cocking its head at me. A quick text to CAIT told me all three bugs were transmitting. I got the hell out of there with a mental, *Thank you for your stamina, Alexander.*

CHAPTER TWENTY-FIVE

The next day, everyone in the office ragged me about how I got the sensors planted and what they heard coming from the bugs. That was the first time I interacted with some of the folks, almost enjoying it, until I remembered who I was and what I did. Retreating to an empty station, I settled in to listen to the recordings with Charlotte and Anderson, happy I accomplished something to move the case forward.

An hour passed before Chief called me and Charlotte into his office. "Good work, Raine. The bugs haven't given us much yet, but we're anticipating some good stuff today. It's important we get solid evidence on Sonia. We need the buyers, and we need the virus's location."

Around 0900, the bug on the phone picked up a bunch of Russian cussing—then it went dead. Sonia already found the surveillance devices and destroyed the phone. I held my breath, waiting for her people to find the one on the puppy's tag. They didn't. Hot damn.

Later that day, Chief pulled a bunch of us into the conference room. Me, Charlotte, Shepherd, Anderson, Harry from CAIT—a few others. He had never invited me to a strategy meeting like that before, and I was nervous about entering the room. Everyone else looked calm and focused like it was any old meeting.

"What have we got so far?" Chief asked once everyone sat.

Charlotte took the lead. "The tracker Raine put on the suspect in Club Dekadent gave us his people's location. We also got a lot off the dog's tag. We've been able to identify one potential buyer, Zaid Mostafa, al Qaeda aligned."

"Good work, Charlotte and Raine," several people said. Everyone had a tablet in their hands and tapped at them furiously. I noticed most shifted or twisted in their seats. Maybe they were as worried as I was about what was happening.

Charlotte tapped the controls on the conference table, and a photo of Mostafa appeared in front of each of us. "The DHS already tagged him and is following him for other reasons," Charlotte said. "This information was new to them though." The screens scrolled through several more photos of the terrorist and some of his associates.

"How'd they miss chatter about smallpox?" I asked.

"Probably not shared knowledge among the sect," Chief said. "What else do you have, Charlotte?"

"There are two more buyers. Sonia believes one of them won't come close to meeting the price. All we know about that one, they're Asian, probably Chinese, and not well known to the Dvornikovs." The photos of the first group disappeared, replaced with a map of China accompanied by a list of two dozen known criminal organizations originating there. "Subtracting the cartels familiar to the Dvornikovs," some names on the list disappeared, "that leaves us with about twelve possibilities. They're a long shot though. I think we can put them on the backburner and focus our energies on the other two buyers."

The table screens went blank when Charlotte tapped her tablet screen again. "That leaves one more buyer to discover, the one

Raine overheard about in the spa. We have an idea who they are, Taliban affiliated, but need a little more information to confirm."

Well, at least my time in the spa wasn't a total bust.

"Thanks, Charlotte," Chief said. "Raine, what else do you have?"

"We uncovered a warehouse the Zhiglovs own on the Baltimore docks." A tap to my tablet sent a 3D rendition of the warehouse to the center of the table. I hit the control, causing the image to rotate 360° for no other reason than it looked cool. "It's close to the edge of the wharf, has large rolling doors on the east end facing the water, and has a regular door on the west end. Harry let me know the security system is pretty basic, though it's tied to a central monitoring service."

"We could hack that system real easy," Harry said.

"I researched the security firm," I added. "They watch remotely, and there's hardly ever a guard on site at night. Ownership on record is a Russian-owned export business. Two tails reported Alexander visits the site maybe once a week. We don't know why." I replaced the building with a drone photo of Alexander exiting a Mercedes in front of the structure.

"We need to find out why he's there," Chief said. "Raine, you'll get cameras and bugs in that warehouse. Charlotte, try to get Raine any recent interior photos. See if our contact at the DHS has any. We need evidence to convince the DHS that the Zhiglovs are key players in this mess."

"Even after the recent intel I brought in?" I asked.

"Yup. Go get what we need to convince them."

I'd be at the warehouse that night.

It was cold outside at 2300 hours. A fog rolled in, bringing a rotting seaweed odor along with the salt. The forecast promised teeming rain, but it hadn't started yet. Anderson was watching the weather radar and would give me an alert. I wore gray mottled tacticals and though damp to the skin and cold, I wasn't dripping wet and wouldn't leave a trail of puddles. I had braided my hair and wore a mask, folded on top of my head for the moment, which protected my ears from the biting winds. Before I went inside, I'd pull it over my face.

I squeezed between two shipping containers thirty feet from the back door of the Zhiglov warehouse. I replayed the stats Charlotte gave me while waiting on the CAIT team to finish hacking the alarm. My mission—set cameras and bugs and root around for anything interesting.

Earlier in the day, Charlotte gave me the basics on the place. "It sits thirty yards from the water and is smaller than most of the warehouses nearby. Fifteen thousand square feet—fifty by three hundred."

From timed runs in training, I knew I could make that distance in about fifteen to sixteen seconds. All the office resources were on hand to back me up—a new thing for me. Chief always said we were a team, and that night, I really felt it. A heavy weight sat on my brain when I considered the implications of smallpox getting loose. All my other jobs had been important, but not internationally or even nationally super critical. Failure on my part might have gotten a few people killed. Someone else would have come in and cleaned up after me. Thing was if I failed on this case, millions of innocents could die. I wanted to ask Chief why he made me lead on this. Why didn't he call in someone else more experienced? Instead of asking, I swallowed my fear and focused.

Overhead, Harry operated a drone outfitted with a heat sensor. He was supposed to fly it over the warehouse's roof and let me know if the drone registered human or large animal heat signatures inside. The high winds coming off the waterfront that night made it difficult to control the drone. At that point, all that was certain was fifteen minutes ago, there were no heat signatures in the east end of the warehouse. Not entirely useful.

Harry spoke into my conduction receiver. "I'll keep timing the gusts and hop the drone over the roof's surface as best I can, okay?"

"Roger that," I replied. What else was there to say?

All the on-duty CAIT team, as well as Charlotte, Anderson, and Chief, were on my com piece. Chief ordered me to wear a body camera which meant that the office would be with me every step of the way. Tech gave me a tiny, flat camera that fit in a hook over my ear with the lens next to my left temple. As I turned my head, the camera moved with me, and everyone back home viewed what I saw.

Five minutes later, CAIT confirmed they rerouted the alarm through our ghost terminal. That meant the off-site security service monitoring the place saw a recording of a quiet and empty warehouse. I could enter, move about, and leave like, well, a ghost.

Even so, I opted to pull on the ninja-type mask with an opening for the camera before going to the back door. The mask had built-in night vision opticals activated with an on/off button. Sewn right into the fabric were two large, flat, alien, bug-eyed shaped lenses. They were huge, giving me a wide field of view even in my peripheral. The hick part of me thought they looked wicked cool.

The techs also gave me an electronic lock pick—easier than the old school way, but the bulky piece of equipment was the size and thickness of my palm and was a pain to carry. Still, with three locks to open, it made sense that night. Besides, I wore a backpack with a bunch of cameras and listening devices. What was one more piece of equipment? My Glock nestled at my waist, and I carried both knives. Two extra magazines sat in pockets on each calf.

I entered, grabbed my gun, and paused to see if anyone inside noticed my arrival. Hopefully, not a dog. After a few moments, I addressed Harry.

"Pilot, I'm inside the east door. Doesn't seem like anyone's here. You have anything?"

"The feds approved our request to redirect their high-altitude drone. They've confirmed the building is clear."

I debated whether I should relock the doors behind me but decided not to. What if I needed a quick escape? The odds of anyone showing up were slim to none, so it seemed a reasonable risk. The interior had a few emergency lights on, and with my night vision lenses, I saw all I needed to see. It took less than a minute to plant the first camera and bug, each placed near the door to record who came in.

Positioned right next to the door, several slender pipes and electrical cables ran from the floor to the roof. I climbed the pipes to set a camera that would give us a nice bird's eye view of most of the space. I would set a camera in the same position at the other end of the warehouse to get the full picture. I moved on to an office with lots of windows that faced the work floor and got things set up there.

"CAIT, can you verify the first three cameras and bugs are operational?"

"Affirmative. All three transmitting."

It took me ten minutes to search the office. A file cabinet held a bunch of manifests, all from the same four ships. The most recent came from a freighter named *Papa's Max*. I found a cargo list from the latest shipment and a few more invoices laying around, all having to do with fish. I sent those to Charlotte, too.

I moved to the warehouse's far end, had just set the first camera and bug to view the rolling doors, when Anderson came on the line. "Raine, a vehicle entered your vicinity. Stand by until we verify its intent."

"Roger that."

I gathered my equipment and faded into the stacks of Econtainers and pallets at the end of the warehouse. They probably weren't even going to come in my warehouse.

Wrong.

"Raine," Charlotte said. "One male exited the vehicle. He's walking in the direction of the door. Hide. We're rearming the alarm in case he goes in."

"Negative." I was already sprinting the length of the warehouse. fifteen seconds. That better be quick enough. "I have to relock those damn doors, or he'll raise an alarm, security system or not." Damn it. I should have relocked the doors after all.

"Affirmative. Get the doors locked and hide A.S.A.P."

Shit. Shit. Shit. I got two locks turned. Outside, the alarm keypad beeped. The third lock wouldn't move. The first deadbolt twisted open. I pushed on the bottom lock again. Second key lock twisting open. The stuck lock finally moved. That end of the warehouse was empty. No place to hide unless I ran for it, and fifteen seconds wasn't fast enough.

I shimmied up the pipes and wires to hide over top the door. What were the chances he'd look up? The tips of my boots found a tiny ledge to hang on to, my hands wrapped around a pipe and an electrical cable. With any luck, he'd leave the door unlocked behind him and move away so I could leave—maybe finish it when he left. Either that or I'd have to climb higher and get near the darker ceiling line.

The door opened, bringing the cold, rainy glow of the outside security light, the sour, salty smell of the wind, and a man on the small side for a bear. Had to be the runt of the family. From my perch, I looked down on the beginnings of a bald spot on the very top of his head.

The man lumbered across the floor toward the office, keys in his paw, swinging them around in a circle. The clumsy shit let the keys fly out of his hand behind him. He turned, grunted when he bent to pick them up, then straightened and looked in my direction. I froze. Pretended I was invisible.

I wasn't.

"Shit!" he yelled in Russian, pulled a gun, and ran forward.

I let go with one hand to grab my gun and shifted my weight. The wire I held with my left gave way a few inches, dropping me some, and I lost the narrow toe perch I had. My right foot swung wide off the tiny ledge. I half-jumped, half fell to the ground. A bullet hit where my chest had been a second before. A second shot missed. I hit the ground hard and didn't have time to recover or make some space. He was on me.

In a fight, speed was one of my best talents. I feinted right, then kicked his gut with my left boot. A throat punch with my right, my left into his temple, another kick into his solar plexus. He staggered back some. While he was off balance, I made a leg sweep that sent him to the ground but threw me off balance too. He lost his grip on his gun, which skittered a few feet away. The ugly shit rolled and got to his feet. Came at me.

Recovering in time to reengage, I blocked his punch, then kicked his groin slowing him down. My gun. One shot to the chest. He fell back and went still. I backed off a few steps to catch my breath, not taking my eyes off him or completely lowering my guard.

Chief's no-nonsense voice came over my com. "Raine, report."

"I'm fine. One bear down. Stand by."

Still huffing, I went around the body in a wide circle to approach the head. Up close, I couldn't detect breathing, though the blood leaking out was minimal. If the bullet hadn't exited, and if I could avoid a second shot, I'd have a chance of cleaning up the mess without leaving behind much evidence.

I approached and felt for a pulse. Nothing. "Problem solved. Hey Charlotte, can you get me an ID?"

I reached inside my backpack for a tampon, stuffing it into the bullet hole to plug the leak. I heard they were first invented like back in World War I to stop blood loss from bullet wounds, which was why all the male field agents had a couple in their kit too. I bunched the fabric of his jacket in my fists to lift one shoulder and checked the floor underneath him. No blood—no exit wound.

Chief's voice came on the line. "Raine, facial recognition ID'd him as lower-level Zhiglov muscle. You need to disappear that body. Do you want back up?"

I thought about what I had to work with. After high school, I had a job in a warehouse using pallet jacks and forklifts. That warehouse had several of each. Since the Zhiglov place was next to the water, it would be a short walk to the wharf's edge to dump the body.

First, I had to weigh it down and get it there. A stack of those pressed wood pallets sat up against the garage door wall. All I had to do was get the body on a pallet, tie the body to the pallet, tie the pallet to the jack, then dump it all off the wharf—without any witnesses. Earlier, I had noted four manual jacks in the space. Maybe they'd forget they had four.

"Raine, copy?" came Chief's voice in a more urgent tone.

"Nah, I got this. Pilot, if I get the body on a pallet, am I clear to push it to the wharf's edge?"

"You get set up, and I'll check the area," Harry replied.

How the hell was I going to lift that body? First things first. I swept my pen light across the floor, and by a miracle, found both his spent bullet casings and mine too. They went in my pocket. I shined the light where the bullets hit. There was a mark in a beam above the door and a tiny hole in the warehouse's metal siding. Hopefully, it wasn't that noticeable. I had no idea how to hide it. Maybe the office would take care of it.

Next, I ran to the other end of the warehouse, grabbed the pallet jack and a pallet, and brought both next to the guy. I tried grabbing the body under the arms and pulling it on to the pallet. Nothing doing. Even though I thought of him as the runt of the litter, he was one heavy son-of-a-bitch. I tugged on his legs. Got one leg on the pallet. Not very useful. I stood back to think. Charlotte came on the line.

"Raine, maybe you'd have better luck loading him onto the pallet forks, then using the jack to get him onto the pallet."

That damn body camera. Everybody watched me struggle. A guy would have already been done. But since Charlotte had a good idea, I said, "I'll give it a try."

I repositioned the pallet forks. By tugging, pulling, pushing, sitting on my ass, and shoving with my feet, I got him positioned over the forks enough to lift him. From there, it was easy enough to slide him on the pallet and reposition the jack. Next, I rifled his pockets, stowing a wallet, keys, cell phone, and miscellaneous shit, then checked his body for tech. Nothing. I took the battery out of the phone. I expected to hear a lot more direction coming in from Chief, but he remained silent and let me go about my work. I guessed I was doing okay since he wasn't nagging at me to go about things differently.

Bunches of tie-down straps with ratchets to tighten them hung on the wall. I grabbed some, threw a tarp over him, and strapped the bear to the pallet. Next, I strapped the pallet to the jack. Damn chore took me nearly thirteen minutes. All I had to do was get out the rolling doors with it, stroll to the edge of the wharf, and get it in the water—undetected.

"Pilot, what's the area look like?"

"Clear."

"Stand by. Making the transfer."

Making the transfer. What a polite way of saying I was dumping a body I murdered. Would I have had the nerve to do that if I hadn't had a drone overhead helping me?

"Here comes the rain," Anderson said into my device. The

metal roof came alive with a driving downpour pelting it. Just great. I'd be wet on top of everything else.

The rolling doors had manual chains to open them. I lifted one just high enough for the pallet handle to clear it then pushed the jack out. I went back in, lowered the door to one foot, and slid out on my belly. Hopefully, if anyone scanned the area, they wouldn't notice the open door. I couldn't close it all the way from the outside and didn't want to leave the jack unattended while I went out the door and ran around the building. Stupid. Like my cargo was going to come back to life and cause trouble.

With buckets of rain soaking me, I pushed the jack to the wharf's edge, and the whole thing tipped into the cold, winter water with a splash. I squatted there, my toes hanging off the edge, to make sure it sank, then ran back to the warehouse, crawled under the door, and lowered it again. I shivered, soaked in icy sleet.

"Seems okay, Raine," Harry said. "Don't see any activity."

I let out a sigh of relief and took a moment to calm myself, watching an ever-widening puddle form around my feet. I leaned on the door with my eyes closed and tried to keep my breathing quiet so everyone in the office wouldn't see how rattled I was. It wasn't my fault. I had no choice. Once I caught my breath, it was back to business. I shucked my mask and jacket to minimize leaving water everywhere and said, "Going to search that second office now. Stand by."

It took me twelve minutes to finish a search of the second office, set my cameras and bugs, then confirm the devices were operational. Time to grab my stuff and return to the west end. I had to go out that door and relock it if I wanted to leave undetected. The keys I lifted off the bear got me in his car. Anderson was already working on a place for me to abandon it in case it had a tracker. A couple of other people from the office would retrieve the SUV I arrived in and had parked two blocks over from where I cut the fence to get in. All in all, a successful night's work.

CHAPTER TWENTY-SIX

Instead of heading into the office after that job, Chief sent me straight home and told me to report at noon. At home, I showered then took a couple of melatonin and fell into a deep sleep. I woke at nine to someone leaning on my doorbell.

The peephole showed Connor's distorted face outside. He twitched and fidgeted while waiting for me to unlock the door and let him in. My hair was a rat's nest of tangles, and I wore only underwear, a tank top, and a pair of white socks. I had wrapped a blanket around me before opening the door.

"Hey," I said with a raspy voice. "How'd you know I'd be home now?"

He took a moment, looking at me in all my puffy-eyed, morning glory before answering. "I took a chance, swinging by and saw your Jeep in the lot. I guess I got lucky. Sorry I woke you."

"Oh. Yeah. Give me a minute, okay?" Without waiting for an answer, I went back into the bedroom and pulled on leggings and a sweatshirt. I winced and looked at the bruises from the previous night. My right hand was swollen and stiff. Back in the main room, I started a pot of coffee.

Connor started off with his doctor thing, asking questions, checking my temperature, and making me move about. I exposed enough skin to show him the scar where he had stitched me but not my new bruises. Then before I even had a chance to pour us each a coffee, he got into it.

"Raine, we're good together. We're alike. I want to be with you. I want to know about your life, your job, your thoughts. Everything." He put his eyes right on mine. His face held an intensity that I'd never seen before.

Both alarm and dread filled me, my skin going cold and goosebumps forming on the backs of my arms. My job? I couldn't tell him about my job. I searched for something to say that would keep the status quo. "You don't really know me. If you did, you'd run for the hills."

"I know you've been hurt in the past—"

How would he know that?

"—but I think I've proven myself loyal, haven't I? You work for the government. I know you're some kind of undercover cop or FBI agent or something. Your work is dangerous. I can handle that."

Some kind of undercover cop. I guess that made sense from what he saw.

"Yeah. You say that now, but I don't work a schedule. I go where I'm sent and for however long it takes. And I can't talk about it."

"I'll stop asking."

I softened my expression a little. "No, you won't."

"Then what's the point of us even seeing each other?"

Huh? "I think we're good together too," I mumbled. What was going on with him?

"So, it's just sex once in a while? That's all?"

I opened my mouth, but nothing came out.

"Oh wait," he said sarcasm taking over his voice, "and come to your rescue when you get yourself hurt? And afterward, get out of your way?"

Who was he to speak to me like that? What the fuck was his problem? I snapped out my next words. "I paid you well each time I asked for help. 'Cash only, up front, sweetheart.' Isn't that what you told me the first time I contacted you?"

"You're going to hold me to something I said before I even knew you?"

My voice doubled in volume. "And what did you say after the first time we had sex? What was it? Oh yeah ...'Don't get any attachment ideas, hon. I don't do the monogamous thing. We can hang out and all, but don't count on me—ever.'"

"Again, I didn't know you. That was a year ago. I was a different person then."

"You're different now? Really? Like I'm the only one you fuck? I've seen you with plenty of women." I went into full battle mode, my hands in fists ready to make a strike. My whole body tingled with the itch to fight.

"How many guys you got?" Connor asked, his eyes blazing.

"What do you care?"

"I would if you'd let me."

That statement hit me like a brick to the teeth, making me drop back to my heels and freeze. I couldn't answer him; couldn't even look at him. He didn't understand. I couldn't be with anyone ever. I was tied to a job that turned me into a murderer for eight and half more years. Even if I broke free of it, who'd want an assassin as a girlfriend? Who could ever trust me?

"I see I'm wasting my time. Don't call me. Find some other schmuck to deal with your injuries. I can't be with you anymore." Connor slammed his hand on the table, grabbed his backpack, and stormed out the door.

I still hadn't moved. Why the hell did he have to go and change the rules? How could Connor break up with me when we were never going out in the first place? 'Couldn't be with me anymore.' What did that mean? By reflex, I reached for my bottle of whiskey then acknowledged it was only a little after 0900. I changed direction and poured a coffee.

He was just a fuck. We both enjoyed it, and I never put any rules or restrictions on him. By the time I finished a cup, I had calmed. He must have had some weird head thing going on. If I gave it a few weeks, he'd call me.

For the next hour, I sulked. I wanted to hit my punching bag, but my hands were too sore. Everyone was getting weird on me. Connor. Charlotte with her stupid request. And those asshole people out there in the world who couldn't act right. Who preyed on the old, the weak, even kids. The office sent me out to hunt them because they wouldn't leave innocent people alone. I paced my apartment then showered, downed some painkillers, and got ready to go into the office for a debrief still angry.

After a hard day of labor in the fields and knowing another was coming, Pappy used to say, "No rest for the weary." That's the way I felt when I arrived at the office just before noon. Stepping off the elevator, I first saw Chief, but I also looked toward Charlotte's station. It was empty and dark as was Anderson's.

"Where's Charlotte?" I asked, approaching Chief just outside his office. She was always at her station by 0800.

"Charlotte and Anderson spent the rest of the night going over the intel you found at the warehouse," Chief said and rubbed his hand over his face. "I sent them home for some sleep." His ringed eyes and yesterday's wrinkled shirt said he hadn't slept at all.

"Did they or CAIT find anything yet?"

"Yes. Seems the Dvornikovs have a freighter on the Baltimore docks not far from that warehouse. The one you found records for last night—Papa's Max, though it's not directly linked to them. The country of origin is Russia, registered to a foodstuff's conglomerate, but I'll bet my favorite shirt the corporate trail leads back to them."

"Have they noticed yet that one of their bodyguards is missing?" I had driven the car to a public parking lot and abandoned it there last night—after CAIT took those security cameras off-line for a few minutes. Flynn met me there and gave me a ride back.

"Yeah, but they're not concerned yet. Maybe that guy has a history of not checking in."

"Here's hoping." The longer they ignored his disappearance, the better.

Chief stifled a yawn, and I fought not to mimic him. At least I had a few hours of rest.

"What do you know about ships? Freighters in particular?" Chief asked.

"Not much." Which meant I knew nothing.

"You need some education on that. Go to CAIT and read up on the rest of the intel. I'll find a way to get you up to speed on freighters and then get myself some rest."

Chief wasn't kidding when he said he'd find a way for me to learn about freighters. He sent me back to Baltimore to the Seagirt Marine Terminal. There, at 1400, I met a man who was Homeland Security and ex-Coast Guard.

He took me on board a ship similar to the Dvornikov freighter and ran me all over the place for an hour. We returned to the main deck, and then I led him wherever he designated. The captain's quarters, the mess, the infirmary, the holds. I had two hours to absorb all I could. An hour more would have been nice. By the time I returned to the office at 1700, Charlotte and Anderson were back at work. When I stepped off the elevator, they waved me over.

"We have two files back from Tech," Charlotte said. "They were able to filter and capture two times when Sonia was on her phone in the background. And believe me, they're very telling." Anderson said nothing but bobbed his head in agreement.

"Not only that, she was also on speakerphone with her father. Here." Charlotte handed me her headset and pushed me into a chair next to her station. Anderson handed me a written translation of the conversation, and I sat to listen. "She doesn't say much and pauses a lot," Charlotte said, "but keep listening to the end."

The first file confirmed what we already knew.

Father, we've been in contact with Feydor Ovechkin and explained we have come back for our territory, and he should get out.

How did you contact him?

We killed his best bodyguards.

How did he know it was you?

I let Oleg take the hands.

Always with the hands, that one. Are you sure you have him in control?

Da, Father.

Make sure you take care of Feydor by the time we're ready to accept the bids.

The audio cut out there, but it was enough to confirm Sonia's relationship with her father, that she was running the Zhiglovs, and that she ordered the deaths of the two goons under the overpass. Hot damn.

Charlotte queued up a second audio file while Anderson handed me a second written translation. "Again," Charlotte said, "she's in the background on speaker phone. She was alone in the room but far enough away from the bug that we missed her voice on the first pass for analysis. This one's harder to hear, but I think we got it."

I put the headphones back on to listen again. First came a man's voice. Her father.

I'd feel better if this were in your brother's hands.

Father, he is six years dead. I have done everything as he would have. I have done well for the family.

You are not a man. You'll never have your own power. Even now you hide behind Alexander as you did Victor.

Da. But now, I have my own success. Now, I have my own respect.

No. Not respect. You have their surprise. You have their attention. You do not yet have their respect. You never will.

You mourn Maximillian, but he is dead, and I am here. I am working hard for you, Father. As hard as Max ever did. You don't even care. Ships are named for women, yet you named your new freighter after your dead son. It should be my name on that ship. My name. I take care of your business.

She paused to listen to her father's reply then made a frustrated sound. We heard a door slam, and the bug didn't pick up any more of her conversation. I sat in the chair rereading the translation and finally said, "That explains some stuff, doesn't it?"

"We have a few more audio files, mostly about spa or hairdresser appointments, shopping and such," Charlotte said. "If anything else turns up, we'll let you know right away."

"Glad that worked out. What else is happening?"

"We're still trying to find an internal layout of *Papa's Max*," Charlotte said.

If they couldn't find anything, I'd have to go in cold and find my way. I sat with both Charlotte and Anderson to study the exterior photos. "What are those?" I pointed to four small platforms on the main deck, two on each side. The ship I toured didn't have them.

"They're gun mounts," Charlotte said.

"Yeah," Anderson said. "A lot of seagoing freighters mount heavy guns against pirates."

Wow. I never really paid attention to the idea of modern-day pirates. "Looks like they stowed the guns."

"Illegal in our ports. Some places in the world allow them," Charlotte said.

An hour later in my next meeting with Chief, he told me, "The

Dvornikovs have three more freighters in Redwood City, California."

"Where's that?"

"So close to San Francisco you could aim your piss and soak them."

"Perfect. Close enough to infect all of San Francisco and its surrounding area in a day." Exposure to that many people couldn't be contained, and trans-continental flights would deliver the virus to the rest of the country within twelve hours.

"We're backing up the DHS there. The CDC also has people on site. They believe that's where all this is going down. They pulled the people assigned to this case out of D.C. and sent them to San Francisco."

"What do I do?"

"Keep collecting intel. Maybe we'll find the one clue that'll give Tony and the rest what they need to end this. It would help if we knew which of the three freighters housed the stolen vials. They're heavily guarded. We're still working on getting someone on board to search without sparking an international incident."

"There was nothing else in the warehouse. Nothing much on Sonia's phone, nothing in the apartment at Nick's Bar. But I haven't gone into her house yet."

"I doubt she has anything at her house. I'll send someone else to check it out. That leaves the freighter. Do you feel up to the task?"

"You made me learn my way around a freighter for a reason."

"To be honest, you're all I've got here on the east coast. Everyone else is either engaged and can't be reprioritized or is in California."

So, all the smart, well-trained people were on this, and the hick rookie was his last choice for anything. Did he really think I was useless? "I get that I'm not your first choice, but can we afford to pass up a chance to check with the deadline for the sale getting closer?"

Chief sat back in his chair and his focus went somewhere else. He grunted and said, "I guess not."

"How many people are on the freighter?"

"According to the intel, seven or eight during the day, including the captain. At night, it's two security guards. Even the captain spends his night ashore."

I gave it some thought. "If I take them out or even just drug or subdue them, it'll tip of the Zhiglovs we're getting close to figuring them out, which in turn tips off the Dvornikovs."

"Exactly. That's why you'll have to avoid them while searching the ship. Leave no trace."

"Great. That'll be easy."

"Never said this job was easy. You'll have the team backing you up and CAIT operating drones. Problem is the drone's heat-seeking sensors can only penetrate the upper levels of the ship. All the metal blocks them from seeing the lower decks. The same goes for your communications and video. Once you're below deck, you're on your own."

"Okay." I didn't like that at all. I'd started becoming used to working with a team, or at least a little company. How would I call for help in a bad situation? I wouldn't. I'd have to take care of myself. Seemed like my rookie days were over.

"Good news is, the DHS shared some of their intel. The two overnight guards mostly stay in the mess, probably playing cards or drinking and don't patrol the whole ship on a regular schedule."

"So, avoiding them shouldn't be impossible."

"Not if you're careful."

It was nice Chief had some confidence in me.

"Go in tonight. Get studying the intel and gather your equipment."

So soon? Maybe he had too much confidence. "Sounds urgent."

"We just heard another phone call Sonia made to her father, picked up on the dog's device, so we only hear her side." Chief pushed a transcript to me in both Russian and English, hit a button on his computer, and Sonia's voice filled the office. I read the transcript as well as listened, not wanting to miss any details.

Yes, we have three buyers lined up. Some silence then, *You want them to make the bids in the next two days? Da.*

More silence then.

All is good. You'll get the money, get rid of the product, then we'll all get out of America. This will soon be a bad place to be.

Sonia listened some more.

Da, Papa. My cousins. They did not deserve to die like that. We have something special for those Ovechkin dogs. They will pay for what they did to Tibor and Pierre.

Pierre? Weird name for a Russian. She must be talking about the two I took out at the strip club. More listening.

Da. It will happen the day after tomorrow. He only leaves his house for medical reasons. We'll kill Fedor Ovechkin at his doctor's appointment.

She listened some more, said love you to daddy, and disconnected.

"Does anyone have the other side of the conversation?" I asked.

"Nope."

"Too bad her father doesn't have a dog. Are we doing anything about Fedor Ovechkin?"

"Nope. He's not worth it, and I won't allow any diversion from this case. Priorities."

Yeah. One nasty old criminal versus a virus that could kill millions. Bye, bye Fedor.

CHAPTER TWENTY-SEVEN

That was the second night in a row a large team stood by to back me up. Up until then, my jobs weren't urgent enough to warrant the use of all the resources. I'd handled less important assignments under Chief's watchful eye, everyone at the DSS knowing if I messed up, it wouldn't be a catastrophe. And now I carried a heavy load on my shoulders, relieved I wasn't completely alone.

Flynn drove me to the site and waited with me in the stacks of containers, though she wouldn't be going on board with me. Harry remote-piloted the drone. Charlotte, Anderson, Chief, and CAIT were online and watching my body camera. I wore the same tacticals and mask as the previous night. Same equipment and weapons. Charlotte hadn't found an exact layout of the ship but gave me her best guess based on similar ships.

Just as I got the countdown to move, I pulled my night vision mask with its bug eyes over my face. Getting on board was easy enough. The freighter's portside faced the wharf with a gangplank in place. The mess was on an upper deck on that freighter, one that the drone sensor could reach. Harry reported two heat signatures there. Flynn moved off to create a minor distraction on the far side of the terminal with a few blasts on an air horn. When the air horn sounded, I scurried up the gangplank then paused at a gate with a padlock that barred the way in. A quick pick, and I was through. CAIT confirmed the two guards on board never left the mess, but anyone else in the yard hopefully threw their attention in the opposite direction. I moved at will.

In the captain's quarters, I picked the lock to the door then the desk and found a laptop. A transfer device allowed me to copy its information directly to the office and disengage without leaving a trace. After I replaced the computer, I searched and relocked the desk. Another five minutes of rummaging, and I came up with nothing else. I set a camera and a listening device then made my way toward the bridge. Harry came on the line. "Guards on the move. Looks like they decided to make rounds."

"Roger that. Hunkering down." I was at the stairs near the holds. I went down a flight and a half, crouching in the dark to watch and wait. Usually, the guard's half-hearted patrol of the upper deck took twenty minutes.

Fifteen minutes in, I heard their voices at the top. I shifted my foot a little to pull further into the shadows and sent something— maybe a screw or bolt—falling to the next level. It made a soft plink, plink sound, but that noise on the silent ship sounded as loud as a shout.

"Grigor, what are you doing?" came a Russian accented voice. Grigor? The same man I met in Club Dekadent with Sonia?

"I heard something."

"Rats. You heard rats."

"Going to look a little. Make sure."

"Da, fine. We go." I had used the noise of their voices to move further down the stairs. I came out in a forward hold area and slipped among several metal barrels to hide, scattering a couple of rats. Ugly little shits.

The two guards descended the stairs casual, stepping hard and shining their flashlights every which way. Amateurs. I risked a swift look at them so my camera could pick up their faces. Yup. Grigor and Georgi from Club Dekadent. If they saw me, even with a mask on, I'd have to kill them.

A scratchy noise to my right. One of those asshole rats got bold and came closer, twitching its whiskers at my boot. Its beady eyes shined in the dark. God, I hated rats. They got into the grain, chewed everything, peed everywhere. Had I been alone, I would have kicked it. As it was, I wiggled my boot to scare it off. The nasty thing came closer, sniffing at my toe and sending the creeps up and down my arms. That foul, diseased creature climbed onto my boot, and a little shake of my foot didn't get rid of it. I couldn't risk a bigger move. My whole body tensed as the rat crawled over to my other boot, dragging its skinny, hairless tail and stretching to reach up my pant leg.

The guards moved to the far side of the room, and the damned rat moved off my foot to the edge of the bulkhead. The men made a cursory inspection, got bored playing cop, and clomped back up the stairs. When their voices faded, I kicked in the direction of that damned rat, making it squeal and run.

Refocusing, I turned my attention to the other end of the hold. The guard's flashlights didn't show them anything, but they showed me something. I called to the team. "You guys see anything when they shined their lights?"

No answer.

"Anyone copy?"

Silence. Then I remembered. All the metal blocked my transmissions. If my audio wasn't working, then my video wasn't transmitting either and no way for anyone to give me a heads up. Damn that metal. I swept my penlight across the hold and paused in front of a heavy metal door with several gauges and digital readouts. A freezer. I made sure my camera recorded the door and the displays. After, I turned to the second thing in the room that caught my eye. Four familiar-looking canisters in a rack.

I set a camera where it would document whoever came down the stairs and put another device near the freezer door, hopefully at an angle to pick up anyone entering a code. A final camera got aimed at the rack of canisters. They wouldn't transmit from down there, so to gather the intelligence, I'd have to come back and retrieve them. One more sweep of my penlight showed another door set back to the left of the freezer, leading to another section of the hold.

Time to report in. I climbed the first staircase and at the landing tried the team.

"HQ copy?"

Silence.

One more landing. "HQ copy?" I received a static-filled reply I couldn't discern. At the top of the stairs, almost at the main deck, I reached them.

Charlotte came through with, "Raine, good to hear your voice."

"Yours too. Harry, copy?"

"Affirmative."

"Hang on. I've got to get somewhere I can show y'all something before I leave."

On the port side, almost at the stern was a comfy little place between a winch and other equipment, far away from the door that led to the mess. I figured being on the side of the ship closest to the wharf where I was sheltered from the wind was safest. There, I transmitted the recording. "Everyone—take a look at this."

Several moments of silence followed before Chief spoke. "Raine, do you know what you found?"

"Yeah. A freezer set at negative eighty Celsius." I wasn't exactly sure what that was in Fahrenheit, but I knew it was damn cold. "Seems awfully excessive for storing fish. Is that normal on a freighter?" Seeing those dials triggered a bad suspicion in my gut.

"That converts to negative one hundred twelve Fahrenheit which is too cold for storing food, but perfect for storing a virus," Chief said. "Shit. The virus isn't in California. It's here."

I had a brain flash. Back in that restaurant when I bugged Alexander he had spoken to the buyer of a false trail for the gov't to follow. He succeeded in convincing everyone that the virus was in San Francisco.

"Can I get into the freezer? Grab the vials and dump them in the harbor? Would that destroy them?" Seemed like a good idea to me.

"Negative," came Anderson's voice. "I'm re-watching the footage. That's an electronic lock, and we don't have the code. You need heavy equipment or explosives to break in and a special suit and gloves to enter and grab the vials, or you'd frostbite your hands beyond repair."

"Roger that," I replied. Damn. So close to ending it. "I saw something else. Did you see what I videoed after the freezer door? You guys know what they are, don't you?"

"Why don't you enlighten us," Chief said.

"They're almost the same as the nitro canisters used to transport livestock semen." I knew then what the buyer in the restaurant asked about when he wanted to know if the 'transport' was ready. "I saw canisters like those in barns back home with bull and horse semen for insemination. These are the same idea but seem ... more high tech."

"And perfect for transporting the virus," Charlotte said. "Running a search. Will confirm." I shivered in the wind listening to the slap of the water against the boat until Charlotte came back on the line about four minutes later. "Confirmed. You're right, Raine."

Usually, it felt good to be right about stuff, but not that night. No matter what tension I was feeling, I had to shake it off and do my job. "Since I can't get in the freezer, can I sabotage those canisters in a way they won't notice? They load the virus, and it dies?"

"Negative," Charlotte said. "There's no guarantee with that. We need a new plan."

"We've got what we need for the moment," Chief said. "Retreat."

Harry cut in. "Wait. Hold position."

"What?"

"The guards are on the main deck at the gangplank having a smoke and talking to someone on the wharf. You'll have to wait them out. I moved the drone closer to pick up their conversation."

"Roger that."

I pushed further into the winch's cover. Charlotte came back on the line within two minutes.

"Raine, stay hidden. A car pulled up. It's Alexander and someone else. He said he's going below deck to check ... something. Sorry, transmission broke up."

"We all know what he's going to check. I've got a bug on me. Maybe I can get it on Alexander."

"Negative," Chief said. "It won't work below deck anyway and too much risk to the overall case."

Okay, he had me there. "Roger that." I leaned out just enough to see Alexander board the ship and disappear down the hold stairs. One of his lower-level muscles went with him. Probably a recent promotion to bodyguard since I'd killed so many. They had to be feeling the pressure of that.

A gap between the structure of the winch allowed me to watch some of the forward deck while Harry and Charlotte fed me intel. They reported the ship's two guards remained on the main deck, looking more alert since Alexander showed up. I couldn't slip past the guards, get down the gangplank, and sneak off.

Harry came back on the line. "Raine, the guards are on the move, traveling along the port rail. How secure is your position?"

I used all the available cover to scramble to the starboard side, slipping into a pile of barrels, ropes, and other crap. "Hiding on the starboard side. I'll look for an op to exit. Going silent." I caught the hum of Harry's drone somewhere over my head. If you weren't listening for it, you wouldn't hear it. Amazing how that stupid piece of plastic made me feel less alone.

"Raine, turn your head toward the rail. I think I saw something on your body cam." Charlotte said.

I turned.

"Is that rope to your left long enough to help?" she asked.

"Maybe. Stand by."

"Guards rounding to the stern," Harry said.

A quick look showed the rope reached almost to the water. It was a crazy but functional idea. I grasped the rope, which even through my gloves felt scratchy. "Going over the starboard side."

"You're clear to move," Harry said.

I popped over the side and lowered myself down approximately ten feet. One leg entwined in the rope, both hands gripped it. I looked at the water. The night vision tech showed everything tinged in green, but I knew the water was as black as the inside of a cave. Black as death. Rope climbing in gym class never prepped me for that.

"They're almost at the rope," Harry said. "Hold position." His voice kept me steady. "Twenty feet past," came his next report.

My arms and wrists ached. The freezing wind blew against a sliver of exposed skin on my neck. I shivered and that reminded me that everything around me was icy cold. The water, the metal, the wind, the air. Cold enough to kill.

"Forty feet," Harry said interrupting my destructive thoughts, "making the turn across the bow. Come back up."

I released one hand to climb up, and the other slipped down the rope a foot. I grabbed it again with both hands, but my hold felt tenuous.

"Raine, report," Chief ordered.

"Slimy rope, bad grip." Even I heard the tension in my voice. I tried again. It was no use. Every few seconds, I slipped a few more inches. Desperate and worried, I tried to grip the rope tighter, realizing I was overusing what strength I had to keep a grip and climb back up. I was still anxiously hoping to figure out how to get back on the ship. Chief was more realistic. "If you enter the water, swim to the stern, and wait to exit until we create a distraction."

"Rog—" I couldn't keep my hold. My hands slid down the rope a few inches at a time, and my heart raced while my mind imagined what it would feel like plunging into the inky water. By that point, no matter what, I was going into the harbor. There was one thing left in my control. I pointed my toes and straightened my body, attempting to enter silently without a splash, and drew a lungful of air. Just as my feet hit, a loud honk from an airhorn sounded. Had to be Flynn covering my splash.

That was the last coherent thought I had for a while. I panicked when I sank. A thousand cold needles pierced my skin. Pain swelled in my head. I kicked to rise to the surface while shrugging off the backpack. That lightened me enough to break the surface and take a gulp of air. I gathered enough wherewithal to look up. No one stood at the starboard rail. Maybe they hadn't heard me.

An ache started in my joints and spread to my entire body. A sharp pain formed in my head, and I couldn't feel my fingers. Chief's last words came back to me.

I yanked the mask off my face, stuffed it down my shirt, and tried to swim. I couldn't make my body stretch to do a forward crawl and ended up doing more of a dog paddle. My conduction receiver still worked. Words filled my head.

"C'mon, Raine. Move your ass. Get to that wharf." Chief sounded stern, military, matter of fact. It helped.

I replied, "Mm hmmm." It was all I managed through the pain and chattering teeth. I couldn't draw a full breath, but I kept going. I rounded the stern—spied a ladder to the top of the wharf. Encouraged, I paddled harder.

At the ladder, I climbed high enough to get most of me out of the water without putting my head over the wharf. To hold on, I hooked my elbow through the rungs. I couldn't control my fingers.

"Chief, on ladder waiting to exit."

"Raine," Charlotte said, "We lost your visual but have audio. Are you okay?"

"I gotta get moving," I said through chattering teeth and a wavering voice. From Pappy's winter hunting lessons, I knew remaining still was a death sentence.

"Stand by. Looks like Alexander's leaving."

"Roger." Ah, shit. Couldn't he have stayed below a little longer?

Harry came on the line. "Hey, Thompson, look up." I did and saw two dim, quick pulses of a soft blue light way above. Harry's drone looking down on me. "I'll hang with you. We'll give you the signal as soon as we can."

"Roger."

In training, they told me that in a physically stressful situation, I needed to distract my mind. The trainer tried teaching me meditation, but I never got the hang of it. Instead, I thought about the stuff I learned during my foray, then my mind drifted to the thousands of dollars of tech I dropped to the bottom of the harbor. Maybe that would come out of my pay. Even though my gun got dunked, it would still work, but only if my fingers defrosted enough to pull the trigger. The ladder shook, I shivered so hard.

The car started and drove away. It was another minute until Harry told me everyone was gone.

"Up the ladder, straight into the containers. Flynn's there," Chief said.

I got myself on the wharf and ran bent over on wobbly ankles and weak knees.

Flynn appeared from the shadows. "C'mon, Raine." She stripped off my jacket and put hers over my shoulders. "Follow me." She took me by the arm, and we ran to her van.

Blessed heater in the van. Blessed Flynn who was nearly the same size as me and threw a navy-blue sweatshirt on the dash. "Get your clothes off. You're better off bare skinned under the heater than in those wet things."

"Got any hot coffee?" I couldn't keep the quaver out of my voice as I pulled off wet clothes and threw them behind my seat.

Flynn fished a blanket from the back then said, "I have a thermos full."

Guess who was my new favorite person? She even gave me her chocolate-frosted donut.

Chief spoke into my receiver. "Raine, report status."

"In Flynn's van. Out of my wet clothes. Standing by for orders."

"Alexander took the canisters with him when he left the ship."

"Do you think he has the virus inside?"

"I'm willing to bet he does."

"Do we know where he went?"

"Affirmative. Not far. The warehouse."

The warehouse was on the far side of the yard from where I was. "Orders?"

"Secure those canisters. You have sanction to use ultimate force on whoever gets in your way."

CHAPTER TWENTY-EIGHT

I turned to Flynn. "Did you pick that up?"

"Yeah, sure did."

"Guess I'm putting on wet clothes." I reached behind me.

"Or you can put on mine."

"You have a change of clothes?"

"Nope," she said, pulling off her shirt.

God damn. She was giving me the clothes off her back just to get that job done. It took a few minutes of wiggling around the front seat to get Flynn's gray sweater and tactical pants on. She gave me her socks, didn't offer her underwear, thank God, but I had to wear my soaked boots.

There was nothing I could do about my wet hair, and the night vision cap was just as drenched. Stuffed in the door bin was a black and white bandana. I snatched it and tied it around my head—it was better than nothing.

"Chief, what intel do you have?"

"I just got word. The bidding happened at 2200 at a hotel near the Newark, New Jersey Airport. It went down too quickly for us to get there. Sonia and the buyer, Mohammad al Bari, upper-level

Hamas, have already headed for the warehouse. We don't have a device or visual on the car, so we don't know how quickly she'll show up there. I've got eyes watching the major roadways and every entrance into the docks."

"Anything else? I need a few more minutes to gear up."

"Yeah. Pay attention. It's more important to secure the virus than it is to capture the buyers. You got that?"

"They're guilty as hell. We already have tons of evidence on them."

"Virus first. Millions of lives are at stake."

"And if the best way to secure the virus is to eliminate all threats ...."

"As I said, Sonia, her people, as well as the buyers, meet all criteria for ultimate action. If it comes to that, upstairs and the DHS prefers this get done under the radar and this mess not make the evening news."

"Fine. I'll be ready in five minutes."

"One more thing. I've got help for you. Another DSS agent."

"Who?" Tony was in California with that other guy. I didn't know any other local agents. Shepherd maybe?

"Jack is on route. He freed up yesterday and has been briefed."

What? Chief had to be kidding. "Fuck no. This is mine."

A year and some ago, the Zhiglovs were Daniel's case. After his murder, it became mine. When I first began working it, I asked Chief why they killed Daniel in the street in plain sight.

Chief had said it was a message to whoever Daniel worked for. "That they were too smart for us to take on." He had made a funny smile. "They wanted us to know that no man we sent would infiltrate them. So, I didn't send another man."

I shook my head to clear the memory. Chief said, "Switching to a secure line." A moment later, he spoke only to me. "You're too inexperienced to do this alone, and Sonia's too well-guarded. It's

Jack or nothing. He'll be professional. And so will you. Jack's prepared to go it alone if need be."

That hurt like a kick from a mule. "It should be me. I should finish this."

"Raine, it's because of your work we have this chance." Chief's voice got softer—and tinged with sadness. "Daniel would be proud of you. He was right. You are a good agent and problem solver. Finish this the right way. Professional—as part of a team."

Honesty made me admit Chief was right. The job loomed too big. That didn't mean I had to like it. "Fine," I said, suppressing the venom in my tone.

Chief opened the line and finished giving everyone his take on the situation. The CDC were also on their way and would hang back to wait for me and Jack to hand off the virus to them. Adrenalin pumped through my body giving me the illusion of warmth.

"Jack's almost here," Flynn said, listening to her receiver.

A moment later, Flynn opened the van's sliding door, and Janky Jack Miller got in the back. He settled on a seat and tossed a jacket at Flynn still in underwear and a sports bra.

"Hey, doll. It's my extra."

"Thanks, Jack." Flynn sounded as if she actually liked him. Maybe she did. Maybe it was only me who hated him.

"Evening," he said to me with a stupid grin. Then he pulled out his weapon, a Glock 17 like mine, and checked the clip. Jack smirked at me. "Bygones. Right, Raindrop?"

What a shit. "I'm only working with you because Chief's forcing me." I leaned toward him. "Get this, Jackass, if you touch me, do anything to piss me off, not only will I break your bones, I'll break your boner. I'll rip it off your body."

"You mean, you'll grab my cock? Who's inappropriate now, Raindrop?"

Fucking asshole.

Jack opened his mike and outlined his plan for getting into the warehouse. Best option—steal the canisters under the gang's noses and get it to the CDC people. Next option—kill as many as we needed to secure the canisters, do our best to escape before two Navy jets blew up the warehouse, the freighter, and our entire end of the wharf. The jets, out of Norfolk, Virginia, were already prepped for the mission and getting ready for takeoff. We had minutes to get in place. Maybe an hour to get it done.

Flynn handed me my Glock grip first. "All cleaned up, full magazine and ready to go," she said.

"Awesome, thanks."

"Here's a spare." She handed me another weapon—also a Glock 17.

Flynn was still my favorite person. "Thanks."

I took inventory. Glock, second Glock, six more magazines, both knives, shivs in my boots. Both guns went into the waistband of the pants I borrowed off Flynn.

"Hey," I asked her, "you don't by chance have anything useful hidden in your waistband or hems, do you?"

"This ain't my first rodeo, girl. The usual stuff is there, razor blade, handcuff keys, mini-compass, lock picks."

I swept my hand along the waistband, locating each item. "Cool. Ready to rock and roll."

CHAPTER TWENTY-NINE

Jack and I left the van and got in his SUV—a shiny, black Ford Expedition. Big and noticeable if you asked me. We moved through the streets to approach the warehouse from the other side of the yard.

"Describe the warehouse to me," he said, slowing down then blowing through a red light. By then, it was 0100 and not much traffic.

I gave him the layout I saw the night before. "Harry will have the drone overhead to feed us intel."

Jack ran another red light. "You ready for this?" he asked. "You ready to do some hard-core, ball-busting work, Raindrop?"

"Fuck off the Raindrop crap."

Jack laughed as he reversed into a descending truck ramp at a warehouse on the outer edge of the docks. The downward angle of the slope hid the SUV. I made note of that trick.

Time to go forward on foot. I showed Jack the cut in the fence I made twenty-four hours earlier to get in undetected, and so far, no one had noticed it. Playing the part of the good team member, I held the chain link back for him to squeeze through first. We paused in the container stacks at the same place I waited last night. Flynn wouldn't join us or hide in the stacks that night. It was too much to ask, hanging in the open, in January, without clothes. Parked near the warehouse door were two vehicles—a Chevy Suburban and a Mercedes sedan.

"Think we should disable those before going in?" I asked.

"What do you think, Raindrop?"

Fucking asshole. "Fine. I'll get the rear tires."

"You get the Mercedes, and I'll get the Chevy. Get under and cut the fuel line too. You'll find it—"

"I know where the damn fuel line is."

"Easy there, Raindrop."

I ignored Jack, slashed the tires, and crawled under the Mercedes. I cut the fuel line without splashing gas on myself and scooted out to see Jack finished with the Chevy. In less than fifteen seconds, we were ready to hit the warehouse.

Harry opened the mike. "I'm overhead. You're clear. No heat signatures outside but yours."

Still behind the car, I asked, "Who's taking lead at the door?"

The door was the only way in. It was a kill box, but our only option. We wouldn't be able to quietly come in the skylights and rappel to the floor or use the rolling doors at the other end. Nine inside. Two of us, four guns. That would be the first time, outside of training, I'd go in with a gun in both hands. Usually, I snuck up on my quarry. That time, there were too many for a sneak attack.

"Hang on a sec." Jack held out his hand with something army green and cylindrical in it. I took it while he pulled out another one.

"What is it?"

"Stun grenade. Also called a flash-bang. It's not for killing anyone, it just knocks them over and lets you get some control. Police use them in riot situations."

"I've never trained on this."

"It ain't rocket science, Raindrop. Just pull the pin and throw it far away from you. Aim for the assholes."

Since Jack knew I considered *him* an asshole, you'd think he'd have been more specific with his where to aim instructions.

"You'll pull the door, then get on the ground behind it," he said. "I'll feign going in, they'll start firing, I'll throw my grenade."

"Yeah. Then you go in, I follow, toss my grenade, and start shooting."

"See? It ain't hard. Don't try to pull the pin with your teeth. That's only in the movies."

Shit. With two hands on the grenade, how was I supposed to hold my guns?

We got in place. I pulled the door and fell to the ground as bullets came our way. Jack made like he would enter then pulled back, tossed his grenade, and got on the ground. Soon as it detonated, Jack ran inside, guns in both hands, firing.

I had the grenade in my right, pulled the pin, and ran inside. Bullets came from the office door. I lobbed the grenade in that direction. It went off, and the bears inside fell over. The shockwave pushed me over too, except I was ready for it, eye shut and behind my arm, then rolling and grabbing the guns out of my waistband. Got the two in the office doorway. Shots fired all around me.

Charlotte's voice said something in my earpiece—had to ignore her.

Two more bears popped up in the office. They shot out the windows, firing on Jack. I got one, the other ducked. I threw myself against the back wall and looked for a head to shoot at.

The rest of the bears retreated to the far end of the warehouse with Alexander. The person in the office popped up. Jack got him before I could. Damn, he was quick. Made a body count. Were nine inside. We got four in the office, and two lay on the warehouse floor near us. Three left. Alexander and two bodyguards.

Again, Charlotte spoke. "Sonia's arrived. Copy?"

Shit. Already? What about the advanced notice we were supposed to get? "How?" I said, loading two new magazines.

"Never mind how," Jack said. "Where?"

"Approaching the rolling doors," came Charlotte's reply.

"Raine, lay cover fire," Jack said, making his move.

I sprayed bullets at the area where I last saw gunfire. Jack made it into the stacks with return fire coming his way too late. My turn. I fired into the stacks again and went forward until I was maybe thirty feet from the rolling doors sheltered against a huge bulk container. I waited for someone to fire on me to know where they were. No shots. Risked a look down one aisle. Empty. Then curses shrieked in Russian followed by Jack calling my name—not from the com devise in my head. I looked in the aisle again to see Jack sprinting along it with a nitro container in each hand. I ducked back as he passed making for the door.

"Hold them off, Raindrop."

Jack was following mission protocol. He secured two of the nitro containers and made off with them. But only two. Where were the other two?

When Jack passed, I turned into the aisle and squeezed my triggers. Only one bear there, and I put him down with four shots to his torso. I moved in on Alexander's position. Alexander and a bear on one side of the rolling door with two canisters—Sonia outside the same door with more firepower.

"How many bodyguards does Sonia have with her?" I asked Charlotte.

"Three and the buyer," she said.

I went one aisle closer to the rolling doors. The last stack of bulk containers shielded me from a hail of bullets. I dropped my empty mags and added two full ones. That left me with one set of full mags left after those. It didn't seem like enough.

Silence. Then a door going up. Stealing a look around the edge of the container, I saw Alexander holding the other canisters, one in each hand. He crouched ready to scoot under the door as soon as there was enough room. Outside, five pairs of legs. Four in trousers and men's shoes and one set of women's legs in red platform shoes.

The inside bodyguard shot at me. I dodged, then aimed and got him. Three shots in the torso. One in the head. Alexander was halfway outside. I got him. Squeezed the triggers of both guns, and at least six bullets entered him, his body jerking before it fell to the ground. I couldn't check for sure, but he had to be dead. I fired more rounds at the erratic movements of panicked legs outside. No hits. Out of ammo again.

Sonia screamed. The three bears outside squatted to shoot inside, and the door continued to rise. I dropped the empty mags, but before I could load my last set of magazines, one bodyguard entered. Sonia grabbed the nitro containers, still screaming over Alexander's death. The buyer and one man stayed outside, pulling on Sonia's arm as they urged her to flee. I ducked behind the bulk container.

"HQ, did you copy all that? Do you have eyes on Sonia?" I couldn't understand the static-filled message that came back. Maybe only six or seven minutes had elapsed. Nine gang members eliminated. Alexander eliminated. Forty minutes until fighter jets passed over.

Damn. I was on my own.

One bear to deal with before I could go after Sonia and the virus. If Jack came back, he'd head straight for the other two containers. I retreated with the bear giving chase. He shot at me so I didn't get a chance to load new mags. I always said my best defense was distance and big weapons. I had lost my best weapon. My guns were useless. So distance then. I could sprint that warehouse end to end in about fifteen seconds. I needed to make it out the door and into the maze of shipping containers to set up an ambush—maybe scoop up a gun from a dead bear on my way. I made my move and sprinted toward the door almost a hundred feet away. The bear followed. I made the door, slamming into it and jarring my whole body. Couldn't get it open. Fucking locked. Who did that?

An arm around my neck, a pistol at my head.

"Stupid bitch." He pulled me back. "Drop your guns."

I hesitated.

He jammed the end of his gun to my skull and said, "Drop them."

I complied.

"You killed my comrades. You killed my family. You will die too."

"Asshole."

He growled. "But before you die, I fuck you. I fuck you hard till you bleed."

He wrenched my neck and dragged me back toward the containers. To save strength, I went limp and looked for a break. When the bear paused to look behind him, I grabbed his arms, raised my body, twisted, and got one leg behind him to trip him. When he fell, his grip loosened. I got free, kicked his groin, and made a second kick to send his gun skittering. He jumped to his feet and caught me in the face right where my conduction receiver sat on my upper gum line. I moved with the punch lessening its impact then made two strikes to his nose. Blinded by tears, he swung without precision. I dodged.

Pulled my knife.

Stabbed him in the neck.

Caught the jugular.

When he fell, I staggered back eight or ten steps, breathing hard and watching his growing pool of blood. I had to recover. Had to go after Sonia and the other two containers. I shook my head hard then tried the team.

"Anyone copy?" No answer. I swept my tongue over my mouthpiece and felt its frayed edges and tasted blood. Damaged. Damn it.

The side of my face was already swelling. I ran my tongue along my teeth to find them all still there but tender as hell. I spit blood off to the side then pulled out my cell. It was wet. Damn, it went into the harbor with me. In the warehouse's office, I dialed Chief, hoping he'd answer the unfamiliar number. One ring.

"Raine? We've got you on the cameras you set."

Oh, right. That's how he knew to answer the call. "Warehouse secured. Jack captured two containers. Are they safe?"

"Yes. In the hands of the CDC."

"Where's Sonia?"

"Headed to the freighter with the two containers. Jack's approaching the warehouse door."

"Right." I hung up then opened the door for Jack. A line of blood ran down his forehead into his eye.

"Sonia's at the freighter," I said. Fumbling in one of the pants pockets, I brought out a tiny first aid kit. "I'll get a steri-strip on your cut. It'll keep the blood out of your eye."

"Sure, Raindrop."

He sat on the concrete floor to let me work. I let the Raindrop shit go by. "Why didn't Sonia leave in the car she arrived in?"

"Because Flynn disabled it."

Damn, but she was one dedicated woman to run almost naked around the docks in January.

"She shadowed them to the freighter but was told to hang back." Jack reached into his pocket. "Here." He handed me four clips for my Glocks. I picked up both my guns, slammed two mags into them, stowed the other two, and we left the warehouse. Twenty-five minutes until the jets passed over. By then, they were airborne.

I led Jack through the maze of containers to the set parked just opposite the freighter. There, we paused to plan.

"Describe the freighter to me," he said. "How many levels?"

"It's small. Bridge Deck, main deck, and two lower decks with the holds, engines, other equipment. The freezer is on the lowest deck. The upper hold is empty. We'll need CAIT to help us out to know where they are when we get there. I'm told the captain comes on board daily. I don't know what time."

"You didn't do much homework for this job, did you, Raindrop?"

"Fuck off the Raindrop crap." I was already berating myself for that oversight. "At the top of the gangplank is a gate with a padlock."

"I'll get that," Jack said. "I'm quicker than you."

I pushed down my irritation. "It's a straight shot to the stairs below."

"Ladders."

"What about ladders?"

"The stairs on a freighter are called ladders."

"What-the-fuck-ever."

"In this game, details matter, Raindrop." He shifted to move forward.

"Hang on. My mouthpiece is dead. Ask Harry if he has any visuals or heat signatures on the upper decks."

Jack asked the question and listened to the reply. "Harry says he has no visuals or heat signatures on the upper decks or captain's quarters. Not exactly useful."

"We know where she isn't."

"Beautiful, Raindrop."

Bastard.

Jack smacked my ass, said, "Let's go, Raindrop," and led the way up the gangplank to the locked gate. He wasn't through it any faster than I would have been. Main deck. Guess who was waiting for us? Those two lazy security guards, Grigor and Georgi. They didn't last long. I got Grigor, and Jack got Georgi. Both bodies went over the side.

"You have any more stun grenades?" I asked.

"Nope, those were my only two. Okay, Raine. We gotta do this the hard way. I'm betting they're below on the lowest level. I'll go down first; you back me up. We'll move ladder by ladder until we flush them out."

Jack was taking the more vulnerable position again. And he called me by my name. Hell must have been freezing over.

CHAPTER THIRTY

Step by step, we made it past the upper hold to the lower hold—me sticking to Jack's six. The first compartment with the freezer was dimly lit and empty. The freezer readout still registered negative eighty Celsius. The hatch to the next compartment appeared shut and sealed. Then, noise on the ladders above us.

"Follow my lead," Jack said. "Wait till I give the signal to begin shooting."

We scrambled to hide—me in the barrels again while Jack faded into the shadows and machinery under the ladder. God damn, I wanted to be anywhere but there in the hold with all of them. I'd rather have gone over the side into the icy harbor again. The captain came down the steps, his huge belly preceding him. He held both rails, treading carefully, pulling his foot back once or twice before committing to the next step. At the bottom, he took a long moment to look around the room before going to the hatch door and opening it.

Loud cussing in Russian drove him a couple of steps back. A man's voice asked, "Have you heard from Grigor? Is the bitch dead yet?"

I guessed bitch meant me.

"I haven't heard," the captain said.

"Then what are you doing down here?"

"I can't find Grigor or his partner."

"Where could they go?"

"I don't know. I came to ask you."

More cussing in Russian—a lot about the captain and his mother. Two bears pushed through the door with Sonia following and Mohammad al Bari bringing up the rear. No canisters. Maybe they left them behind in the other hold? Put them back in the freezer?

They crowded around the freezer door. At first, the captain tried to stand with Sonia, but she ordered him away. He came to where I hid behind the barrels, holding his arms out from his sides, I guessed for balance though the ship barely moved. I was freaking out with him so close to my hiding spot, but then he belched. Had to be drunk. No smell but unwashed body, so probably vodka, of course. Shit, but when was Jack going to bust a move? How long were we going to wait?

The captain leaned on a barrel and shifted it back a couple of inches, leaving a bigger gap in my hiding spot, damn that drunk asshole. He struggled for balance pivoting on one foot and ended up facing me. At first, he could only point and stutter for words. As the first fluttering of panic hit me, I decided no point in waiting. I raised my arm and shot him through the eye.

The bears pulled pistols and shot in my direction. Jack came out firing, got the attention off me, and took a hit on his side. He crumpled but didn't fall and retreated behind the ladders. The bears fled through the hatch with Sonia. Before the smaller dude got through, I nailed him—one bullet in the back—hopefully a lung shot. The door slammed shut.

I went to Jack. His wound bled freely but didn't seem critical.

"Can you get topside to the infirmary?" I asked Jack. "I'll hold them here."

He nodded through the pain with tight eyes and gritted teeth while keeping a grip on his side. "There's no cavalry, Raindrop. We need to confirm we've secured the canisters to cancel the bombing run."

"I know. Go." His soft footfalls faded up the ladder. I had to fight not to follow him. Not to run into the night, far away from the ship, and never look back. But I wasn't a quitter. I wasn't a coward. I turned my gaze to the hatch.

The ship I had toured had two ways out of the holds, so I assumed the same held true for this ship. There was no help for it—I had to go through that hatch and into the second hold to stop Sonia from escaping. I opened it, waited to the side to listen, then entered the second hold. No lights. I went to the side of the hatch and crouched to allow my eyes to acclimate. Movement on the other side. I fired three shots. When the bullets ricocheted off the bulkhead and made sparks, I knew I missed whoever it was.

Someone tackled me from the right. Sonia slammed me into the bulkhead and wrestled me for my gun. Pressure from her hands made me squeeze off two shots which made more sparks when they ricocheted off the bulkhead. Intent on keeping my gun, I fucked up. I allowed her to grab my hair and bang my head against a pipe. My knees hit the deck while stars popped in my eyes and warm blood slid down my neck. My gun slipped from my hand. Sonia let go of me, seeming off balance too.

The buyer, al Bari, used the flashlight on his phone to locate and grab the canisters then raced toward the hatch I just came through. He'd make it out before I could find my gun. Through blurry vision, I had just enough wherewithal to twist my feet in front of me and kick at the hatch to slam it closed. It only moved partway, but that was enough. In his panic, al Bari ran smack into the hatch's edge and fell back stunned or unconscious—I wasn't sure which. With the roll of the ship, the canisters skittered to different places on the bulkhead and came to a stop. My vision cleared enough to show me their digital readouts hadn't changed. I hoped that meant the canisters weren't damaged and leaking.

Before I could move, Sonia kicked me in the gut with her platform shoes. I slumped to the floor and curled in a ball. Yeah, it was easy to hurt someone who was already beat up. Another kick to my forearm covering my guts.

I had to distract her and Chief's words and the emotions they stirred up a few minutes ago still echoed in my head. I couldn't resist the things I spewed. Still on the floor, I spat out, "Your precious Victor. Do you know who killed him? Put three bullets in him? I did. I shot him and all the others."

She froze for a moment digesting my words. The ship moved again, and Sonia's ridiculous platform shoes affected her equilibrium. She wobbled, taking two steps back and windmilled her arms to regain her balance.

That was all I needed. Ignoring the pain, I pushed to my feet and made a hook kick into her gut. Yeah, bitch. My boots were made for that. When she bent forward, instead of lowering my foot, I kicked her face. Blood gushed from her nose, and she cried out. Two strikes to her head from my left and she went unconscious.

I stood over Sonia, hands on my thighs, catching my breath. Dizzy. So dizzy. The idea of the greater good versus dealing with Sonia warred within me. The canisters. Though Sonia, the source of all my troubles, lay vulnerable before me, I had to forgo vengeance and get those damn canisters to the CDC. I made two steps in the direction of the closest one when a noise froze my progress.

The door in the farthest section of the hold creaked open. The bear who escaped in that direction with Sonia appeared. He made soft footfalls, but his breaths came like a wheezy old drunk.

He had shed his jacket and wore a T-shirt too tight for his chest and arms. Those arms. I had just found the 'young Arnold Schwarzenegger' who carried the Ovechkin bodies for dumping. A chill then a sweat passed over my skin. I needed an Uzi or a tank or something big like that. He hadn't pulled a gun yet. I guess he thought he could easily take me with his bare hands. I was thinking in that direction too. That one was massive enough to have been the one who cut off all those hands with one swing of a hatchet—the one Sonia called Oleg.

He reached behind him and pulled a weapon from his waistband. Fucking hatchet. Identity confirmed, and his crazy eyes suggested he enjoyed using his hatchet too much. Oh, hell no. I didn't want to die without my hands. For a split-second, I was disappointed it wasn't a gun. At least I knew what to expect from a bullet. He stood there with that hatchet in his huge left hand and grinned at me. A southpaw to boot. I didn't have much experience fighting lefties. The Arnold-bear grinned. We both knew it wasn't going to be a fair fight.

I darted my eyes to the hatch opening, both of us moving at the same time. He reached with a long gorilla arm and grabbed me at the bicep. Arnold-bear flung me across the hold like I was a toy. I tucked and braced as I hit the wall. Dazed, my rubbery legs barely let me stand. He came at me. The hatchet hovered over his head, and he swung downward toward my neck and shoulder area.

I had just enough sense left to throw myself to the side. Sparks flew off the hatchet's edge where it hit the metal bulkhead. He swung again, not even aiming, trying to hack into or cut off anything he could. I dropped to the deck and rolled. How long could I keep that up? Had to get to my feet and run. He gave me no chance, swinging and chopping—me rolling and scrambling.

He got me. Grabbed my ankle and pulled me a few feet across the floor before straddling my waist and holding my arm to the floor with his hand crossed over his body. His elbow pressed into my chest, and he grinned over brown-stained teeth. So much weight and pressure; I could hardly breathe. I couldn't move my arm or pull a knife. My other hand struck anywhere I could reach—with no effect. My arm wasn't long enough for my fingers to reach his damn eyes.

He raised the hatchet. He was going to cut off my hand at the wrist just like the others. Without enough air, I wouldn't even be able to scream when he chopped into me. Ah damn, I didn't want to go to hell without my hands. The blade's edge made a small glint in the dim lighting when his body shifted to bring the hatchet down. I couldn't move my eyes from the sharp cutting edge.

An attack from the left. Jack—deflecting the downward stroke. He pushed the goon to the side just as the ship rolled and the canisters skittered under Arnold Bear's feet when he tried to stand. He tripped, and the hatchet flew out of the asshole's hand.

Jack came back.

He saved me, and while grateful, I didn't have time to say so or dwell on it. I drew in air, filling my oxygen-starved lungs. Jack all the while gripped him in a hug and pinned his arm to his side but couldn't get his arms all the way around Arnold-bear's bulk. The giant shook Jack who held on. Arnold-bear was too big for Jack and would soon break free. Lifting Jack with him, he got to his feet, which let me scramble to my feet.

I had to help Jack. Gulping air, I raced for my knife.

Arnold-bear howled as my blade sliced into his ribs. Neither a killing, nor stopping injury, but something. I tried to get behind him. Jack still hugged his one arm, keeping him from a full range of motion. Arnold-bear thrust his right hand forward and hit me between my shoulder blades, slamming me to the deck. I sprawled on my front and scraped my chin on a metal seam. The knife flew from my hand. Through the stinging pain and hot, dripping blood, I scrambled on all fours, re-secured my knife, and positioned to stab his neck, chest, belly, anything. The beast spun and used Jack as a shield between us with Jack's legs swinging like a rag doll. New tactic.

First, a feint to the right, then I dropped the knife to dodge left to grab the hatchet. Made a pirouette, then chopped the hatchet into the goon's left hamstring. He roared with pain, thrusting his pelvis forward and throwing his head back. I repositioned as Jack jumped off, and I hacked into his right hamstring. Deep grooves.

The goon fell to the floor on his stomach, howling and screaming, beating the deck with his fists. I stepped back and held the blood-stained hatchet in front of me while more blood spread over the deck. Jack, a crazed look on his face, ran for the knife I lost, grabbed Arnold-bear by the hair, and stabbed him through the eye. Like an ass, I froze and held the hatchet as Jack finished him. I dropped the hatchet but for a moment couldn't move. All I did was stand there catching my breath, holding my ribs, and staring at the body.

Jack pulled a rag from his pocket. He ran the rag over the blade once, twice, displaying no emotion, no panting for air. "You okay there, Raindrop?"

Raindrop. That motivated me. "Got a clean cloth?" I asked, forcing a nasty attitude that I didn't feel into my voice.

He jerked his chin to the floor. There, the black and white bandana from my head lay abandoned. Must have come off during the fight. I used it to staunch the cut on the back of my scalp. I pulled my sleeve over the heel of my hand and pressed it to the cut on my chin.

A shadow caught our eyes. The buyer. We heard his footfalls on the ladder in the other hold. I searched the deck. Only one canister lay there. He must have regained consciousness, grabbed a canister while we were distracted, and made a break for it. Jack, clutching his side, smacked my ass again and went after him, yelling, "Grab that other canister and c'mon, Raindrop."

He disappeared through the hatch. I took two more breaths

then turned to fetch the fourth canister before following him, knowing the virus was all that mattered. A howling shriek came from behind me. Sonia ran at me, screaming, "Victor!"

Before I could turn all the way to meet her, she slammed my ribs with a crowbar. Pain spiked through my ribcage and echoed up my spine.

"It was you! You kill my Victor. Take him from me."

Sonia pulled back the crowbar for another swing. Instinct made me stumble back a few steps, my feet unsteady and my vision cloudy. The bitch was horror-movie bloody, and her crazed eyes stared into mine.

"He–the only man I love. He–the only man I respect, and you murder him," Sonia screeched.

"Because you ordered him to kill Daniel," I screamed right back at her.

For a moment, we were both too winded and injured to move, panting, our eyes locked, planning our next move.

"Who this Daniel?" Sonia asked with a puzzled expression on her face.

She didn't even remember him. My voice became a growl when I said, "My boyfriend, who you ordered Victor to shoot on the street. You murdered Daniel."

She bared her teeth. "It is you. You are the silly girl at the Club Dekadent with us. Now you think you can hurt me? Hurt my family? You are stupid like the man who thought he could hurt my family. The stupid, stupid man who thought he could arrest us."

"Guess what, bitch? I was the stupid masseuse at the spa. I was in your house when you and Alexander were screwing on the sofa. And I killed your cousins in that alley. It was all me." I kept my gaze on her, holding my ribs, fighting to slow my gasps.

Her expression changed from rage to calm. Sonia's eyes focused on me, and her breath slowed. At that moment, I knew she would do anything to kill me.

I began edging across the hold toward my gun, never taking my eyes off her. She rushed me with the crowbar over her head. In defense, I ran at her, and we collided, both falling hard to the deck.

I wanted to get up. I wanted to grab the canister and run, but I couldn't move. My legs wouldn't respond. Sonia, a few feet away from me, lay on her back limp and not moving. I struggled to stay conscious. The memories played like a movie in my mind.

Daniel took me on that job as his lookout, hidden in the back of a commercial-style van. No one followed him down that alley. However, at the forty-minute mark two guys, huge and bald, dragged him to the street. Blood had streamed down his face, dripping to the sidewalk. I reached for the van's rear door handle.

Through my earpiece Daniel, using my real name, had said, "Sarah, don't move. Don't." He looked at the ground and not at the van, protecting me. I knew Daniel would be okay. He'd been in worse situations. He'd figure a way out. Like he always did. A third man appeared, smaller than the first two. He wasted no time. In one fluid motion he pulled a gun and shot Daniel in the head. Once. Twice.

I saw that horrible night as if I were there again. It was my fault that Daniel died. I had done nothing to help him, protect him. Still inside the van, I screamed into my hands. The men on the sidewalk startled but couldn't tell where the noise came from. I fell to the van's floor holding in my screams, hands over my mouth, rocking. When I looked out the back window again, Daniel lay alone on the sidewalk, his murderers already gone. I opened the door and ran to him. Maybe I could save Daniel. The craters in his skull convinced me he was dead. I dropped to hold Daniel and sob. A voice from down the block shouted, "Call the police!"

A strange clarity overcame me then. I remembered all that Daniel had taught me. I grabbed his wallet and other stuff and ran. Instead of entering his apartment, I hid in the one next door and watched the Zhiglovs come and ransack his place. The shooter,

Victor, never considered that someone might be coming after him. I showed him how wrong he was when I shot him dead in his own bar. Moments later, the door burst open and a second set of armed men captured me. Later, I learned they were from Domestic Security Services, and my future co-workers. All my training and compliance with the DSS orders and regulations had led me to this moment. My chance for vengeance.

Movement to the side pulled me away from those memories and back into the ship's hold. Sonia had regained her feet. Raised the crowbar over her head again. I scrambled to my feet knowing I had one advantage over her. Though taller than me, she was soft and untrained. Problem was, I didn't have much strength left. Still holding my ribs, I knew I only had one last, good kick—a front snap square into her gut. When she doubled over, I grabbed the switchblade from my boot, hit the button, and screamed all my pain and frustration. I let her raise her head then swept the blade across her throat.

Hot, red liquid splashed on my face and splattered to the floor. Sonia's eyes widened in surprise. Her blood made a gurgling sound and the crowbar clanked to the deck, making a sound that echoed in my head. My vision blurred, and my head spun as I watched her knees buckle and hit the deck. The rest of her body flopped forward with her eyes facing me.

Dead. By my hand. The one who took Daniel from me. The one who set me on the path to becoming a killer. And the satisfaction I thought I'd feel at that moment wasn't there. I was glad she was dead, but I didn't feel any better about anything.

The ship moved again, and that damn canister rolled to my feet. When I bent to pick it up, a wave of dizziness passed over me. The switchblade slipped from my hand, and my knees buckled. I collapsed to the deck. My ribs had shrieked with that last twist, and the pain had not let up. Black appeared at the edge of my vision, and I sank to the floor near Sonia with my body curled around the canister. I watched her blood seep closer like it would engulf and drown me. Even so, I couldn't move. No energy, and the cold, metal deck felt too good against my cheek.

I wasn't sure how long I lay there. Jack came to hover over me as armed people wearing respirators pushed their way into the hold. People in white spacesuits with air tanks on their back followed them. The CDC, I assumed.

My breaths game in gasps. "The canisters okay? Not leaking?"

"Secured," Jack gently took the one I held and looked at it. "They're fine. And don't worry, Raindrop. I canceled the bombing run too."

My last coherent thoughts as more people in white spacesuits entered the hold was that Sonia was dead, we contained the virus, and I wasn't going to get blown up.

CHAPTER THIRTY-ONE

I ended up admitted to University Hospital with a concussion, all battered and bruised. The doctors also put staples in the back of my skull and sutures on my chin. X-rays showed fractures on two ribs while a constant ringing in my ears drove me crazy. The doctor told me I had to stay in the hospital for forty-eight hours. While lying there, I thought about Connor and the way he had taken care of me back when Lamas stabbed me. I missed him. If we hadn't fought, I would have called him, and he would have cared. At least a little.

The next morning, I lay with the head of the bed raised partway, half-heartedly looking at the TV. The major news outlets had picked up the story of the battle at the warehouse and the freighter. A national news anchor was reporting the activity on the docks was gang-related, that officials seized thousands of dollars of drugs and made many arrests. HAZMAT was on the scene because several bags of heroin and fentanyl burst open, polluting the air. Yeah, right. Of course, there was no mention of Russians, terrorists, or the smallpox virus.

Someone let it slip to the doctors and nurses that I was part of that bust and injured in the raid. They were being especially nice to me—extra pillows, more Jell-O, almost anything I wanted. They patted my hand and called me a hero. All I wanted was to be at home.

Though not sleeping, I had my eyes closed when Shepherd showed up with his FBI badge to keep the doctors and nurses from asking too many questions or talking to outsiders about my injuries. He called my name softly, and I smiled when I saw him.

"Hey. Come to check up on me?"

"You're the talk of the DSS, girl," he said, squeezing my hand ever so gently. "The analysts and CAIT have been replaying parts of your fights on the big screen. They can't wait for you to come in and commentate it for them."

"But my body cam broke early on."

"Yeah, but Jack's and the ones you planted in that hold were still filming. They didn't catch everything, which is why you need to fill in the gaps for everyone."

I just shook my head.

He leaned closer and took my hand in both of his. "You did well. Better than well."

"Thanks." I would have squeezed his hand, but mine hurt too much. It was nice he came, but I had been hoping to hear from Chief. His opinion mattered a lot to me. So far, there hadn't even been a phone call.

As if reading my mind, Shepherd said, "Chief wants you to know he's real happy too. He would have come himself, but he's doing some damage control and managing the fallout." I couldn't hide the small smile that crept over my mouth. Shepherd turned and pulled up a chair.

He told me the ER treated Jack, and he left without being admitted. Damn him. That janky old coot even managed to make it look like Mohammad al Bari 'escaped.' Jack left him alive and running with a GPS capsule floating inside his stomach. How he got the dude to swallow a GPS capsule was a mystery to me. I was nowhere near Jack's level of talent yet. With luck, the capsule would remain in al Bari's digestive system for three days—maybe as long as six days so CAIT could track his movements back to his sect. al Bari's people would want their money back from Sonia's father. Maybe that would keep Dvonikov's attention from hunting me down. It would give the office time to clean up our involvement, at least.

After Shepherd left, I took some time to reflect on what happened. I was alive because that jackass Jack Miller saved me. Twice. He didn't let them kill me and took injuries in the process. I hated him and was in his debt. Pretty soon, I'd have to face him, say thanks, and make it real. Best I did it on an empty stomach so I wouldn't puke on the words.

Flowers arrived. Two dozen tiny, white roses. The card read *Thank you* with no signature or ID. From the office I assumed ... though it was weird for them to send me flowers. Did the guys get flowers when they were injured on the job?

On my second day, at lunchtime, Charlotte came. She brought a turkey sandwich from Kramer's and some chips. "Thought you'd prefer this to the hospital food," she said. "Wow! Shepherd was right. Your face is a collage of purple and bandages."

I didn't answer Charlotte at first. She walked in, leaning on a cane, which caught my attention as did the dark circles under her eyes. Her skin looked ... thin. "Why the cane? Is your ankle bothering you?" I wanted that to be the answer, but my gut told me different.

Her face took on a bittersweet countenance. "I find myself stumbling a bit. This helps. I told the office I twisted my ankle again." She changed the subject. "How are you? Much pain?"

"Yeah, some, and I am hungry." I smiled at her the best I was able. That one came easy. She didn't mention her request that I help her die, and I didn't go there either. Maybe she had changed her mind. I hoped so.

Charlotte set my lunch on the tray as I raised the bed some more. She stayed with me while I ate, picking small bits off the sandwich and only chewing on one side of my mouth. After an hour, she admonished me to take a nap and left. First thing the next morning, Shepherd came to pick me up.

"Ready to go home, Raine?"

"Ready to go to the office."

"You sure you're up for that?"

I gave him one of those looks and limped to the elevator. I needed my debrief before I could go home.

Chief waited for me in his doorway. First thing I said was, "I lost the backpack into the harbor—the rest of the equipment–and I broke my body cam."

"Yeah, I noticed."

"Sorry."

"Nah. Part of the job."

I took that to mean the cost wouldn't come out of my pay. He motioned me into his office, closed the door, and darkened the glass walls to make them opaque. Holding my elbows, he helped me sink into a chair then paced as he spoke.

"The Dvornikovs know a dark-haired woman was involved and killed Sonia. They don't know who you are or where you're from, but you are their enemy. Sooner or later, they'll find out."

I figured that much. Chief went on to tell me that Anatoly Dvornikov already fled back to Russia where I couldn't touch him, and the CIA chose not to act. They had bigger fish to fry, I guessed.

Dvornikov lost a daughter, a lot of money, and plenty of street cred when we killed Sonia and captured the virus. He wasn't done, though. Not even close. Just a little wounded. His motivation to find me included a father's desire to find his daughter's killer. Something like that doesn't fade away as I well knew.

Someday, he'd find out who I was. Someday, he'd come for me. Both sides of the war had traitors. Moles. Sooner or later, someone would realize they could make a lot of money selling my name and location.

Eight and a half more years to go before I could leave the office, take a new identity, and hide. Eight and a half more years to save up money, learn a skill I could make a living with, and make a new life for myself.

If I survived that long.

"About those severed hands ..." Chief began.

"What about them?"

"We found a dozen or so sets in the freezer. Our best guess right now is they download the prints and used the hands to leave evidence behind to cover up their trail. They stored other body parts in there too."

"That's disgusting. Inhuman."

"It's why our side has to fight as hard as we do."

"Yeah."

"You did well, Raine. I'm proud of you."

I dipped my head. I wasn't sure how I felt about working for the DSS. I had tried not to think about it while I was in the hospital. It was my fault Daniel died. How could I ever be worthy to be anyone's friend or girlfriend? I didn't have the skills then that I had learned from Chief, but I could have done something, anything, to save Daniel. I hated myself for hesitating that night.

For the last year and a half, I had embraced my love and grief for Daniel like a treasure. It had defined who I was from the moment it happened and gave me purpose. Sonia, his murderer, was dead—by my hand. The Zhiglovs were finished. I felt empty. Adrift.

So, who was I? I took the DSS job to save my own ass and avenge Daniel's death. I allowed Chief to shape me into a killer. It still felt wrong, like a mask I wore to survive. How would I go forward?

"Thanks, Chief." I couldn't think of anything else to say.

"I got word the doctors want you off work for at least a month."

"Yeah."

"You think you'll stick around here?" Chief was doing his best to sound casual but worry came through.

"Probably. I'll let you know if I go anywhere."

"I'm always here if you want to talk."

"Thanks, Chief."

As I left his office, Andrea called me over to hand me a little gift bag.

"What's this?"

"Chocolates. To help you feel better. Hey, you helped save the world, right? You deserve something for that. Anyway, they say chocolate has healing properties."

"Uh, okay."

"Even if it doesn't, it's good for the soul, right?"

"Thanks." I stood there a moment, knowing I should be more effusive in my gratitude but didn't know the words.

"Do you need anything, Raine?"

For all the times I was bitchy to her, she was still being nice to me, damn it. "Nothing, but thanks. Appreciate it."

I turned away from her desk and looked out to the theater to see Charlotte watching me. If I could say thanks to Andrea for some chocolate, I could say more to the people who had my back and took care of me when the bullets flew. I walked down the theater ramp and to Charlotte's station.

"Hey, Charlotte. Hey, Anderson," I called to him one row lower. "Thanks for keeping me informed and safe. I couldn't have done it without both of you. Harry and Flynn too."

Charlotte laid her hand on my arm. I didn't flinch from it as hard as before. "We're just happy you're fine."

"Thanks. Am I clear to enter CAIT?"

"Actually, no," Charlotte said. "We're getting in a lot of sensitive stuff just now. Busy day."

A glance at the other techs and analysts showed they all had their head in their screens while typing or talking into mics. Up on the main screen was an agent's body camera. He appeared to be copying files from a computer. It never stopped. Put one bad guy down, there was another to take his ... or her place.

"Yeah, okay. I'll talk to Harry later."

I went home to rest.

CHAPTER THIRTY-TWO

About two weeks later, Charlotte invited me to her apartment for dinner and a movie. "Wouldn't it be nice for just us girls to sit and be comfortable?" she asked.

"Yeah. Okay. I guess." No not really, but I'd make an effort for her. It'd been so long since I hung out with anyone, I felt something like a social anxiety creep over me beyond her request that I kill her.

"Come over tomorrow—about six thirty? I'll make us a nice dinner and we'll watch something on TV."

I nodded and agreed to go even though I didn't want to. She had maneuvered me out of my comfort zone and shifted me onto her turf. Smart woman. That would make it harder to make excuses or escape answering her questions. She had let certain things lie with so much happening at the office, but now she would press me for a solution to her problem.

I remembered the layout and security systems in Charlotte's building from when I picked her up in the emergency room. The one security guard sat in the lobby in the evenings, and he didn't bother to make rounds. Only the parking garage and lobby cameras were operational. The rest were for the illusion of security.

On Tuesday, I put on decent clothes to visit Charlotte. Nothing fancy, just clean because it seemed the respectful thing to do. Charlotte greeted me with a kiss on the cheek. I resisted the urge to swipe my hand over it. I couldn't remember the last time someone kissed me in friendship.

"Here." I thrust a bottle of wine at her.

"Raine, how thoughtful." Charlotte chattered while I took off my jacket, a black wool pea coat instead of my leather, and threw it and my gym bag on the floor. I wore my Glock on my belt but figured she was used to seeing it, so I didn't move or hide it. Her apartment had comfortable furnishings in soft feminine tones. Not too crowded or fussy. I ran my eyes over the expanse of thick, cream carpeting. Not a stain or speck of dirt on it, and Charlotte's feet were bare.

"Should I take off my boots?"

"Only if you want to. I don't care either way."

I opted to keep my boots. Better if I wanted to get away in a hurry—not that I expected any trouble. I studied her face. Eyes, dark circles; hands, trembled a bit; bare feet, yet walked as if she was drunk or dizzy. Her coloring was off too—gray and sickly. Focused on myself, I missed the advancement of her illness, but there in her apartment, it was all too apparent. Even her hair seemed to be losing color and volume.

She invited me into the tiny kitchen for a glass of wine and some cheese while she finished preparing dinner. Thick porterhouse steaks sizzled in the broiler, and she served them with baked potatoes and carrots. I made a face at the carrots.

"I sweetened them with a little honey."

Honey. That might not be so bad. "Sounds good," I said, doing my best to be a nice guest. That was the first dinner invitation I'd ever accepted. All I knew about being a guest was from television, and I didn't watch much TV.

Despite my fears, the dinner was more comfortable than the lunch at the fancy French restaurant. We had stuff to talk about, and she served the meal with an expensive and tasty red wine. I almost relaxed. Charlotte had made a warm peach cobbler served with French vanilla ice cream for dessert. If I didn't know better, I'd think she was trying to seduce me. I guess in a way, she was.

After dinner and the dishes, Charlotte made popcorn. We settled ourselves on the sofa and started the movie. When the movie got to a slow part, she paused it.

"Have you decided?" she asked without looking at me. Her voice sounded detached and quiet.

"I guess so." I didn't look at her either. For a moment, the silence was as loud as a gunshot.

"Well?"

"I'll do it."

"How much?"

"Nothing."

"C'mon. I have money. I want to save some for my son, for college, but I can offer you five thousand. Do you want a key to my apartment?"

"Nah. Don't want your money. Don't need a key." I stared at the paused television screen.

"I suppose not," she said with a quirk of her lips. "And it will be quick? Like a bullet?"

"Is that how you want it?"

"Yes. I want to be going about my business and then ... nothing."

"There are gentler ways." It was surreal to me—discussing the method of death with my target.

"If you can, put a bullet into the part of my brain with the tumor. Destroy the damn thing."

"That won't make for a pretty funeral."

"I don't really want that anyway."

"When do you want it to happen?"

"Anytime between now and real soon. I'm already forgetting people, tasks, other stuff. I stumble when I walk and can't wear heels anymore. I don't have much time before I become helpless."

I had noticed her stumbling and dropping things even more lately. Yeah. It was happening. "I gotta use your bathroom." My hands shook, which was stupid.

Those months of working with and studying alongside her changed me. Charlotte, like me, was a person who needed control over her environment. Like me, she lived alone. Her family wasn't dead like mine, but they were far away and didn't seem to have close ties.

Charlotte obsessed over almost everything. Her clothes, hair, apartment—most especially her job. Her attention to detail kept me and other agents safe. She took pride in her work and in her independence. Losing that autonomy would be worse than death. For her, nursing care for everything from eating to wiping her ass would become a long humiliation that only death would relieve. Charlotte would suffer more from the indignity of it all than the pain—than even the awareness of her mortality. Until I thought that through, I didn't realize how much Charlotte and I had in common.

When I returned, she said, "Me too," and headed for the bathroom.

Earlier in the day, I had made up my mind to help her. I didn't think she'd ask for a bullet. Bullets killed Daniel. Bullets hurt. Even if they're quick, there's still a moment of pain. And bullets don't always kill immediately. That's why I always went for the double tap. Besides, it was hard to make a shot to the head look like an accident or suicide, but I wasn't going to tell her. That part was my problem to solve.

She had a sweet tea on the table, and I had some tranquilizer in my pocket. One of my street thug acquaintances got it for me—his brother worked security in a hospital. I poured it into her tea, gave it a swirl with my finger, and sat back. The tranquilizer wouldn't kill her. Just make her sleepy and relaxed. The lethal dose rested in my pocket heavy as a brick. She could change her mind. I'd find out how serious she was.

When Charlotte returned, I said, "We'll talk about it later."

She resumed the movie, ate more popcorn, and took a big sip. Then another. I kept my eyes on the screen. A moment later, she turned to me with effort.

"Now? I thought we agreed on a bullet." Her words slurred a little.

"Bullets are for criminal shits. You can still back out. Still say stop. You don't have a lethal dose yet."

"No This is fine. I guess here on my sofa is ... fine."

I stood and held out my hands. "Come." I helped her to stand and walked her to her bed. I put her in the middle, then got on the bed and lay next to her.

"You won't die alone," I said. I put my arm under her head and embraced her. "Just let yourself fall asleep."

She made a dreamy sort of smile while her unfocused eyes tried to meet mine. "You're a good friend, Raine. A blessing to me. Thank you."

"Shhh," I whispered. "I promise sweet dreams when you fall asleep."

Her next words came out weak and breathy. "Be good to Connor. He loves you."

A lot she knew. I counted to twenty, and her breathing became soft and shallow. To make sure, I shook her. "Charlotte?" I called a little louder, "Charlotte?" No response. Not even a flicker of an eyelash. I eased my arm from under her head and kneeled on the bed next to her. From my pocket, I retrieved the lethal syringe.

I touched Charlotte's face with my fingertips, so calm and peaceful. When I lifted her arm, it felt warm with life though heavier than I expected. The skin inside her elbow was almost translucent in its paleness—her veins were delicate blue lines. I eased the needle's tip into a vein, depressed the plunger, and let the liquid disappear into her body. I stayed next to Charlotte and held her hand. It felt warm in my grip, or maybe my hands were cold. I monitored her pulse. The beats weakened and came further apart. Two minutes later, her pulse faded and stopped.

I didn't move and held her hand for maybe another two or three minutes before laying it on the duvet. Then I eased myself off the bed as if trying not to disturb a sleeping baby.

Surgical gloves helped me take on a professional persona. I wiped the cap, syringe, and tranquilizer vial, then pressed each to her fingertips, messy and overlapping. I left the items near her hands like I had seen in photos of suicides. I fluffed the pillow my head indented and smoothed the comforter. There'd be fewer questions if her death looked self-inflicted.

Tears prickled my eyes, but then I remembered there was no reason for that. Training took over. I left the room and wiped down any surface I had touched. I was careful about touching things that evening. You'd think an analyst would have noticed how cautious I was or asked why I had brought a gym bag with me. Next, I cleaned the kitchen, bathroom and living room. I vacuumed, especially in the bedroom and on the bed, even though my hair was in a braid to minimize shedding strands.

At her door, Charlotte's vacuum in tow, I put on the wig, hat, and scarf from my gym bag and reversed my coat to the green wool side. That was how the security cameras saw me going in and how they'd see me leaving. I slipped out the door with the vacuum and made for the service stairs and parking garage. The vacuum cleaner would soon disappear into the river.

I walked away alone like I always did. But I couldn't help the thought that popped into my mind, and that time it hurt.

I had a friend. But not anymore. I didn't have any friends.

ACKNOWLEDGMENTS

A great deal of the writing process happens alone in front of a computer screen. Without support, writers flounder—especially me. I've received a ton of support along the way, and I am grateful.

Thank you to my husband and daughter for putting up with me sticking my face into a computer screen for hours on end. I love you.

Thank you to my sisters, Nancy and Joan, my awesome cheering section. Thank you also to my parents—voracious readers—who instilled a love of books in me at an early age.

An abundance of appreciation to my two writing buddies Sandra M. Bush and Jeanne Moran, both awesome authors, who encouraged this book from its very early stages. Your support has been invaluable. And thanks to my awesome critique group: Hermina, Thorne, Sue, Ron, and Deb. I appreciate all of you.

To my editor, Aimee Hardy. Thank you for your insights and for guiding me through the editing process. You showed me how to really make this book shine.

A special call out to Pennwriters.org. You are a wonderful group of people who give your time and expertise to all the members to help us become better writers.

Running Wild Press publishes stories that cross genres with great stories and writing. RIZE publishes great genre stories written by people of color and by authors who identify with other marginalized groups. Our team consists of:

Lisa Diane Kastner, Founder and Executive Editor
Joelle Mitchell, Licensing and Strategy Lead
Cody Sisco, Acquisition Editor, RIZE
Benjamin White, Acquisition Editor, Running Wild
Peter A. Wright, Acquisition Editor, Running Wild
Resa Alboher, Editor
Angela Andrews, Editor
Sandra Bush, Editor
Ashley Crantas, Editor
Rebecca Dimyan, Editor
Abigail Efird, Editor
Aimee Hardy, Editor
Henry L. Herz, Editor
Cecilia Kennedy, Editor
Barbara Lockwood, Editor
AE Williams, Editor
Scott Schultz, Editor
Rod Gilley, Editor
Kelly Ottiano, Editor
Carolyn Banks, Editor

Evangeline Estropia, Product Manager
Kimberly Ligutan, Product Manager
Pulp Art Studios, Cover Design
Standout Books, Interior Design
Polgarus Studios, Interior Design

ABOUT RUNNING WILD PRESS

Learn more about us and our stories at www.runningwildpublishing.com

Loved this story and want more? Follow us at www.runningwildpublishing.com, www.facebook.com/runningwildpress, on Twitter @lisadkastner @RunWildBooks